Ghost Writer

Ghost Writer

By Lorna Collins

Oak Tree Press Taylorville, IL

Oak Tree Press

Oak Tree Press books may be purchased for educational, business or sales promotional purposes. Contact Publisher for quantity discounts.

First Edition, July 2012

Cover by Karen Phillips

Interior Pages by Linda W. Rigsbee

ISBN 978-1-61009-202-9
LCCN 2012936887

Dedication

~To Larry, my best friend, husband and soul mate.
If I could, I'd do it all again with you.~

Acknowledgements

WITH MUCH LOVE AND GRATITUDE TO THE FOLLOWING FOR their contributions to the writing of this book:

- ❤ **Letha Collins**, my late mother-in-love, whose passion for old movies helped me recreate the world of glamorous old-time Hollywood described in the book.
- ❤ **Lagunita Writers**, who listened to each iteration of every chapter and helped make the final work better.
- ❤ **Bob Schwenck**, who introduced me to Anna Hills and the California Impressionist painters, and who gave me suggestions on the manuscript.
- ❤ **The Missiles of October** for wonderful music.
- ❤ **Billie** and **Sunny** and everyone at Oak Tree for their support and encouragement.
- ❤ And, as always, **Larry.**

"I DON'T BELIEVE IN GHOSTS," I USED TO TELL ANYONE WHO'D ask. I'm a 'techie,' a computer programmer. I deal with data and facts, not fiction and fantasy.

So how did I get mixed up with a temperamental, egotistical, rude, smart, funny, aggravating, self-centered, loveable... uh... spirit? Okay, if you insist, ghost.

It all started the day I moved into my house.

Well, it's not really a house, more of a cottage on the sand south of Laguna Beach, California.

This place was the one blessing I received in a whole series of otherwise disastrous events, starting with losing my job.

I worked in the mortgage industry for five years following my college graduation. It was all I knew until I became another victim of the banking industry collapse. I went to work one day, and the company was gone. *Pffft.* Taken over by the government. The assets were sold and I got two weeks' severance.

Of course, at the end of the first week, not only was my job gone, but so was Jeff, my live-in boyfriend, taking all the cash in my wallet with him. Since he hadn't worked in over a year, I figured he'd found another gainfully employed female to support him. I was really ticked off that he split the minute he lost me as his meal ticket. I needed his help.

It had been kinda nice coming home to a human being after work. Well, not always, but he was there most of the time waiting for me to nuke his dinner. And he was sort of cute, with long dark hair and big brown eyes. I thought we looked pretty good together. Besides, he was the first guy who really paid any attention to me. I'd hoped it was because of my personality and not my paycheck, but after he took off, I wasn't so sure.

I got the eviction notice the day after Jeff moved out. The building was in foreclosure. It was probably just as well because I couldn't afford the apartment on unemployment insurance anyway.

So learning I'd inherited a house couldn't have come at a better time.

My great-great-aunt, Nanette Burton, for whom I was named, died at one hundred and four years old in the mansion where she'd lived for years and loved so much. She'd never married and never had children. I heard rumors of several passionate affairs in her younger days, although I wasn't supposed to know about them.

A week later, her attorney invited us to the reading of her will.

"Mr. and Mrs. Burton, and Miss Burton, please take a seat," he said as we entered his Santa Monica office.

Since the rest of Aunt Netta's family had died, Dad and I were her only surviving relatives, but, to our surprise, there were a few others already there.

Albert William Spencer, Esq. (according to the sign on his door) was a throwback to another era, courtly and tall, with a full head of wavy white hair. His charcoal pinstriped suit, vest, and white shirt were impeccably pressed. I wouldn't have been surprised if he wore a pocket watch, but his jacket was buttoned, so I couldn't tell.

His inner sanctum looked like it had come from the 1950s. I've watched lots of movies from that era, and all the attorneys' offices were the same. Before the window, stood an impressive highly-polished wooden desk, a monument to old money. The walls were lined with matching bookcases holding leather-bound volumes from floor to ceiling.

We took our seats.

"Since everyone has now arrived, I shall begin."

I spaced out during some of the preliminaries. It wasn't until we reached the bequests that I gave the attorney my full attention. I was hoping for a little help out of the pit my life had become.

"My real estate holdings and personal property, with the exceptions listed herein, are to be sold immediately. I have asked my attorney to manage the sale and have given him all the particulars."

Mr. Spencer turned to us. "As Ms. Burton requested, the estate is already on the market and I anticipate several offers shortly. It is a rare and exceptionally large property. Buyers remain plentiful. I shall arrange for an auction of her personal belongings not specifically listed in her will to be held soon."

He returned to the papers in his hand and described a few rings and other items that had belonged to family members, which she left to Dad. Then he looked up again to make sure we all understood.

We nodded in unison like bobble heads.

"Half the proceeds of the sale, after expenses, are to go to several animal shelters and rescue organizations listed herein in the proportions designated." He read the names of six or seven groups and their respective percentages. That explained the other people in the room. Their representatives smiled and nodded.

I wasn't really too surprised. For a very wealthy woman, Aunt Netta seemed to collect more than her share of strays. She converted an old chicken coop on her property and its surrounding yard into a pretty nice temporary residence for the dogs. Then she hired someone to come every day to feed, exercise, groom, and clean up after them. But she worked hard to find each one a new home. She was so persuasive that she only had five mutts left when she died. Plus Mitzi, her own favorite and much-pampered Shih Tzu.

"The animals currently in my care, with the exception of my pet, Mitzi, are to be entrusted to 'Homes for All,' until suitable arrangements can be made for their permanent placement."

I was sure the organization would be more than happy to take the dogs since a sizeable bequest came along with them.

"My beloved Mitzi, I leave to my great-grandniece, Nanette."

Oh joy, I get the dog. Just what I always wanted—but not much.

Not only was I named for Aunt Netta, I was born on her birthday. I think that may be why she tolerated me, even though she was quite outspoken about not liking children in general. It probably also helped that I was an only child, as was my dad. She seemed better able to be around kids one at a time.

Mr. Spencer looked over the top of his wire-rimmed reading glasses to be sure I understood. "My secretary, Mrs. Owens, has been caring for Mitzi. The dog and all her belongings are in the outer office."

I wanted to say, "But I have nowhere to live myself, and I don't have a job. How can I take on a dog? Besides, even as a kid, I never wanted a dog." But instead I smiled, said nothing, and resumed my head-bobbing.

Mr. Spencer cleared his throat and went back to his paper. "Let me see. Where was I? Oh, yes," he continued. "The remainder of my estate is to be disposed of in the following manner. One half, I leave to my great nephew Craig William Burton. One quarter will remain in trust for my great-grandniece Nanette Louise Burton to be held until her thirtieth birthday, at which time, she will have access to the annual income. On her fortieth birthday, she will be given complete control. My attorney has specific instructions on how the trust is to be invested and managed."

Okay, so I'll have some income at thirty, and if there's anything left, I'll actually get to spend it at forty. Three years before I get anything. Great.

Mr. Spencer continued reading. "The final quarter is to be managed by my attorney for the care of my precious Mitzi. I trust that my great-grandniece will provide food and shelter as well as loving care to my darling companion. When my pet meets her final end, I have arranged for a thorough examination to be certain no foul play was involved. At that time, the balance of Mitzi's bequest will become the property of my great-grandniece, Nanette Louise Burton. However, if there is any question about the cause of the dog's demise, all remaining funds, other than those left to Craig William Burton, including Nanette Louise Burton's trust fund, are to be liquidated immediately and given to the organizations named herein."

Mr. Spencer removed his glasses and stared at me. "You do understand Ms. Burton's wishes." It was a statement, not a question.

"Yes, sir. If the dog dies of anything other than old age, I lose everything. I think that about sums it up."

This is going to be the most pampered pooch in history.

He cleared his throat. I don't think he was used to such direct answers. "Yes, that is correct."

He returned to the papers in his hand. "There is one last bequest. The property on Seashell Cove, I leave to my great-grandniece, Nanette Louise Burton, along with the contents therein."

Holy crap! Her beach cottage is mine! My heart pounded so loudly I was sure the rest of them could hear. *I'll take really good care of the dog as long as I can live there.*

I gasped and he glanced up at me.

"The house, indeed, is yours. I took the liberty of arranging for it to be cleaned and having the deed transferred to your name."

My life suddenly looked a lot brighter. Even with a dog in it.

CHAPTER

"GET OUT OF MY HOUSE!"

I turned from the gorgeous view of the ocean to find out who the rude guy with the British accent was. I wasn't scared, just startled and annoyed that my exploration of the new digs had been interrupted.

I didn't see anyone.

"It's not your house. It's mine," I replied, looking behind the living room furniture for someone hiding there. Since most of it was wicker, it didn't seem a likely possibility.

"This is my home. Now remove yourself!" he roared. His voice echoed off the white plaster walls like he was right there with me.

"Who are you? And what are you doing here?" I walked back toward the archway to the entry hall to see if someone was lurking. No one there either.

"What the..."

"I live here," came the voice from the same location as before.

I nearly tripped over Mitzi who had her fanny firmly planted in the doorway staring into space toward the location of the voice, somewhere near the stone fireplace. I was starting to adjust to the shaggy little black-and white mop but hadn't gotten used to her always being underfoot.

"Is this a joke? Am I being punked?" I began searching around the room for hidden microphones or cameras. I couldn't see anything that looked suspicious or out of place.

"What sort of claptrap are you speaking?"

"It's perfectly good American English, and if you don't like it, leave." I was getting annoyed. I couldn't think of anyone who'd play this kind of joke.

Maybe it's one of those reality TV shows with a prize or even payment if they run the episode. Guess I'll play along.

I walked back toward the window with the killer view of the Pacific. "Nice weather we're having," I began.

"I don't give a fig about the bloody weather," the voice raged. It seemed a little nearer, but still in the same room. "This is California. The sunshine is storied, famous throughout the world. I just want your person anywhere other than here."

My dad is half Irish and Mom is nearly full-blooded. I blame my temper on both of them. "Now, listen, whoever you are, wherever you are, I own this place. My name's on the deed. I belong here and you don't. So scram."

I know there are really small electronics, but I don't see anything even remotely resembling a recording device or speakers of any kind. I got down on my hands and knees and hunted along the floor.

"Believe me, dear girl, if I could depart, I would. I have no tolerance for useless females and as for that mutt..."

I turned my head in the direction of the voice. "Hey, leave Mitzi out of this. It's between the two of us." I glanced at the fur ball still planted in the doorway staring into space. "I'm not useless, and I'm not going anywhere." *There. That told him. This joke is getting really old.*

"Very well. I've tried civility. From now on, I won't be as pleasant."

"Pleasant? You call that pleasant?" I nearly shouted. "You're one rude, crude dude!"

"I will not have my reputation besmirched by an uncouth upstart such as yourself. I'll have you know..."

"I don't want to hear whatever it is you have to say. Just take your hidden camera and microphone and—and whatever other gear you brought in here—and get out before I call a cop!"

A deep laugh boomed across the room. "Please do so," he said. "I would enjoy watching their faces while you describe your experience. I've seen others try. Although, come to think of it, I can't recall anyone else actually hearing my voice. My clanking and banging, yes, but..." He grew silent for a moment. "Hmmm. Perhaps there is a reason for your presence after all. That may be the answer..."

"The answer to what?"

He didn't reply. The moment of quiet was really nice, especially since I could hear the waves breaking on the sandy beach outside.

I decided I'd get back to what I'd intended to do when my dad dropped me off, along with all my stuff. Move in. I hoped he'd get bored and go away.

Dad had helped me pile my boxes in the small one-car space attached to the cottage. Since my car had died right after I lost my job and couldn't be repaired, I didn't own a vehicle at the moment. There was lots of room. I was surprised to see another small stack of cartons in the back corner and figured I'd go through them later on. After all, I owned the house as well as the contents.

I actually liked most of the furniture and other decorations inside. The white wicker in the living room was in good shape. The flowered pillows looked a bit faded and old-ladyish, but it was a definite improvement over the castoffs and broken-down, mismatched stuff in my last unlamented apartment. I'd already discovered actual matching sets of dishes, silverware, and glassware. The plates had daisies on them to match the yellow kitchen. A step up from the mismatched and chipped dishes and silverware I'd been using.

Mom had insisted on buying me some groceries and other 'necessities' so I wouldn't have to shop for a while. I'd already unloaded most of those, enjoying the sunny yellow paint on the kitchen walls, sheer curtains framing the window, and of course, the view. I was glad Mr. Spencer had arranged to have the place cleaned before I moved in since he'd said it had stood empty for a long time. The rooms smelled fresh.

I walked through my new home and realized the tiny one-bedroom house had everything I needed to be comfortable, except maybe enough storage space.

Of course, the dog's needs were covered. Mitzi had come to me complete with her own bed, several blankets, a coat, raincoat, rain boots, brushes, combs, shampoo, leashes, bowls, additional clothing and assorted other items, some of which I hadn't even figured out yet.

"This is one spoiled dog," I'd muttered as I'd unpacked all of it.

She also came with a rather thick manual. It included detailed instructions for her care. I'd begun reading it on the way back to my folks' house from the lawyer's office. I had to protect my future.

"What?" I'd yelped when I reached the second chapter on 'Feeding.' "I have to make all her food? And look what goes into it. Yecch!"

At that point, I didn't boil water unless it was in a microwave. I was afraid the cottage was so small it wouldn't have one of those. Or a dishwasher either.

"I'll teach you how to cook," Mom volunteered when she realized my predicament. I handed her the book and she looked over the recipes.

Did I mention there were different ones for every day of the week?

"These aren't difficult," she said. "We'll make them together when we get home."

Mom helped me with the first couple, and they weren't too hard, once I got the hang of them. The ingredients were different, but the process was pretty much the same.

"Multiply each recipe and freeze some. That way, you won't need to cook every day," Mom had suggested.

We'd run into a snag when we got to the recipes for the weekend.

"You may have to go to a specialty store for some of the ingredients," Mom had announced, shaking her head.

"What about the cost?" I wailed. Unemployment wouldn't get me very far, especially now that I had the dog.

"Dad and I'll help this time. But you have to talk to Mr. Spencer about an allowance to take care of Mitzi. She has her own inheritance, remember?"

"Oh, yeah." I glanced at the clock and groaned. "It's too late today and tomorrow's Saturday. They probably won't be open. Besides, I'm moving. I'll call him first thing Monday morning," I said.

I sighed when I thought about my financial situation. It was pretty dismal. I wouldn't have rent to pay, but there would still be utility bills and the other housing expenses on top of my personal ones.

As soon as my job ended, I'd visited the nice folks at EDD and filed my claim. The reality of my situation hit hard. Unemployment insurance wouldn't pay very much. Oh, don't get me wrong, I was glad to have it.

"I really need a new job," I'd muttered as I left the unemployment office. In my head, I started to plan.

Luckily, I could extend my medical benefits through something called COBRA, but that would take a big chunk of my bi-weekly checks. On the other hand, I was afraid not to have coverage since I wouldn't be able to pay the cost of doctor visits or prescriptions or an accident without it.

I'm pretty healthy. I don't smoke or drink, other than a glass of wine or beer if someone else is paying and usually with a meal. I love to run and walk and was looking forward to jogs on the beach with Mitzi.

When I'd arrived at the cottage, I'd unpacked the frozen and refrigerated food first thing. Unfortunately, my fears about the kitchen were realized. No microwave. And the refrigerator was really old and small. It had a freezer about the size of a toaster. The dog's entrees took up the whole thing, plus part of the refrigerator. By the time I finished storing Mitzi's dinners, there wasn't much room left for my food.

"Are you going to stand there staring all day, or do you plan on getting down to business?" the annoying British voice sounded from behind me.

"Don't do that!" I said.

"Precisely what did I do?" he asked.

"You snuck up and scared me. I thought you'd gone."

I heard him sigh. "No. I'm still here. Believe me, dear girl, I'd love to depart from this place. But I seem to be stuck."

"What do you mean 'stuck'?"

"I simply must remain in this location until—well—I'm not exactly certain what must occur for that to happen."

"Who are you? And why are you here?"

"My publisher had recommended America as a more receptive market for an author writing in my genre."

"Wait a minute. Are you the 'famous author' Aunt Netta told me about?"

"One and the same."

Aunt Netta had explained that she'd once owned a great deal of real estate throughout Southern California and had made a huge profit on each investment she made. However, in order to acquire her mansion, she'd sold it all. Well, all but one house: this tiny cottage on the beach.

I never knew exactly why she kept it. When I asked, she answered, "A famous author lived there." But she wouldn't divulge the person's name, even when I begged. In fact, I wasn't sure whether it was a man or a woman. As a romantic teenager, I secretly suspected she might have visited a lover there.

Once when I was in high school, some friends and I drove to Seashell Cove and jogged along the sand just to get a glimpse of the house. I knew instantly which one it was. My emotional response came as a surprise. I loved it at first sight.

Of course, I didn't have the nerve to knock on the door, even to find out more about the 'famous author,' but I never forgot the little green clapboard building with the fresh white trim. It whispered, "Home." So when I heard that it was mine, it was as if I'd always known it would be.

But at that moment I needed to find out who the crazy Brit was, why he'd bugged my house, and how I could get rid of him and his electronics.

I decided to start with a few personal details. "How long have you lived here?"

"Let me see... I arrived in California in 1939. War seemed imminent in London at the time, and both my parents had succumbed to the influenza epidemic. I moved into this house in 1942."

"Well, how old are you?" I still couldn't see anyone or anything responsible for the annoying voice, and he didn't sound ancient.

"I died in 1977 when I was seventy-five. So, I guess I'm still that age."

"What do you mean you died?" Okay, so now I was starting to get a little creeped out.

"I died here in this room, seated at my desk before the window."

"Eeew. So that means you're a..."

"I believe the term is 'ghost' or 'disembodied spirit' in the common vernacular. Personally, I prefer 'specter.' It's much more poetic, don't you think?"

"You died right here, sitting in that chair?" I pointed to the one at the desk.

"Indeed. That's where my sweet Nanette discovered me."

"Aunt Netta found you?"

"If Nanette Burton is your aunt, then, yes. She discovered my earthly remains."

This is getting way too weird and a little too spooky.

I glanced at the chair. It looked okay, but I wasn't about to sit in it. I moved it across the room and set it next to the fireplace.

I really don't believe in ghosts, but this conversation is shaking me up.

"What on earth are you doing?" he demanded, outrage once again in his tone.

"I'll use one of the kitchen chairs. They seem more—uh—comfortable."

"A writer can't be concerned about comfort. If you are going to finish my novel..."

"Finish your novel? Just what makes you think I'll do that? I'm a programmer, not a writer. I deal with bits and bytes, not words. You're delusional."

"Everyone deals with words, my dear girl. All conversation uses them. We are, in fact, making use of words at this moment."

"Stop calling me your 'dear girl.' I'm a grown woman, not a girl, and I'm not yours, or anyone's. *And* I don't do words. Period."

"Well, you shall now."

"And why would I?" He'd gotten my Irish up, to use the cliché. And in my case, it applied.

"Because I believe it may be the only means by which I shall be able to depart from this locale." He suddenly sounded calm and rational.

"And just how do you see that happening?"

"If you simply look in the bottom left-hand drawer of my desk, you will discover the beginning of the novel I was writing at the time of my demise. I believe it is your purpose to assist me with its completion."

I opened the drawer, and sure enough, there was a stack of yellow tablets about an inch thick covered with chicken scratches. I picked them up.

"Where's the file?" I asked.

"You are currently holding it in your hand," he replied, sounding as if he thought I was an idiot.

"I mean, the digital file," I answered in much the same tone.

"I am certain I have no idea of your reference. The pages you discovered are the only record extant of this work. We must begin with those."

"Do you mean I'll have to copy all of this onto the computer before we can even start?" I looked at the carefully-numbered pages, turned to the last one, and stared. The number '175' stared back. "No way, Jose." I threw the stack back into the drawer and slammed it shut.

"Do you wish me to waken you in the night with creaking? Or would you prefer banging on the wall? Perhaps you'd rather I rattle windows. I've become rather adept at all of those. But I'm certain I could add to my repertoire if need be."

"You'd really do that?" *What a jerk!*

"Young lady, I shall do whatever is required in order to find peace. And you shall have none until I do."

I sighed. *Great. First the dog and now a ghost with a mission. What next?*

"HEY, WHAT'S YOUR NAME?" I FINALLY ASKED. I FIGURED IT WOULD be easier to carry on a conversation with my resident spirit, assuming that's what he was, if I knew what to call him. But I wasn't going to tell him I had no intention of doing anything with his stupid yellow tablets. At least not yet.

"Maximilian Alexander Murdoch."

"I thought you were a famous writer. How come I've never heard of you?"

"Because, dear child, my books were in fashion long before you were born and because no sane novelist would publish using his Christian name. Like the most highly revered scribes, I assumed a nom de plume." He sounded arrogant and stuffy.

"So, what was your pen name?" I asked as I sat down on the loveseat.

I was answered with silence.

"Are you ashamed of it?" It was a little unnerving to be carrying on a conversation with the wall. But, what the heck...

"Certainly not!" he blustered.

"Then tell me what it is." I didn't know whether he thought I'd give up or what, but now I was really curious.

"I must preface that disclosure with the information that I wrote in a genre not usual for a male author at the time."

"And just what was that?"

"Women's fiction."

"Do you mean romance?"

"Well, perhaps it might be characterized with that appellation," he answered, but sounded reluctant to admit it.

I started to laugh. I couldn't help myself. "You were a romance writer?"

"It is an honorable undertaking. And it provided me with a comfortable living."

"Okay, so what name did you use?"

Another pause was followed with, "Maxine du Bois."

"Really?" I remembered that Aunt Netta had loved romance novels. I'd seen shelves filled with them in her house. And the author who appeared most often was Maxine du Bois.

"I read one of your books when I was in high school."

"Did you enjoy it?"

"Well, actually, I thought it was kind of lame."

"Lame! And exactly what is the current interpretation of that particular word?"

"Uh, kind of dumb." I figured if he could, he'd probably have hit me. As it was…

"Dumb? Those tomes are masterpieces! They reside in the finest collections of twentieth-century fiction." His voice seemed to change directions, moving behind me as though he was pacing. "Dumb! What utter cheek!"

"See, the problem is that this is the twenty-first century. Tastes have changed. I'm sure your books were good for their time, but people today want fast reads."

"My work was heralded during my lifetime. Critics raved." He seemed to have stopped his pacing and returned to the place where he'd started.

"Uh, I'm sure it was."

"Well, like it or not, I have a final masterpiece to complete and you, my girl, will assist me with the task."

"Listen, Max, no one tells me what to do. I make my own decisions."

"So you want me to spoil your rest? Generate so much chaos you'll not find peace? Listen to this: *Whoooo*."

He did a bad imitation of a movie ghost. That is, a ghost from one of those stupid old black-and-white pictures that never really frightened anyone. My friends and I used to watch them on TV and giggle at how hokey they were.

I probably should have tried to stop myself, but I laughed again. "I haven't been scared of those sounds since, well, I never was. In fact, I don't believe in you. You're a figment of my imagination."

I left the room to get a kitchen chair to use at the desk. When I returned, I thought I heard the 'death chair' creak.

"You might not be frightened at this moment, but you will not enjoy being awakened numerous times during the night. I have discovered I no longer require slumber. And since you seem to hear me, I can experiment with my entire repertoire of vocalizations. This may prove to be most amusing." I heard another creak.

I happened to look at Mitzi. She'd changed position and was now sitting directly in front of 'that' chair.

"I think Mitzi can see you," I observed.

"Most curious," he replied. "You have the auditory sensitivity while your animal has the visual. Quite fascinating."

I thought I saw Mitzi's coat move and she lifted her head and closed her eyes. It kind of sounded like she was purring. That is, if dogs purr.

"Are you petting my dog?"

"Apparently the canine is also able to receive tactile stimulation. Interesting. Perhaps this mutt will prove an ally."

"If you're trying to spook me, it's not working. It'll take more than a little fluffed fur to frighten me." Actually, though his voice was annoying, I wondered just how much he was able to move stuff or if he could see through walls.

Not going there...

Mitzi's coat ruffled again and this time I was sure I hadn't imagined it.

"If you'll excuse me, I still need to unpack," I announced as I started to leave without any further argument from my 'tenant.'

My turncoat dog remained with the person—uh—one who gave her attention. "Traitor," I muttered under my breath as I went to the garage.

I brought in the last carton of food, and it didn't take long to put away.

Cereal and spices and the basics I'd need for the dog's gourmet meals. Mitzi's stuff took up most of the space.

Then I stowed what little makeup I owned in the bathroom but decided to deal with my clothes later.

I was pretty low maintenance. I got my hair cut a couple of times a year, when Mom bugged me enough. I kept my own bangs trimmed in between. Fortunately, I have thick, wavy hair, so little mistakes didn't show up too much. It was pretty long, and most of the time, I kept it in a ponytail. It was easier.

When I was younger, people said I looked like Aunt Netta. I'd seen pictures of her, of course, and our features were pretty much the same. We both had oval faces, high foreheads, the big blue Burton eyes, and blonde hair. Well, mine was blonde when I was a kid. As I got older, it got darker. Now it was kind of dishwater.

Aunt Netta was high maintenance. Very high maintenance. She was 'blonde' until the day she died. And she still had her hair styled and her nails done every week. She was beautiful, and she knew it. No one had ever called me that. At least not seriously.

What she spent on one casual outfit would have covered my entire wardrobe for a few years. At work, I'd worn polo shirts with the bank's name and logo on them. But I didn't have to buy them. They also gave us labeled windbreakers. Those were my only jackets and were warm enough for Southern California. I still had all those work clothes. I figured I'd keep wearing them until they wore out. The only things I'd bought since college were underwear, jeans, t-shirts, and shoes. As gifts, Mom had bought me a few sweaters and a couple of skirts I almost never wore.

At that moment I sported my oldest khaki shorts, a faded bank polo shirt, and flip-flops.

I glanced out the window. After being in the house all day, the afternoon sunshine and the beach called to me. Besides, Max made me nervous, and I needed a change of scenery. "Hey, Mitzi," I called. "Want to take a walk?" I figured that would tempt her away from her new 'playmate.'

The little dog came running. I found her leash and quickly clipped it to her matching harness. Did I mention that the dog had jeweled harnesses instead of collars? The manual said, "Small dogs should never wear collars because their windpipes can be constricted from the pressure."

Mitzi had harnesses, with matching leashes, in every color, to coordinate with every outfit, suitable for every occasion. I couldn't figure out why since they disappeared beneath her thick fur.

"Let's go, girl," I said, although she didn't really need any encouragement. I have to admit, she was pretty well-behaved. She didn't jump or yap. I suspected she'd been trained, or maybe it was from living with an old lady. The dog seemed really gentle. I always think of little dogs as hyper and mouthy, but Mitzi wasn't.

We went out the back door. I left my shoes on the porch. She headed straight for the little patch of grass next to the house and did her 'business.' Then she matched her pace to mine as we jogged along the sand. She must have been trained to heel because she stayed right with me on my left.

It felt wonderful to move with the salty breeze in my face, the sound of the breakers, and the feel of the warm sand on my bare feet. I wondered if the sky really was bluer near the ocean or if it just seemed that way.

I looked out at the small waves and saw a few kids near shore with boogie boards. Beyond them, the larger waves broke, and about a dozen surfers waited their turn. As the ocean rose, a couple paddled like crazy, and usually one managed to stand up and ride. It looked like fun. But I sure wasn't going to try it!

Once when I was little, Dad took me beyond the breakers. He didn't realize there was a riptide until I got snatched from him and started being pulled out to sea. The lifeguard saw what happened and raced to me.

I was sure I was going to drown, but he caught my arm and pulled me up. Even though he was a strong swimmer, it felt like a long time before we reached the sand. I still remember what he looked like with water dripping off his curly blond hair onto the golden tan of his muscles. He'd been my image of a hero ever since.

Dad got to shore just ahead of us, and boy, was he glad to see me.

I've never wanted to try it again, although I can swim and enjoy a nice clean, chlorinated pool once in a while. I used to love the one at Aunt Netta's estate. Mom and I swam laps together on those rare occasions when we were invited to visit.

When I was about ten, we house sat for her for about a month while she was traveling in Europe. Or Asia. Or Australia. Or somewhere exotic. Just Mom and me.

We lived about an hour and a half away, and the daily commute would have been too far for Dad. But he came on the weekends. I was out of school for the summer, and Mom had a lot of accrued paid time off, so we enjoyed our luxurious vacation.

I was a princess.

Aunt Netta had live-in servants. The cook, Bertie, was a plump lady with a round face and smiling eyes. She kept saying, "I just love having a child in the house." Of course she pronounced 'child' as 'chil.' When I asked about it, Aunt Netta told me Bertie was born in New Orleans. I always loved her accent. It sounded like music.

Bertie baked the best cookies. When she discovered that I adored chocolate chip and iced sugar ones, she made sure both kinds were always fresh and available.

Bertie's husband, Arthur, was the chauffer, butler, and all-around handyman. When Aunt Netta entertained, they both served the guests, Bertie in her black uniform with the starched white apron and Arthur in his dark tuxedo with crisp white shirt and black bow tie.

But when we stayed there, they dressed casually and treated me more like a grandchild than a guest. Arthur played games with me. He taught me to play tennis. There were two courts behind the garage.

Meanwhile, Bertie took care of my every need and want.

"Bertie, you're spoiling her," Mom scolded. But the twinkle in her eye told both of us she wasn't angry.

"It's one of the few simple pleasures of this job, Ms. Burton."

"Fiona, please," Mom requested for the umpteenth time.

"Yes, ma'am," Bertie replied. But all three of us knew she'd never be that informal. Besides, Aunt Netta wouldn't have liked it.

"Do you have any kids?" I asked Bertie one day while helping her cut out cookies with animal-shaped cutters. I was covered with flour and as completely happy as I can ever remember being.

"No, honey. Arthur and I were never blessed with our own. But God's put many other people's babies in our lives. So we just love them like they were ours. Same as you." Her coffee-colored skin crinkled around her eyes when she smiled at me.

I never was sure exactly what her ethnic background was, or Arthur's either, for that matter. I don't think I ever heard their last names, so I had no clue.

Besides, those kinds of labels don't matter. I figured out early that everyone was a person just like me. Some I liked. Some I didn't. And the color of their skin or their accents or anything else like that had nothing to do with it.

Staying at Aunt Netta's was one of the highlights of my childhood. I loved exploring the grounds and the buildings, spending time with Mom, playing with Arthur, cooking with Bertie, and swimming. But even though I enjoyed the pool, I didn't change my mind about the ocean. I had no intention of going back in there again.

MITZI AND I TOOK A LONG RUN AND IT FELT GREAT. AFTER ABOUT twenty minutes, we turned to head back. I slowed for the return trip since I didn't want to wear the little Shih Tzu out the first day.

Along the way, I was fascinated by all the sea birds, as they congregated on the sand and flew overhead. I recognized the gulls and pelicans, and there were other smaller ones, too.

The ocean was a gorgeous shade of dark blue at the horizon, but changed into a mosaic of color as the waves rose, and then turned into white foam as they reached the shore. Running was easier on the wet sand, and occasionally a wave would lap at our toes.

We saw several people out on their decks and walking on the beach. They waved, and I waved back.

At least the neighbors are friendly.

When we slowed our pace and neared my cottage, the last place on the point before the cove ended in a cliff, we passed the house two doors down. I noticed a girl on the deck. She was tall and had glorious red hair, which looked like golden flames whipped by the sea breeze. In her turquoise bikini, she could have been a model.

As we got closer, she was joined by an amazing-looking guy. He was the absolute image of my lifeguard hero-of-the sea from so long ago. The afternoon sun made his bronzed skin and wavy blond hair glow. He wore a red Speedo. I could barely breathe.

They both waved, I guess, but I could only stare at him. Somehow I had enough wits about me to wave back.

Later, I found myself standing in my kitchen with no memory of entering the house or removing Mitzi's leash.

Enough daydreaming about Mr. Gorgeous.

"Want some dinner?" I asked the dog.

"As a matter of fact," I heard the by-now too familiar baritone, "I no longer require nourishment. Although, the memory of dining in the company of a charming lady is a most pleasant one."

"I told you, don't do that!" I watched where Mitzi was looking and assumed that Max was in the doorway. "Don't sneak up on me!"

"I did no such thing," he replied indignantly.

I tried to ignore him as I dumped one of Mitzi's carefully-prepared meals into a pan and turned on the burner. It didn't light.

"What's the matter with this thing?" I asked.

"It requires the use of a match, of course," Max replied. Once again it sounded as though he thought I was an idiot.

"You mean it doesn't light by itself?" I was used to Mom's electric stove with the smooth cook top. This was something else altogether.

Max laughed. "Ridiculous."

"Well, all the modern ones do," I grumbled.

"You will find the kitchen matches in that holder on the wall,"

I looked up to see a strange metal box painted with daisies. "I thought this was just a decoration."

"Au contraire, it is quite functional."

I noticed the rounded open section on the bottom, reached in, and pulled out a big wooden match. "So how do I light this thing?"

Max harrumphed. "Absurd," he mumbled.

Yep, he thinks I'm retarded.

"Turn on the gas, then strike the match, and hold it near the outlets."

I did as he said, but when I lit the match, I must have held it too close or turned the gas up too high or something because I saw a flash, and flames whooshed up at me.

"Whoa!" I said, jumping back. I checked to be sure my eyebrows were still there. They were. And I was glad I'd pulled my hair into the pony tail.

"Is anything amiss?" Max asked, his voice oozing false concern. Then he chuckled.

"Glad I amused you," I said as I adjusted the flame and put the pot on the burner to warm. "At least the stove works."

"Of course it does. Everything is always in proper working order."

"I suppose you were a great handyman as well as a writer."

"Nothing of the kind," he harrumphed. "That sort of manual labor was well beneath me. However, my sweet Nanette saw to it that my existence was comfortable. For my art, you know."

"Uh, yeah," I said as I unwrapped one of Mitzi's bowls and set the chrome stand on the tile floor. I glanced at the stamp on the bottom and recognized the name.

Expensive.

I don't care about it myself, but Mom loves dinnerware. She dragged me into the china department whenever we went shopping. This was one of the brands she'd always coveted but said she couldn't afford.

Maybe Dad'll get her some. I'll suggest it next time I talk to him if Mom hasn't already.

After giving Mitzi her water, I tested the warm dog food, just like the manual said. Then I poured it into her other dish and placed it in its holder next to the water bowl. Mitzi gobbled it up.

"I guess the exercise gave you an appetite," I said as I rinsed the pot.

"Have you completed your domestic chores?" Max sounded testy.

"Do you mind if I make myself something to eat?" I really didn't care if he did mind, but smelling the dog's food reminded me I hadn't eaten since early morning and it was now after five o'clock in the afternoon.

I located the bread, peanut butter, and jelly and began making a sandwich. Then I poured myself a glass of milk.

"How can you ingest such a revolting combination?" he asked.

I guess he never learned the joys of PB and J.

I ignored him and took a big bite.

Max harrumphed. "Well, don't take all night. We have work to do."

"You're right," I answered. "I still have a couple more boxes to unpack."

"Rubbish! You need to begin typing my manuscript."

"Not tonight, Max, old pal. I'm tired and want to go to bed early. Dad got me up at six this morning."

"The sooner you complete the manuscript, the sooner I can move on to whatever plane I'm meant to inhabit."

Maybe he had a point. But I had to start my job hunt and figured he needed to know who was in charge right from the beginning.

"Maxie, *if* I agree to your harebrained scheme in order to keep you from making my life miserable, and I'm not saying I will, I'll call the shots. Understood?"

"And just why should I concede to your wishes?"

"Because you need me more than I need you." I didn't realize it until I'd said it, but I was right.

"What makes you believe this to be true?"

"You said yourself that I'm the only one who can hear you. I could get rid of your unreadable yellow pads, and no one would be the wiser."

I was greeted by blessed silence for a moment.

I finished my sandwich and put the plate in the sink. Then I refilled Mitzi's water again and washed her dish and mine.

"Very well," Max said behind me. "What are your terms?"

"I have to job hunt, so I couldn't spend more than about an hour a day, tops, working on your little story."

"My what? This is my masterpiece, my *magnum opus*. It is my finest work. It deserves more of your precious time."

"Nevertheless, you might get an hour, if I can spare it. That's all. Take it or leave it."

No one else can hear him, and I'm the only one who knows about the tablets stashed in the bottom drawer. I figure I hold most of the cards.

"Well... I..." He didn't sound happy, but I think he knew I had him. "Very well. But you must telephone my publisher immediately."

I headed back to the living room. I thought he'd been standing in the doorway, and I tried not to think about walking through him. But I was going to live in the house—*my* house—and he'd have to adapt.

"Max, it's Saturday. Your publisher won't be in his office until Monday morning."

"I don't recall mentioning an office." His voice seemed to come from the chair near the fireplace. Since Mitzi had plopped down next to it, I figured that's where he was. "John Peterson and I are more than publisher and author. We are friends. Bosom buddies. He'll want to be informed about this."

"Oh, yeah? And just what do I say? 'Excuse me, Mr. Peterson, but I was just having a chat with your pal Max, and he asked me to let you know he has a new book.—Well, no, it's not exactly finished, but I'm helping him get it done.' Ya think? He'll hang up on me. At least he will if he has a brain in his head."

"Of course, you can't approach him in that manner. But it is imperative that John be made aware of my final work's existence. His private number is in the center drawer of my desk."

"Are you totally nuts? Even if I agreed with your scheme, which I don't, do you have any idea what a call to New York costs? I'm broke, at least until I can get hold of the lawyer on Monday. So unless you have a pile of cash stashed around here somewhere, I have no intention of making a fool of myself, especially on my dime."

I walked to the desk, trying to decide if I was ready to set up my computer. I decided against it for the moment. A bunch of Max's clutter covered the top, including a humungous metal typewriter, and I wasn't ready to start World War III over changing it, yet.

"As a matter of fact, there is a bit of currency in the house," he said quietly.

I whirled around as if I were facing him, even though I couldn't see him. "What?"

He sighed. "I have a small amount of cash hidden in the kitchen for just such emergencies."

"Why didn't anyone find it in all these years?" This made no sense at all. *It looks like the furniture's never been moved, but surely someone would have found something.*

"My hiding places were exquisitely selected and concealed." He was back to sounding pompous again.

"Well, tell me where to look," I said, starting for the kitchen.

"Only if you agree to telephone my publisher."

I whirled back to where he still seemed to be. "Okay, okay. Now where is it?"

"On the top shelf in the cabinet over the refrigerator, you will find a rather charming ceramic container in the shape of a strawberry."

I pulled a chair over to reach the cupboard and climbed up. "This better not be a joke, Max," I warned him.

"I do not often indulge in humor," was his reply.

"I believe that," I muttered under my breath.

I opened the cupboard, moved a couple of plastic containers, and located the strawberry.

"This looks like it should hold jam," I said as I lifted it down.

"I believe that was its original purpose. A gift from a fan."

"Great," I said. I pulled on the top, but it didn't come off. "Max, this is stuck."

"Of course it is, my dear. I didn't want to risk having someone accidentally discover its secret."

"Well, how do I get it open?"

"I believe if you take the blade of a sharp knife and insert it beneath the lid, you should be able to weaken the glue."

"Are you telling me you glued the lid on?"

"Indeed."

Great. Thirty-year-old glue. This should be fun.

I got out a paring knife and started working it under the cover. It didn't budge. "Max, how attached are you to this thing?" I asked.

"Not particularly..." he began.

That's all I needed to hear. I threw the red berry to the floor. It landed near the sink where it shattered. Mitzi, who'd been standing in the doorway next to her 'friend' ran into the other room.

"Sorry, girl," I called after her. "Stay there." I hadn't thought about the death-of-the-dog clause in the will before I smashed the jar. I hadn't thought of my own bare feet, either. I'd left my flip-flops outside the back door before our run.

"Idiot," I said under my breath.

"Precisely," Max commented.

Then, among the shards of pottery, I spotted a roll of bills.

"Hey, Max, have any more strawberries stashed around here?"

Now this might be okay.

Five

"MITZI, STAY!"

The little dog had returned and planted her bottom in the doorway leading to the living room. She tilted her head as if to say, "Okay, but why?"

"Must you shriek at that poor animal?" Max asked.

"I don't want her to get cut," I answered. Then I contemplated my own situation.

I still sat on the chair where I'd been at the time of 'the shattered strawberry incident.' Pottery shards littered the floor. I was thankful that my feet had been on the rungs.

"Perhaps you should have considered the potential damage to your pet and your person before you performed that ridiculous stunt."

"Yeah, well I didn't."

"So, what is your proposed solution? If I were the hero of one of my novels, I would gallantly carry you from your perch. However, my physical resources are currently severely limited."

I watched the fur ruffle on Mitzi's head as she looked lovingly above her.

"Thanks for the thought, Max, and thanks for keeping Mitzi busy." I figured if I acknowledged him, he might stay in a good mood. But I wasn't counting on it.

"I've never cared for domesticated animals, but this one appears to be exceptionally well-behaved."

"Right now my entire future rests on that little dog, and it helps that she's pretty easy to handle."

As I spoke, I was trying to figure out how to make my escape. I hoped my thongs were still on the porch. But how could I get there?

I couldn't walk across the floor, even if I was really careful. It was old-fashioned, made of little pieces of black and white tile. Some of the smaller pottery shards sat sharp-edge-up in the spaces between. Then I spotted an escape route.

I stood up and moved as close to the side of the seat as I could, wishing I'd put it closer to the countertop. Then I held onto the top of the refrigerator and stretched one leg out as far as possible. My toe touched the cool tile surface.

"Precisely what are you intending to accomplish with these acrobatics?" Max asked.

"I'm going to walk across the counter to that end." I pointed at the doorway leading into the small service porch. "It looks like the cabinet stopped the pieces from leaving this room. When I get there, I should be able to jump across to the floor, open the door, and get my shoes."

"Very observant," he said. It sounded like he'd moved into the kitchen.

I glanced at Mitzi. She remained motionless where she'd been, staring at the spot where the voice originated.

"Good girl," I repeated. "Just stay a little longer."

The dog tilted her head and lifted her ears, but didn't move.

I grabbed the top of the refrigerator with both hands and pushed off, which allowed more of my foot to contact the countertop, at least as far as the instep. I shifted some of my weight to that foot, gave one last shove, and found myself teetering with both feet on the edge of the tile countertop. I wind-milled my arms for balance and managed to remain upright. Then I took a step.

"See, that wasn't too bad."

I walked down the counter and stepped over the sink.

Piece of cake. So far, so good.

Now all I had to do was jump diagonally into the other room. I took a deep breath and leapt.

I came down pretty hard, lost my balance and rolled toward the door, figuring it was safer than into the kitchen. I'd be bruised in the morning. But I wouldn't be cut.

"You'd not receive high marks for that landing." Max sounded close to me.

"I wasn't going for style points," I replied, pretending that I'd planned it that way. I opened the door, reached for my flip-flops, and put them on. "There," I said and closed the door.

"I believe you will find a serviceable broom, dust pan, and other cleaning implements in that tall cupboard."

Everything in the closet was covered with a thick layer of grime, and spiders had apparently enjoyed a few parties in there. Cobwebs clung to everything. I had visions of "Little Miss Muffet." I hated that nursery rhyme.

"Eeew. I hate spiders. I don't even like Halloween because of the bats and fake webs. And these are real."

"Well, my dear, arachnids exist in your world, so buck up. Conquer your fears. Stiff upper lip. Be brave."

"Knock it off, Max."

I took a deep breath, held it, reached in, and grabbed the broom handle with two fingers. It came out dripping with stringy white stuff. So did the dust pan. I'd stirred up a cloud of dust and started to sneeze.

Holding the tools away from me, I crunched into the kitchen over some of the broken strawberry. The dustpan went into the sink with the water running while I took the wet dishrag and wiped down the broom.

Once the janitorial equipment was clean—at least clean enough—I swept up most of the debris and poured it into the trash can. Then I reached toward the money.

"Dear girl, I would recommend you use a damp cloth or towel to wipe the floor in order to be certain no dangerous slivers remain." Max was being obnoxiously 'helpful' as usual. But I looked at Mitzi and realized he had a point.

"Okay." I was anxious to get to the wad of bills, but I grabbed a paper towel, wet it and did as he'd instructed.

I was surprised to see quite a few sharp little red pieces when I turned the towel over.

I decided to wipe the bundle of money, too, just to be safe.

"Satisfied?"

"Hardly. But at least you have done no permanent damage to your body. You'd be unable to complete your assignment if you are injured. You must remain in good health."

"Thanks for your concern. I'll mop later, but right now I want to get to this. How much is in here?" I asked as the rubber band that held the wad of bills disintegrated in my hand.

"I'm not entirely certain. I retained it as an emergency household fund, set aside in the event some small matter arose."

I began to unroll the greenbacks. They all looked like the old ones I got occasionally in change. "Just how long ago did you put these in there?"

"Sometime in the late 1960s, I would surmise."

The bills had probably been crisp when they were rolled. Lots of them. Many were ones, but not all. I began counting.

"... four hundred and eight, four hundred and nine. Max, there's four hundred and nine dollars here."

"I believe you counted correctly. I presume that will be adequate to pay for the telephone call."

"What call?"

"You agreed to phone my publisher. If you fail to honor our agreement, I shall be forced to take extreme measures."

"Okay, okay, don't get excited. This should cover it." *It would probably pay the whole phone bill and a few others for a while.*

"As I recall, there is a public telephone at the small shop some four blocks or so along the highway. The nice young gentleman behind the counter was always quite gracious about exchanging currency for coins."

Max sounded like he'd moved back toward the living room. The dog followed her 'friend,' and I heard the chair by the fireplace squeak.

I joined them and looked around.

"Don't you have one here?" Come to think of it, I hadn't seen a phone, even an old-fashioned one, anywhere in the house.

"I never felt the need."

"Then how did you get hold of your publisher, your friends, Aunt Netta?"

"I made use of the instrument down the highway, just as I informed you. It was very convenient."

I wasn't sure there were actually any pay phones left, and I didn't intend to find out. But I wasn't going to start another argument. "So how did other people reach you?"

"Anyone who wished to contact me was welcome to enjoy a nice excursion to this glorious sliver of paradise or make use of the United States Post Office. Your aunt provided John and a few others her telephone number. She often relayed their messages when she arrived for a visit."

I shook my head. *This guy's so out of touch.*

"Besides," he continued, "I felt it would compromise my sense of well-being to have one of those devices invading my small private island of serenity here."

"Well, I don't need to go anywhere else to make the call," I replied.

"And why not, pray tell?"

I ignored him.

"Come on, Mitzi."

The dog's fur ruffled and she stayed with her 'buddy.'

"Suit yourself," I said over my shoulder to the little deserter as I headed for the bedroom. My cell phone sat on the bed where I'd left it when I got ready for my run on the beach. I picked it up and went back to the living room, opened the desk drawer, and located the publisher's business card. A number was neatly printed on the back.

"Obviously you didn't write this," I said.

I heard a harrumph. I ignored that as well. Then I turned on my phone.

"What do you intend to do with that?"

"Call this number as soon as we figure out what I'm going to tell him."

"That insubstantial toy will reach New York?" He laughed heartily. "Where are the wires?"

"Times have changed, Max, old pal. We don't need wires."

He harrumphed again.

I was starting to realize he did it whenever he was annoyed or confused.

"Then please enlighten me as to how you will be able to make a connection." Then he mumbled, "That is the most ridiculous device."

The chair by the fireplace scraped. I assumed I'd gotten his interest if not his confidence.

"It works better than those clunky old things you used."

I looked around the room and noticed something else was missing.

"Hey, where's your TV?" I asked as I flopped down on the loveseat. I couldn't imagine being without one.

"I had no need to be entertained by one of those absurd machines. I created fantasies in my imagination and recorded them on those tablets you scoffed at."

Bummer. But I'll deal with that later.

"Well, you'd better come up with a script in a hurry if you want me to talk to your publisher. I have no idea what to say to him. Besides, is he still alive? He's got to be really old by now."

"John Peterson was considerably younger than I. His father, James, was my first American publisher after I arrived on these shores. I entered into a contract with him in nineteen-thirty-nine. At that time, he must have been in his thirties, approximately ten years my junior. He married subsequent to our meeting. His wife gave birth to a daughter and then to a son sometime later. Just before I expired, John assumed responsibility for my work. The young man must be... let me see. What year is this?"

"Two-thousand ten."

"My. Has that much time passed? I had no idea. Well, John must now be in his fifties. Still a young man."

"Let's hope he's not smart enough to hang up on me when I call," I muttered. I held my phone in one hand and the card in the other. "You still haven't told me what to say. I'm waiting."

"Oh, rot. Just tell him you are currently residing in my abode and discovered that I had written one more volume—my final masterpiece."

"Okay, okay. I'll say I found your dumb scribbling and ask him what I should do with it. He'll probably say, 'Make yourself a nice fire.' And I'll answer, 'Thanks a lot. It gets chilly at the beach.' He'll think I'm a total nut case, but what the heck..."

"Just connect with John and I will guide you."

I'd promised, and I always keep my promises, although I wasn't sure how binding they'd be to my invisible 'guest.' I pushed number one for long distance. "Wait a minute. What's the area code?"

"The what?"

"Each city has an area code. Some have more than one. What's his?"

"I am sure I have no idea."

I dialed long distance information and found out there were several for New York City. I wrote them down.

"Max, did he live right in the city?"

"Certainly. He was proud that he could walk to his office from his home."

I looked at the numbers I'd written. "Well, 718 looks like it might be a good one." In truth, it was a random choice. But I punched it in along with the number on the card. I figured I'd have to try them all, and I still didn't expect to be able to get to the publisher. At least I hoped not. Then I'd be off the hook.

I was amazed when a male voice answered, "Hello."

I prayed that the family had moved away and I'd gotten hold of someone else. "Uh, yes. I'm trying to reach John Peterson, the publisher."

"How did you get this number?" He didn't sound too friendly.

"Well, you see, I just moved into the cottage where Max Murdoch used to live. You know, Maxine du Bois? I found your card in his desk. And, uh, I discovered some yellow tablets, too. They look like the beginning of a book and he... I wondered if you were interested in them." *Max, you owe me for this embarrassment!*

"You say you discovered some of Max's writing? Maybe it's a draft of one of his published works."

"Oh, no." I knew I had to lie, and I hate lying. Besides, I'm lousy at it. "See, I read the beginning and I didn't recognize any of it. I know his books pretty well." I not only had my fingers crossed, but also my toes. *God will surely get me for this!*

I heard Max chuckle. I shot a dirty look toward where I thought he was and stuck my tongue out.

"Interesting," Mr. Peterson—at least I assumed it was Mr. Peterson—said. "Never cared much for his stuff myself, but he was Dad's friend. I kept putting out his books even though public tastes were changing. Still, he usually made back his advances. Sometimes a bit more."

There was a long silence. I didn't want to push, but I was hoping he'd just say, "No," and get it over with.

He finally spoke. "I've turned over most of the business, including acquisitions, to my son, Steven. I only manage long-time clients and our top sellers these days. Steven is there in California near you. At least, I assume that's where you are since you're living in Max's house."

I bit my tongue to keep from correcting him. It was *my* house and had belonged to Aunt Netta when Max lived here. Instead, I said, "Yes. I'm in Orange County."

I heard rustling on the other end of the line, then, "Give me your name and number. I'll have Steven contact you. He can decide if he's interested."

I had the feeling Dad was passing the buck and would let Junior be the hatchet man. But it was better than laughing at me or hanging up. I settled for that.

I gave him my contact information. "Thank you very much, Mr. Peterson."

"You're welcome." And he hung up.

"Well, you weren't very enthusiastic."

"Listen, buddy, you're lucky he didn't slam the phone down or worse. He'll have his son call me. But don't hold your breath. Oops, I forgot. You can't do that. You can't breathe." I laughed at my own joke.

He didn't. "John should have been overjoyed at the thought of one last work from my pen," he grumbled.

"I hate to break it to you, but he said your books barely broke even. He didn't even like them and just published them because you were his father's friend. And I'm going to rot in hell for the lies I just told. So I suggest you back off."

He was uncharacteristically silent.

"Come on, Mitzi. Let's get the last of our stuff put away."

To my great surprise, the little mutt followed me into the bedroom.

So there, Maximilian Murdoch or Maxine du Bois or whoever the heck you are!

THE RED NUMBERS ON MY CLOCK READ '2:00.' I LOOKED AROUND for the source of the noise that had awakened me. It wasn't Mitzi. She was sleeping soundly at the foot of the bed.

Okay, I was going to make her sleep on her fancy pillow on the floor, but she must have sneaked up after I fell asleep.

I heard the noise again—that same weird ghost imitation he'd threatened me with earlier in the day. Correction—the day before, since it was now early the next morning.

"Knock it off, Max!" I felt Mitzi stir. Then she padded up and licked my hand. I petted her.

"Would you prefer that I sing? I know several wonderful operatic works."

"Just shut up and let me sleep. I'm tired."

Mitzi settled down right next to me and closed her eyes again.

"But you haven't begun the work on my manuscript."

"I called your darn publisher. Wasn't that enough?"

"You agreed to spend one hour each day typing. It is inadequate, to be sure, but you failed to do even that paltry amount."

"I said *if* I agreed to do it. I didn't say I would. And I also said you'd get no more than one hour a day, maximum, *if* I had time. That's not the same as agreeing."

"And I recall a commitment on my part to experiment with my skills at waking you during the night if you did not. I, at least, fulfill my promises. *Whooo.*"

"That's not funny, Max."

"Your shirking your responsibilities is not amusing to me, either."

"Listen, you, I am a responsible person. I take care of this animal I didn't ask for, don't I?"

"The creature seems to be rather well-behaved and nicely groomed. For how long have you been her caretaker?"

"Well, only two days. But so far, she's doing okay."

"Except for the pottery you shattered in the kitchen..."

"Hey, I made sure she stayed out."

"She was not your priority when you indulged in your childish behavior, was she?"

"That's not the point. I'm entirely too tired to spend all night arguing with a ghost."

"I believe I told you I prefer *specter*. However, *ethereal being* or *apparition* would be acceptable."

"Whatever. Go away like a good boy. We can discuss this in the morning." I punched my pillow.

"I'm terribly sorry, but until you agree to my plan, I am unable to comply with your wishes." Then he tried an evil cackle.

"I told you, Max, those dumb old sounds don't scare me."

"But they do not allow you to slumber either."

He had a point, but I couldn't let him win.

Note to self: Get earplugs.

I buried my head beneath my pillow, but he just got louder.

Mitzi didn't stir.

Then he began singing. It was off-key and noisy. It sounded like opera. I hate opera.

After about an hour, I gave up and went to the closet.

"What on earth are you doing?"

"None of your business. You're just a ghost and I don't have to explain anything to you."

For once, there was no answer.

I located my college sweats and threw them on over the t-shirt and panties I'd worn to bed. Then I took a spare blanket from the shelf, grabbed my pillow and called to Mitzi. "Come on, girl. We're leaving."

"And just where do you plan to go?"

"Anywhere that's not here," I replied. I hadn't thought it through. But Max had indicated he couldn't leave the house. I hoped he was right.

Most of the places on the crescent of beach along Seashell Cove had been remodeled and enlarged or rebuilt during the last fifty years or so. Not mine. That was part of its charm. But it was small and had no deck, just a small covered porch.

I hooked Mitzi's leash and led her out the door. I heard a window rattle as I left.

"Oh, no you don't, Maxie. I'm getting far enough away that I can't hear you," I said under my breath, although I hoped he hadn't heard me.

The sound dimmed a little as I moved away from the cottage.

I was exhausted. I laid the blanket on the sand, still slightly warm from the day before, put my pillow on it, and lay down. Then I pulled the loose edge over me and patted a spot next to me. Mitzi curled up and was asleep long before I was.

I could still hear a window or door rattle once in a while, but I wasn't about to let Max know. I assumed Mitzi couldn't hear him at all.

Finally, just before dawn, I fell asleep.

I'd barely gotten any rest before the sound of voices reached my ears. Folks were starting to stir and a couple of surfers were headed for the breakers.

I yawned. "Okay, dog, let's go back in."

Mitzi made a stop on the way.

"Sleep well?" came a familiar voice as I entered the back door.

"Oh, yeah," I answered. "Best rest I've had in ages."

Okay, that was a lie. For more than a month before, I'd slept on my parents' sofa.

When I moved out of my old apartment, I naturally went home. I hadn't expected to be with my folks for long. Just until I found a new job and another place to live. But I didn't know the job hunt would be so difficult. And when my car died a week later, leaving me without reliable transportation, I had even fewer options. Unlike the rest of the country, or the world, for that matter, it's nearly impossible to get anywhere in Southern California without a car. So I extended my stay.

When I'd left for college, they'd turned my bedroom into Dad's den, complete with leather recliner and big-screen TV. He wasn't giving it up, so I was left with the couch in the living room.

Not the coziest, since it was Victorian style with a lot of wood trim.

Now I had a real bed. It may have been a little lumpy and old, but at least it had a mattress I could stretch out on. The only drawback was my resident ghost, who made it impossible to sleep there. I wondered what God or whoever was doing to me. I'd tried to live a good life. What had I done to deserve all this bad luck?

I heated up Mitzi's breakfast and made myself a cup of instant coffee. I had to boil the water on the stove since there was no alternative. I hate instant coffee and I loathed having to use the stove.

Note to self: Buy a cheap coffeemaker and microwave! The TV will have to wait until I get another job.

Of course, there was still the problem of not having a car. It was seven o'clock, still too early to call the lawyer.

I jumped into the shower and got dressed. Then I surveyed the living room. I still had to hook up my computer. Thank God, I had wireless Internet service with the same carrier as my phone.

"First thing, this has to go," I said as I picked up the huge, heavy typewriter, which dominated the landscape of the desk.

"Just what do you think you are doing with that fine piece of office equipment?" Max shouted.

I figured he'd probably give me a hard time about it, but I was too tired to care.

"Taking it to the garage," I answered.

"I'll have you know, that is the ultimate machine available. It is an IBM Selectric II Correctable, and it is practically new. There is no earthly reason to remove it. Besides, how do you intend to type my manuscript?"

I kept right on walking and his voice followed me to the door into the garage.

"Watch and learn, Max. Watch and learn."

He harrumphed just as the garage door slammed closed behind me.

I had no idea what I'd do with the hulking machine, so I set it down carefully. The thing was heavy.

Maybe some charity organization wants it. Or maybe not...

Then I recovered my laptop case and returned to the house.

"Are we planning a trip?" Max asked.

"Nope," I answered. "I'm planning to update my résumé and do some job hunting."

"And how, pray tell, do you intend to accomplish those objectives? I see no newspapers in evidence with the latest classified ads."

"No one uses those anymore," I replied as I removed the laptop and cords.

"Then how is it possible to become informed as to what career opportunities are available?" It sounded as though he was breathing down my neck, that is, if he could breathe.

"Online," I answered as I crawled under the desk to plug in the power cord.

"On what line?" he asked. I could have sworn that he was down there with me.

"The Internet," I replied impatiently.

"What is an Internet?"

I sighed. "It's the vehicle for twenty-first century communications. Just be quiet and I'll show you."

He actually shut up. I wasn't going to question why.

I powered up the computer, amazed that the screen actually came up. The way things were going, anything could have happened without my being surprised.

"Now watch," I said as I clicked the browser icon.

"What does that do?" He sounded like he was next to my right ear.

"It accesses the Internet. Through this browser, I can get to millions of sites around the world."

"And why would one wish to do so?"

"Max, I can find out anything about anybody just by using the browser."

"How is that possible?"

"I'll show you."

I typed in: *"Max Murdoch"* and hit *Enter*.

Pages of listings came up.

"What on earth?"

"Don't worry, Max. These aren't all about you, but I can narrow the search down."

I added: *writer* and *"Maxine du Bois"* to the string.

Suddenly, there he was. And there were lots of sites.

"These are all about you," I said.

"What information do they contain?" I could have sworn he was sitting on my shoulder.

"Well, here's a list of all your books. And here's a biography." I clicked the link. "See, it says you were born in April of 1902, and your death date is listed as August twenty-second 1977. It also says you died of a heart attack and a friend discovered your body."

I scrolled down and read some more.

"Wow. It says you died without leaving a will and that you had no living relatives. They never discovered what happened to all your wealth, although you made a fortune during your lifetime. You had no bank accounts or stocks or bonds. Guess they didn't find the strawberry." I laughed.

"I never trusted financial institutions after my parents' savings were lost in the great worldwide financial collapse," he said, ignoring my reference to his stash of cash.

"I wish I'd learned that lesson," I muttered.

"Do you mean to say you are invested in stocks and bonds and savings accounts?" He sounded horrified.

"No," I grumbled. "I worked for a bank that failed. I lost my job and most of my retirement savings. I bought bank stock. Stupid mistake."

"Indeed!"

"So, Max, if you didn't put your money in stocks or bonds or savings, what happened to it?"

He was silent for a moment. "Perhaps I shall reveal that information in time. Or perhaps not."

Now I was really curious. "You mean you still had some money left when you died?"

"I was frugal, my dear, not like so many others. I lived simply and my wants were few. I existed for my art."

Okay, this is one mystery I intend to solve. But I'd better not push him right now. I won't forget either!

"You didn't have any living relatives?"

"None at all. My parents passed away prior to my arrival in this country. As I told you, they succumbed to an unfortunate influenza epidemic. I was in London at the time meeting with my publisher, so I avoided it. They had no living relatives of whom I was aware. Both were only children, as was I."

"Sounds like my family," I said. I kind of felt sorry for him for a moment. I know how lonely it can be without siblings or cousins.

Max didn't reply.

* * * *

Nanette Louise Burton

1 Seashell Cove

That's as far as I'd gotten on my updated resume when my phone rang. I'd already checked Monster, Career Builder, CalJOBS, and the other sites the unemployment people had recommended and had come up pretty empty. Either the listed jobs required experience I didn't have, or they were too far away, like more than a couple of blocks.

I have to get a car.

My heart hadn't been in writing the darn resume, so I'd kept putting it off.

I'd only had one job since college, and I'd lost it through no fault of my own. The resume I'd written to get that first one wouldn't do now. But I didn't know how to present my skills so an employer would be interested.

I picked up my phone when it rang and saw that the time was ten thirty-five. "Well, that was a pretty wasted morning," I mumbled as I answered.

"Ms. Burton, this is Steven Peterson. My father said you thought you'd discovered an unknown manuscript by Maxine du Bois, or Max Murdoch. He asked me to phone you."

The guy sounded young and had a sexy voice.

"Yes, Mr. Peterson. There are a bunch of yellow tablets covered with nearly indecipherable scrawl."

"I was going to suggest you send me the first chapter."

"I'd have to convert it into an electronic document file to do that since I don't have a scanner." *Please say, "Don't bother."*

"How long before you could do that?"

"It depends. It might take a while to make out the words." I hoped he'd be discouraged.

"Tell him you will complete the work soon," Max said in a loud voice.

"*Shhh,*" I said, covering the mike on the phone.

"What was that?" Steven asked.

"Uh, I was just telling my dog to be quiet," I lied. Actually, Mitzi had been dozing at my feet. At least *she* was making up for no sleep the night before!

"Where exactly are you?" the sexy voice asked.

I gave him my address. "Max used to live here," I explained.

"I just happen to have an appointment in that area tomorrow morning. Another of our authors lives in Laguna, and I am always anxious to drive down. I love the area. Would it be okay if I drop by afterward, say around eleven o'clock?"

"I guess so," I answered.

"I'd like to see what you've found. I can imagine the marketing angle already. Maybe it would boost interest in all the old Maxine du Bois books. I could take you to lunch afterward so we can discuss it, if you'd like." The last sounded like an afterthought.

Would I like? Lunch I don't have to pay for? You bet! "That would be great," I said in my most professional-sounding voice.

"Fine. I'll see you tomorrow."

I heard the dial tone.

"Did you discourage him? Why weren't you more forceful, more complimentary? Why didn't you say it was a masterpiece?" Max sounded impatient and sort of mad.

"Hold your horses, pal. He's coming here tomorrow morning because he wants to take a look at your scribbling. So back off!"

"Very well." Then he harrumphed as usual, and I heard the chair by the fireplace creak. Mitzi got up and settled herself in front of Max, at least where I thought he was.

"That's right. Don't say, 'Thank you.' I got your publisher to come to see your stupid writing, but, of course, I didn't do enough. Geez."

There was no response from the other side of the room, and I started to wonder what the next day would bring and to imagine what Steven Peterson was like.

OBJECTIVE: TO USE MY PROGRAMMING SKILLS TO...

Now what?

I still couldn't get a handle on how to write a résumé that would grab a potential employer. All the job listings I found required very specific skills, usually with at least three to five years of experience. And none of them were in the banking industry, the only kind of business in which I'd worked.

After college graduation, I took a job with a small, local savings and loan, the same one my folks had used for as long as I could remember. It seemed safe and conservative, if a little stodgy and old-fashioned. The pay wasn't great, but they were the only ones who offered me a position.

The Information Technology Department was in the headquarters building near my folks' house. I found an apartment I could afford within a twenty-minute drive. In south Orange County, California, that's really close.

We only serviced ten branches, all of them local.

The company was using an out-of-date proprietary computer system (otherwise known as 'home-grown software'), so that's probably why they were willing to take me. Anyone they hired would've had to learn it.

When I started, my boss told me they were going to upgrade to the industry-standard system in the near future and that I would help them make the transition. Along with the switch, I could expect a healthy raise.

Of course, banking started having problems before any of that could happen. For over a year, we knew the company was in trouble, but our management kept telling us we'd make it through. They said it until the day the FDIC arrived to lock the doors.

One of the well-known banks took over, but since my expertise was on the old system, they didn't need me.

It was now three years since I'd used most of the skills I'd learned in school. And programmers from the financial industry with much more experience were readily available. What chance did I have?

I sighed, saved the document, such as it was, then leaned back and stretched.

"Ah, now that you have completed whatever it was that held you in such rapt attention, are you prepared to make the effort to transform my manuscript into a form suitable for presentation to my publisher?" Max asked next to my ear.

"Will you stop doing that?"

"Stop doing what? Speaking to you?"

"No, sneaking up on me."

"I have remained steadfastly by your side, like your faithful furry companion, throughout the morning."

"Well, I didn't know you were there."

"My humble apologies. I shall try to make witty observations from time to time in the future."

I ignored him and glanced at the clock on the computer. It was nearly noon and I still hadn't contacted Mr. Spencer, the attorney.

"I have a very important call to make."

"More important than experiencing a refreshing repose tonight?"

Max had a point, but getting the money I needed was more pressing. His four hundred nine dollars and my unemployment check wouldn't go far.

"After I take care of this, I'll *think* about starting on your project."

"Just be aware that I have absolutely no qualms about preventing your slumber for as long as is required to achieve my ends."

I watched Mitzi head across the room and settle next to the chair I'd come to think of as Max's. I was sure she could see him. She always seemed to know right where he was.

I didn't have the lawyer's number, so I looked it up in my browser, then dialed.

"Spencer and Stewart," a woman answered. I recognized the voice of his receptionist.

"This is Nan Burton. Is Mr. Spencer there?"

"I'm very sorry, but he's scheduled to be in court all day. I can have him call you when he returns."

"Okay," I said and gave her my number. I was disappointed, but what choice did I have?

"How is Ms. Burton's adorable little dog?"

I'd forgotten she'd taken care of Aunt Netta's 'baby' from the time of her death until I got her. "She's fine. Actually, that's why..."

Before I could say anything else, she broke in. "I'll be sure to let Mr. Spencer know that you phoned. Please excuse me. I have another call." With that, she hung up.

"Sheesh," I said as I stared at the phone.

"Now that you have completed your vitally important communication, will you commence typing?"

"Nope. I'm going to make myself lunch. I'm starving."

I got up and went into the kitchen, where I took out the peanut butter, jelly, and bread. I hadn't eaten breakfast, and the last meal I'd had was a late lunch the day before.

I slathered on the PB and J and poured a large glass of milk. The carton was only about a quarter full. *I definitely have to make a grocery run.*

Just to annoy Max, I sat at the table and took my time eating, chewing each bite well and sharing the corners of the bread with Mitzi. *I don't care what her manual says about not feeding her people food or midday snacks, she likes it. And this one time won't hurt. Besides, giving her treats may be the only way I can get her away from Max.*

After my meal, I carefully washed my plate and glass, dried them, and put them away.

"*Now* are you prepared to begin?" Max's voice came from the doorway. I was fairly certain he'd been there all along watching me.

"Don't think so. Come on, Mitzi, let's take a run."

I heard Max harrumph as I clipped the dog's leash on and headed out the door.

I've always enjoyed running. Mom used to say I had the long legs and lean build of a runner. I get those from Dad, but Mom is thin as well.

I ended up five-foot seven-inches tall, the same height as my mother. My parents thought I might be even taller. Dad's six-one, even though the few women on his side tended to be short. I'd have liked being taller, but I'm okay as I am.

That's another way Aunt Netta and I are different. I'll bet she never even made five feet. She was a little bird of a woman, flitting from one thing to another with lots of energy. Although she had the Olympic-size pool and tennis courts, I don't ever remember her using them. She didn't need to. Just living and breathing seemed to give her enough exercise.

In grammar school, I joined the track team and kept at it through high school and college. I even won a few races. But it wasn't about winning. I enjoyed being outside with the wind in my face, my legs pumping. Even though the sand made it harder, I must admit, I preferred the beach to the track. I don't like shoes. Any shoes. Here, I could go barefoot.

I slowed the pace a little on the way back, but Mitzi seemed willing to keep up with me.

As we neared the cottage, I spotted my hero on his deck. A red-striped surfboard leaned against the wooden stairs. The blond god toweled himself off. I figured he'd just gotten out of the water, and I was sorry I hadn't paid attention to the surfers when I started my run.

He waved, and I waved back, just as a dark-haired beauty stepped through the sliding door and wrapped herself around him. Like the girl the day before, this one was a knockout. And from the body language, they knew each other very well.

Okay, Nan. Give up your daydreams. The guy is a real stud, but he'd never notice you. Not with those other gorgeous examples of female perfection around.

I couldn't think of anything better to do when I got back, so I dragged the stack of yellow tablets out of the bottom drawer.

"Boy, Max, I'm glad you numbered these pages since I doubt I'd have known where to start."

"My long-time secretary, Helen, insisted I do so. It became a habit, and I am prone to observe ritual."

"Lucky for me," I said as I tried to read his handwriting. "How on earth did Helen manage to figure out what this says? It's like ancient hieroglyphics and I don't have the key."

I wasn't exaggerating. The letters were cramped and there was little to make one word stand out from another. "What's this first sentence?"

"I certainly don't recall."

"What do you mean, you don't remember? You wrote it, didn't you?"

"Of course I did. But once the words are on the paper, my mind races on to the next scene. I never return to previously-written text."

"But you had to edit the thing or proof it or something, didn't you? And you had to have read your books when they were published."

"Actually, once the burst of inspiration was spilled out onto the tablets, I never read another word. Instead, my fertile imagination began to work on the next tale."

"Max, you can't be serious. How did you know that everything was the way you wanted it?" I guess I'm more of a control freak than my resident house-ghost. At work, I'd never have let anything go into production without thoroughly going over it from every angle. I personally tested and retested every code change I made. If my name was on it, it had to be right.

"I delegated all the tedious editing chores to my typist after I discovered Helen's attention to detail surpassed even my own. Since my works continued to be enjoyed by the masses, the arrangement was apparently a success."

He had a point. It sounded as though they'd managed to find a good method of working together.

"How long was Helen with you?"

"She came to me directly as a graduate of a highly-regarded secretarial school around 1950. So, we worked together for well over twenty years."

Now I was really curious. "How old was she when she started working for you?"

"Let me think. She must have been about twenty."

"So she'd be close to eighty today. I wonder if she's still around. What was her last name?" *Maybe I can pawn this little job off on the old lady. It's worth a try.*

"I believe it was Zeblinsky."

"Was that her married name?"

"The woman was not married during her tenure in my employ."

"Where did she live?"

"You have wasted entirely too much time asking questions. In the meantime, you have exerted no effort in typing my manuscript. Your delaying tactics will only result in another fitful slumber. But the decision is yours and yours alone." In a second, I heard the Max chair squeak, and his 'pet' settled next to it.

"Okay, okay." I couldn't avoid it any longer.

I tried to follow the strokes to see if any of the letters were recognizable. About halfway down the page I found a single character that looked like the letter 'c'. It was repeated several more times. *That must be how he wrote the letter 'a.' Okay. One down.*

I spent the next two hours trying to decode the marks on the page. Using deductive logic, I figured out what some of the phrases probably were. It was grueling, but at last I had a couple of sentences that made grammatical sense.

Then I read what I'd typed into my document.

"Max, this stinks! If I read this as the first paragraph of a book, I'd throw it away. As a matter of fact, I probably wouldn't get beyond the first sentence."

"My dear girl." He sounded even more patronizing than before, and I didn't think that was possible. "You must have made a mistake. In addition, you already admitted you were not a connoisseur of women's fiction. So I would hardly give much credence to your opinion. Now, read aloud what you have typed."

I thought about telling him he sure was bossy, but figured it wouldn't make any difference to the jerk. So I began to read.

"Mrs. Mildred Murchison contemplated her kitchen. The once-yellow walls had darkened from several years of grease and smoke. Her range and refrigerator

suffered from the same ghastly neglect. She had not perceived, prior to Willard's untimely death, how horribly she had failed to maintain a proper house, especially when she prepared food there every day."

"That sounds quite acceptable. You might just do after all."

"When does this story take place?"

"It is a contemporary romance, of course."

"And how old is this woman?"

"I believe she would probably be about your age."

"Not a chance, Max, old pal. In the first place, absolutely no one my age would be called 'Mildred.' And if that was her real name, she'd have changed it as soon as she could or, at the very least, used a nickname. And no woman uses 'Mrs.' any more, they use 'Ms.' In the second place, no modern woman would take sole responsibility for how the kitchen looked. Where was good old Willard when the place got dirty? Third, I haven't heard that name for a guy, at least not in my lifetime and especially not for anyone I'd consider marrying. Then, there's the matter of her doing all the cooking and the names of the appliances and..."

"How dare you criticize my composition? You yourself informed me that you, '...didn't work in words.' I believe that was your precise verbiage. I, on the other hand, am a master with a phrase."

"Maxie, I'm trying to say you've been dead a long time. You're out of touch with today's world."

"I see no reason why I should compromise my literary standards for an uneducated and unsophisticated reading public. My reputation is well-established. I'm sure discerning readers continue to purchase my volumes. Perhaps you have seen ladies perusing them during your travels."

"Uh, I don't know quite how to break it to you, but most people, especially the ones my age, don't lug around books anymore."

"Then precisely how do these modern people you speak of receive the necessary information for daily life?"

"We watch TV or listen to the radio in the car. We read blogs and get updates as they happen on our phones. And, if we do read books, they're digital."

I thought his voice had been close as I was reading, but I heard a loud protest from the chair as he apparently dropped back into it.

"I believe I am fortunate to have perished before this insane age. It would have perplexed and outraged all my sensibilities."

"I'm sure it would."

He was silent.

I wondered if maybe he'd give up the idea of having me type up his dumb story. On the other hand, if he did give up, how the heck was I going to get rid of him?

Eight

OF COURSE, MAX DIDN'T FORGET HIS PLAN TO USE ME AS HIS PER-sonal slave. I spent another somewhat sleepless night. At least I went to bed early, and he waited until four o'clock to start his banging and singing. He'd figured out that his attempts at opera were much more annoying than his ghost imitations.

Since it was drizzling out, I stayed in bed and suffered until six. Then I got up and took Mitzi for a run. The rain had stopped, leaving only the usual 'June gloom.' That's pretty typical for the early summer months along the coast. The morning fog hangs around until about noon. Then the sun comes out and the temperature rises.

The little dog seemed to enjoy the exercise. She'd spent her life with Aunt Netta sitting or sleeping. Now she was out in the fresh air and acted much younger. I think Mr. Spencer's secretary said she was two or three, but running by my side, she behaved more like a puppy.

No sign of Mr. Gorgeous. I was kind of disappointed, but I figured he had to work sometime. I remembered to look for the surfers as soon as I hit the sand, but the fog obscured the waves. If anyone was out, I couldn't see them.

When we got back inside, I fixed Mitzi's breakfast. I'd have liked a bowl of cereal, but the milk situation worried me. I ended up with a couple of scrambled eggs, toast, and a cup of horrible instant coffee.

Thank goodness there's a toaster. But there has to be some way to get a coffee maker and microwave.

I could have asked Mom to take me shopping, but she was working. Dad, too. Besides, it was important to prove I could take care of myself, not just to them but to myself as well.

I showered and changed into a pair of shorts and a t-shirt. Then I decided to rearrange the bathroom. A lot of old stuff remained in the medicine chest and in the cabinet below the sink. I didn't like the clutter, and some of it kinda scared me. I was sure everything was out-of-date—way out-of-date!

Max had been quiet since I left for my run. I hoped he'd stay that way. He didn't.

"Now, what do you think you are doing? You have an obligation, young lady, and I intend to assure you fulfill it."

"Oh, Max, stuff a sock in it. Enough, already. I said one hour. Yesterday you got two." I continued emptying the medicine chest.

"Just because you made a small, preliminary effort does not mean you may choose to lollygag today."

I turned to the sound of his voice in the doorway. "Max, we need to talk. What I read yesterday is junk. It won't sell. No one today would read it. If the rest is that bad, I'm not going to do any more. It's nearly impossible to figure out your writing, and you're no help."

He huffed and puffed. I think he was speechless for once. Finally he said, "I am nothing if not flexible. I admit times seem to have changed in the world since my absence from it. However, the basic story of love has not."

"And how do you define the 'basic story of love'?"

"It's elementary, my dear. Boy meets girl. Boy loses girl. Girl gets herself into a threatening situation. Boy rescues her. Love blooms. And finally, happily ever after."

I laughed so hard I had to sit down on the toilet seat. "Max, today's woman doesn't need rescuing. She saves herself and sometimes the guy as well. Oh and she doesn't get herself into difficult spots she can't handle, either."

"What about marriage? A life partner, soul mate? Surely young ladies still long for that security." He sounded genuinely confused and not quite so sure of himself.

"Some do, but it's not at the top of many of our priority lists. We make our own livings, handle all our own problems, take care of ourselves. And if we get married, we do it later than when you were around and expect more from it."

"But what about children? Surely you need a husband for that."

"Not necessarily. Lots of women raise children without partners. And they have them after their careers are established and they're financially comfortable."

I could tell that threw him for a loop because he was quiet again, so I continued my organizing. Surprisingly, the medicine cabinet contained a bunch of outdated prescriptions. I wondered why the cleaning crew hadn't tossed them. I decided to trash everything.

"Assuming you are correct, and I seriously doubt you are, just how is parenthood accomplished without a husband?"

"Oh, there are lots of ways. Some women pick a good genetic specimen and have sex with him long enough to get pregnant. Or they can be artificially inseminated." I filled the sink and grabbed the sponge I'd put in the cabinet beneath it when I moved in.

"I am quite certain I do not wish to be told the details."

"You can go to a sperm bank and pick the donor, then have the sperm used to make you pregnant."

"That is outrageous! What about the ethical and moral issues? Ridiculous! And what about a father figure in the child's life? Or is that passé as well?"

I finished washing out the cabinets, even though I knew they were already supposed to be clean, then quickly refilled them with my own stuff.

I'll have to paint over the pink walls. I wonder how Max lived with them. But then again, would he even have noticed?

I made the bed, taking note that the worn flowered quilt had to go.

"Well?"

I sighed and sat down. "Women who choose to raise children alone make every effort to expose them to men. Same with men who raise children alone."

"Why would a man be forced to raise a child alone? Surely there are still women who are willing to marry a man with offspring."

I'm not about to go into same-sex couples adopting kids. He'd really flip. Although his reaction might be fun...

"Oh, Max, men with children don't require wives either. And lots of older guys date younger gals as 'arm candy.' For them, parenting skills aren't as important as looks."

He seemed to think about that for a second. "I must admit, I always selected attractive young women as my companions. However, I chose not to sire any progeny. The need never arose."

"I'll bet the longer you dated, the younger the women got."

"Well..."

"Just as I suspected. You were commitment-phobic."

"Not at all. I committed myself to my art. I didn't have enough energy to sustain a monogamous relationship and my career. I chose the career."

"Sure, Max."

I went to the living room. The night before, I'd tried the radio I brought from my bedroom at the apartment. There was no reception. I finally settled for streaming media on my computer, but soon grew bored.

I'll need a TV soon or I'll go crazy. But I bet I also need cable and I can't afford it at the moment.

Then I looked at my computer and had a brilliant idea.

I can order the basic stuff I need online. I still have my charge card.

Once the computer booted up, I compared prices for a coffee pot and microwave. Both were cheaper than I expected, so I ordered them. The delivery dates were a week or so out if I took the 'Standard Shipping' option. But saving money was more important than time right then.

I began comparing TV prices, but they were a little beyond my budget. I'd just decided to postpone that purchase and try to find a grocery store that delivered when the bell rang.

Who can that be? Not a peep from Mitzi. Some watchdog!

I opened the door. There stood a guy who looked like a nerdy Clark Kent, but I was sure he wouldn't turn into Superman when he took off his black-framed glasses. His eyes looked like light blue, but it was hard to be sure. He was tall enough, a couple of inches taller than I was, but he looked like a rumpled college professor whose dark hair was long overdue for a cut. He had on tan pants that probably hadn't seen an iron in their lifetime, a faded striped polo shirt in green and orange, and dirty tennis shoes.

"Yes?" I said.

He held out his hand. "Hi. I'm Steve Peterson."

Oh my God! I forgot he was coming today!

He glanced at his watch. "I guess I'm a little early."

"Come on in. I'll be ready in a sec."

I ran to the bedroom, changed into white cotton slacks and a clean t-shirt I knew made my eyes look bluer, ran a brush through my hair, and slapped on some lip gloss. After all, the guy was buying me lunch.

When I picked up my phone, I noted the time. He wasn't early. It was already eleven-fifteen.

Oh, well...

"Sorry I kept you waiting," I said as I returned to the living room. "I was so fascinated with the manuscript, I forgot the time."

"Wonderful! Continue to pique his interest," Max said. Mitzi lay snoozing next to the infamous chair. She hadn't uttered a sound.

Steve was looking out the window at the view. "This is incredible."

"It certainly is. Now, would you like to see the manuscript, I mean what seems to be a manuscript?" I continued to the desk where Mr. Messy stood.

He nodded. I opened the bottom drawer and handed him the tablets.

I watched as he frowned and squinted. Then he fanned through the pages.

"I wish I could figure this out," he said finally.

"That's what I'm working on, but it isn't easy."

Max butted in. "Don't infer that my cursive is difficult to read. You are just not used to observing properly written language in this day and age of mechanized living. Simply point out the genius of the words, the creativity of the plot, the..."

I threw a dirty look toward the Max chair, hoping Steve hadn't noticed. Then I cut off his suggestions with, "I'm starting to make out some of it and I hope to get better with time. You know how it is. The more you do, the easier it gets." I tried to smile confidently.

"I understand, but I'm glad you're doing the work. If you get a first chapter translated, please email it to me. I can't make a definitive decision about publication until I've seen something concrete. Here's my card." He fished in his pocket.

I guess I'd expected it to be wrinkled, like his clothes. Even upside down, I could see the card was printed on heavy stock with the name and logo of the company in gold raised lettering. His name and title, Vice President of Acquisitions, were neatly printed in the same font as the corporate information.

"Wait," he said before I could take it. "Let me give you my cell number. I'm away from the office a lot." He pulled out a pen, quickly printed on the back of the card, and handed it to me.

I stuck it in the top desk drawer.

"Where would you like to go for lunch?" he asked. "There are lots of good places in the area."

"I'm not sure. I haven't tried too many yet since I just moved in."

"How about *Las Brisas*? I love the food and the view."

"Sounds good to me."

I remember Dad took Mom and me there once to celebrate a promotion or something, and I loved it. I know it's pretty expensive, but, after all, it's his dime.

I followed him out and locked the door. A dark blue Jaguar convertible sat at the curb. Steve went to the passenger door and held it open for me.

Okay, he gets points for the car and for manners.

"Thanks." I tucked in my legs, and he went around and slid into the driver's seat.

"Would you like the top down?" he asked.

"Let me get a scrunchie for my hair," I said, and put my hand on the door handle.

"Open the glove box. There may be something in there you can use. That is, if you want the top down."

"Oh, I do," I answered. The compartment was surprisingly neat. I found a regular rubber band and decided it was worth tearing out a few strands to drive with the wind blowing. Besides I was hungry and didn't want to wait any longer in case he changed his mind.

I pulled my hair back and wrapped it. "Okay, let's go topless!"

I swear, the guy blushed, but he laughed. He pushed a button, and the top retracted. Then he put the car in gear, and we pulled away from the curb.

I didn't get the chance to ride in a convertible very often, and I loved it! The fog had burned off, and the heat had started to move in. But the breeze took care of that.

"This is great!" I had to raise my voice a little to be heard.

Then I noticed the song playing through his speakers. "You know, that sounds like... But it couldn't be."

"Couldn't be who?"

"The Missiles of October."

"Yep, it is. How do you know them?"

"You're kidding! My boyfriend—that is, my former boyfriend and I used to go to the Marine Room to hear them. The lead singer is great and the other guitarist is amazing!"

"Yeah, I like them, too."

Okay, nice car and good taste in music.

We pulled into the restaurant lot, and he handed his keys to the attendant.

"I've always loved the view from here. You can look a long way down the coast," Steve said as we walked along the cliff top.

I nodded in agreement.

I thought he might try to take my hand, but he didn't. He pulled the door open, stepped back and waited for me to go through first.

No guys open doors any more. At least, none I've ever dated. This one did it in the car and now here. Then again, he probably has to be really polite with his clients. Especially when they make him money.

Within five minutes, the waiter showed us to a table with an ocean view, even though the place was packed, and more people waited outside.

After we sat down and ordered our drinks (iced tea for both of us), I asked, "How did you do that?"

He seemed intent on studying the menu. "Do what?" he asked without raising his head.

"Get us a table that fast," I answered.

He looked up and grinned at me. It was kind of lopsided, but reminded me of a little kid who got caught being naughty.

"I just guessed you'd agree to come here, so I made a reservation ahead of time."

"But you didn't tell them your name."

"They know me pretty well. When I'm in the area, I try to eat here. It's my favorite."

"I thought you lived in L.A."

"I do. But a number of my clients and several friends are here in Orange County."

I don't know why, but when he said 'friends,' all I could picture were girls. The sort my dreamy neighbor, Mr. Muscles, entertained. For some strange reason, I didn't like picturing Clark Kent with one of them, even though he wasn't my type.

Nine

LUNCH WITH STEVE WAS A SURPRISE. THE FOOD WAS GREAT, AS I'd expected, but the conversation was interesting and easy. It seemed as though we'd known each other for a long time.

I found out we had quite a few interests in common. He'd been a runner in school like I had. We both ran middle-distance during track season and cross-country during the off-season. Although his degree was in English, he was very interested in technology and using it to make his job easier.

He told me a lot about the publishing industry. Since I'd committed to typing Max's dumb book, I figured the more I knew about the business the better. When Steve mentioned ebooks, I was fascinated. I asked lots of questions and he answered them in simple terms.

The guy could have been a teacher.

We took our time at the restaurant and even had dessert. I almost never eat sweets, but since he was ordering, I decided to join him. The choices were amazing. Steve finally settled on the chocolate mousse and I had the raspberry tostada. He even suggested sharing, so we each got to taste both. Jeff, my recently-departed boyfriend, never shared. Ever.

We ordered coffee—real coffee—and lingered over it. The waiter kept refilling our cups.

Before we realized it, the time had flown and the dinner crowd was starting to arrive.

"I guess we should go," I said halfheartedly.

"Yeah. I think they need this table," he replied. "Want to take a walk along the beach?"

"Sure."

This time, he did take my hand after a couple of minutes. It didn't feel romantic, just friendly.

We continued to talk while we strolled. Before long, we were laughing. We discovered we found the same silly things funny.

We walked several blocks before returning to the parking lot where Steve reclaimed his car.

"Could I ask a favor?" I asked when we were ready to start back.

"Of course," he replied.

"Can we make a stop on the way? I need to get a few groceries."

"There's a Whole Foods on Broadway. It's not far."

"Sounds perfect."

And it was.

I nearly went crazy until I remembered his Jag didn't have a huge trunk. Still, I picked up milk, coffee, peanut butter, bread, salad dressing, chicken, sliced sandwich meat and some dog treats I thought Mitzi might like. After all, I was still trying to woo her away from Max.

When I saw the produce, I got really excited. "Look at this gorgeous fruit! And the vegetables..."

He grinned. "I love coming here. Everything is so fresh."

I stocked up on bananas, strawberries, half a melon, lettuce, tomatoes and a few other things.

It took a bite out of my cash. Well, Max's cash, really. But I knew it would be worth it. And I was delighted to have some choices at last.

We carried my bags to his car. "Aren't you getting anything?" I asked.

"Not today," he answered.

As we stuffed my purchases into the cramped space, it occurred to me I hadn't left room for anything Steve might have bought. He seemed good-natured about it.

When we got back to my place, he offered to help me carry the bags inside. I was glad for the extra hands.

Once again, my crack watchdog sat at the door wagging her tail, but didn't bark.

After dropping the sacks he carried on the table, Steve bent down and petted her on the head. "Cute dog," he said.

"Her name is Mitzi."

"Well hello, Mitzi."

I opened a box of the doggie treats. "Want one?" I asked, holding it out to her.

She looked up but didn't come. It was obvious she preferred Steve to me, even with a bribe.

I finally walked over and gave it to her. She swallowed it in one bite, and her tail wagged like crazy.

"She's been in the house a long time," I said as I finished putting everything away. "Maybe I should take her out. We usually go for a run in the morning and afternoon." I didn't mention that this routine was recent.

"Would it be okay if I went with you?" he asked.

"Sure. We'd love the company, wouldn't we, Mitzi?"

The dog wagged her tail and danced around. I think she recognized the word 'run.'

I slipped out of my shoes and got the dog leash from the hook near the back door. By the time I clipped it onto her harness, Steve had removed his own shoes and socks and looked ready to go.

We made the usual stop for the dog to do her 'business,' then started across the sand.

I set a pretty quick pace, and Steve and Mitzi stayed right with me. I must admit, the little mutt looked like she was grinning as she ran.

Maybe she gets the same joy from running as I do.

Steve looked happy, too.

We ran down the strand farther than I'd ventured before. Finally, I slowed to a stroll.

"Don't want to wear the dog out," I said.

"She's pretty small, but she kept up well." Steve stooped down and gave her a good rub under her chin. Mitzi purred.

"She sounds like a cat," he said.

"I've noticed that, too. Strange isn't it?"

He nodded. "Never heard a dog do that before."

We turned to go back, but we kept our pace to an easy jog. It wasn't until we reached my door that I realized I hadn't remembered to look for Mr. Greek God.

"I just love to run on the beach." Steve opened the door for Mitzi and me.

"So do I," I answered. "Come down anytime." I don't know why I added the last part, but it had been more fun with human company.

As soon as we got inside, I unhooked Mitzi's leash and refilled her water bowl. She drank as though she was a camel and had to refill her hump.

"Wow, you were thirsty," I said and topped it off again. "I'll bet you're thirsty, too." I looked at Steve.

"Well..." he said.

"I'm sorry there's nothing cool but water. I have ice, though." I grabbed a couple of glasses from the cabinet and the one small ice tray from the freezer. I'd stuffed Mitzi's food around it, but figured I might need the ice, so I left the tray in place.

After filling two tumblers, I handed Steve one. He drank with nearly the same enthusiasm as the dog. I joined him, and the cool liquid made me realize I'd been dry.

"I should get Mitzi something to eat." I removed her food and dumped it in a pot.

"No microwave?" Steve asked.

"Not yet, but I've ordered one." I was pleased to realize I'd have it before too long.

As soon as the dog's dinner was warm, I poured it into her bowl.

"Well, I guess I'd better get going," he said finally, setting his empty glass in the sink.

"I didn't think I'd be hungry again for a week, but the run must have stimulated my appetite. Want to stay?" I didn't want to be alone with just Max, afraid of a lecture on how I'd wasted my day. Since Steve arrived, my ghost-in-residence had been quiet. Maybe too quiet. But it was nice.

"Actually, that sounds great," Steve said. "Traffic's pretty heavy about now. And maybe you can tell me a little about the manuscript."

Oh, yeah. The manuscript. I forgot why he's really here.

"I'm afraid I haven't gotten far enough into it to be able to get a feel for the plot."

"Tell him it's wonderful. Tell him it's brilliant. Remind him what a genius I am," Max's voice boomed across the room. Mitzi looked at the doorway and started toward her friend. As long as Steve petted her, she forgot the annoying spirit haunting my house.

Steve didn't notice her desertion because he was watching as I took the package of chicken breasts out of the refrigerator.

"I think I saw a small grill in the closet in there." I pointed to the one where I'd found the mop and broom.

Before I could warn him, Steve had yanked the door open and discovered the cobwebs and dust. He sneezed and sneezed and kept sneezing.

"Sorry about that. It's been closed up for a long time. I did the same thing when I first went in there."

He backed away and his reaction grew less intense.

"Let me," I said. I dampened a dishtowel, wrapped it around my nose and mouth and tied it in the back. Then I took a deep breath and held it while I reached down and pulled the grill out. I dropped it in the sink, then returned for the small bag of charcoal.

Meanwhile, Steve wet a sponge and wiped down the barbeque.

I removed my damp face covering and dusted off the charcoal bag, only sneezing a couple of times in the process.

Steve slammed the closet door.

"I'm going to have to vacuum that out soon," I muttered. "The place was supposed to have been thoroughly cleaned before I moved in, but it looks like they missed all the cabinets and drawers. I keep stumbling on unpleasant surprises whenever I open anything."

"Looks like you could use some help cleaning up." He sounded eager to volunteer.

"Oh, I should have lots of time to get it all done," I assured him. "It's kind of like a treasure hunt." I remembered Max's ceramic strawberry and the mystery of where the rest of his fortune was. If it was still in the house, I wanted to be the one to find it.

"How are you at starting fires?" I asked.

"Uh, not an expert," he admitted.

"That makes you better than I am," I said. I reached for a couple of matches from the holder on the wall and handed them to him. "I guess you're elected. I can throw together a decent salad, but my cooking skills are somewhat limited."

Steve took the grill and charcoal outside to my small porch. As soon as he left, I removed some of the chicken from the package before returning the rest to the refrigerator. There were three breasts, but I figured we could cook them all, and maybe there'd be leftovers. Besides, I didn't know how much Steve ate. I sprinkled a little salt and pepper on them.

What else? What the heck does Mom use?

I opened the cupboard next to the sink and looked at the spices.

Paprika? Is that it? This looks kind of dark brown. I thought hers was closer to red.

I took a whiff. It smelled okay, so I sprinkled a little on each piece.

How does Dad barbeque chicken? Melted butter? I think he sometimes brushes that on. I don't have any barbeque sauce and don't know how to make it, so maybe I'll try something else.

I got out a small pan and put some margarine in it. Then I lit the burner for the third time that day without causing myself any serious harm.

Hey, I'm starting to get the hang of this thing.

I turned the flame down.

Don't want to burn the stuff. Hope it works the same as butter.

I opened a couple of drawers and managed to unearth the kind of brush I'd seen Dad use.

Now for a salad.

Before I could start that, I smelled smoke from outside and went to see how Steve was doing. The charcoal sat in the grill. Smoke billowed from the pile along with lit paper pieces. They danced in the air, lifted by the slight breeze. Fortunately none of them reached the roof.

Steve jumped back to let the burning ashes land. Most fell harmlessly on the sand. But a couple hit the porch. He moved quickly to toss sand on them before they could do any harm.

"What happened?" I asked.

"Uh, this wasn't the kind with the starter built in," he said. "So I just lit the bag. There wasn't a whole lot left, but it should be enough. It still took two matches to get it to catch, and it was probably damp. That may be why it's smoking."

"Very resourceful. And you avoided burning down the house, too," I teased him. "Left to my own resources, I'd probably have managed a four-alarm fire."

"Well, if they get going okay, the coals should be ready in about half an hour or so," he said.

"The meat is ready when the grill is. I was going to throw together a salad with some of those great veggies we got today."

"Need some help?"

"Nope. I think I can manage that on my own."

"Guess I'd better stay out here to keep an eye on this."

"Good idea." I could just picture a couple more stray embers setting the place ablaze.

"What are you doing now?" a familiar voice demanded. "You have a great deal of work to do."

"Max, I'm trying to be nice to your publisher, so knock it off and get out of here."

He didn't answer, but I figured I'd hear about it later.

I washed the produce and put the salad together. Everything looked so good. I could hardly wait to try it.

Then I set the table, grateful that everything matched. For once, I actually enjoyed that particular task. Jeff never wanted to sit down to a meal. He usually piled his food on a plate and took it to the living room so he could watch TV.

There may be an advantage to not having that particular distraction here.

When Steve announced the coals were ready, we put the chicken on the fire, and he basted the pieces with the melted margarine as they cooked. I had to admit, he did a good job.

We enjoyed our simple meal, laughing at Mitzi as she danced around the room, trying to get us to toss her a bite. In the end, I gave her my last one.

Steve helped clear the table and wash dishes.

"Guess I'd better get going," he said when the last plate and extra chicken were put away. "Traffic should be better by now."

"Thanks for a great lunch," I said.

"And thank you for a good run and for dinner."

"I'll be in touch as soon as I get a chapter finished."

I walked him to the door where he leaned down to pat the dog. "See ya, Mitzi."

I watched as he got into his car and drove off.

He wasn't my type romantically, but I hoped we'd be friends. I'd lost touch with most of the ones I'd had in school and I was never very close to anyone on the job. They'd all worked together for so long, it was hard to break into the circle. Besides, I didn't make friends easily.

It's kind of nice to have a buddy to run and talk with, I thought as I went back into the house and prepared to face Max.

Ten

"I BELIEVE YOU OWE ME THE COURTESY OF EXPLAINING PRE-cisely why you were wasting time flirting with *my* publisher," Max boomed as soon as Steve was gone.

"First, I wasn't flirting. Second, since you roped me into this stupid project of yours, he's now *our* publisher. And third, I need to develop a good relationship with him if you ever hope to get him to actually publish your book. Besides, you should be grateful that I'm willing to schmooze with him on my own time." I wasn't going to let Max get away with making it sound like I'd been fooling around all afternoon. True, I'd had a pretty good time, but I did it for him and his precious manuscript.

"It certainly appeared to be flirting to me. And why was it necessary to squander the entire day when you could have been more productively occupied?"

I settled into the chair at the desk and booted up my computer. "Max, you may not have to eat any more, but we do. After lunch, Steve was nice enough to stop by the store so I could pick up some groceries. When we got here, you heard him ask to go for a run with me. Then we had dinner. I don't call that wasting time."

He harrumphed and I heard his chair squeak. I figured he was going to sulk for a while.

I checked my email, but there wasn't anything too interesting. Then I checked the job boards, but nothing in my area was listed. I widened my search, but no related openings showed up.

I'd just closed the last site when my phone rang. The caller ID said it was Mr. Spencer. *Thank God!*

"Hello," I answered.

"Ms. Burton, my secretary said you called."

"Yes. You see, for me to take care of Mitzi according to her manual, I need to buy a lot of expensive food. And I'm supposed to take her for grooming every other week. I don't have the money to do either, and I don't have a car to take her. Besides, I'm worried about what I'd do if she gets sick and needs medical attention..."

He didn't let me finish my carefully-prepared laundry list of concerns. "I understand. I'll have my secretary arrange for a credit line at a local grocery that delivers. I'm sure there must be a groomer in the area who will come to you. We'll arrange for an account. If transporting the dog is necessary, please call a taxi and then call the office. We will manage the payment. Is there anything else?"

I wasn't prepared for his abrupt answers. "Well, no..."

"Then expect a call from my secretary with all the necessary information." And he hung up.

"*Sheesh!*" I looked at the cell in my hand. "He could have at least listened for a minute."

So much for my plan to get some financial help.

I considered taking another stab at my résumé, but before I could open the file, Max said, "*Now* are you prepared to attend to my manuscript?"

"I've told you not to do that! Don't sneak up on me! Got it?"

"I was unaware that simple conversation constituted 'sneaking up.' I merely inquired if you would like to continue typing the pages."

"Would I like to? Not on your life! Will I?" I paused. "Only because I said I would. But, Max, before we go any further, I need to decide if this story is even worth telling. I know what modern people want to read and the stuff I saw yesterday isn't it!"

"Please elucidate. In what is the modern reader interested? Of course, I have no intention of altering the sort of storytelling that made me famous."

"Then why should we even discuss it?" I started to close the laptop.

"Very well," he said quickly. "How can I persuade you that this final work is worthy of your valuable, albeit currently unoccupied, time?"

"Just tell me the story, Max."

The chair creaked. "Very well."

For the next hour or so he described the plot of the novel he'd begun. I asked questions and thought of ways to make it more up-to-date, although I wasn't going to suggest them right then.

When he was finished, I said, "I hate to admit it, but this thing just might work."

"Not particularly glowing praise, but far superior to what I had expected."

"What did you expect?"

"I was prepared to be told how outdated my ideas were and how no modern reader would waste time with a 'dumb' tale such as the one I propose to convey."

I really hated to admit the book sounded interesting. I could have just told him it was stupid. But it wasn't. In fact, without too much tweaking, I thought it had promise. "The story might work, but it'll take adjustment. Are you willing to update it?"

"I shall take your recommendations under advisement."

"That means, I'll suggest something and you'll have a fit and carry on about how you're the successful writer and I don't know anything."

"It's 'author' not 'writer.' Writers just write. Authors are published and I, my dear girl, am published many times over."

I rolled my eyes.

He continued, "If you are not willing to use accurate terms, this project will be extremely difficult for both of us."

"Okay, Max. But you have to listen to me, or I'll quit."

There was a long silence. Mitzi sat on the floor, looking up. I was glad the dog could see him. It helped me know where my 'houseguest' was.

Finally, Max said, "Oh, very well."

"Good. Now that we understand each other, let's start with the paragraph I worked on yesterday." I opened the file. "First, we have to change her name."

"What would you suggest?" he asked. I could tell he was trying to use a friendly voice, but it still came across as a challenge.

"Well, there were lots of Jennifers when I went to school. How about that?"

"Jennifer," he said slowly as if he was trying it on for size. "No, I think not."

"What about Jessica?"

"I'm not fond of appellations commencing with the 'J' sound. It is too strident on the ear. She is a sensitive soul. Her name should reflect her personality."

For some reason, it made sense. The woman he'd told me about was gentle, if a little too innocent for my taste. "How about Sara? That was the name of my best friend in grammar school." I remembered her dark red hair, the freckles across her nose, green-gold eyes and gap-toothed smile. I wondered where she was now and if she still had freckles.

"Sarah," he said slowly. "S-A-R-A-H. I like it."

"I was thinking of the modern spelling without the 'h.'"

"What? Do you people really corrupt a time-honored name by truncating it? The traditional spelling is from the Bible and should be respected…"

Before he could carry on any more, I interrupted. "Okay, Max. You win. Sarah with an 'h.'" I wondered how many more of these kinds of fights I was in for.

We argued over her last name and that of her husband. He'd originally intended for him to die suddenly in an auto accident, but I thought a long illness made more sense.

"That way, we start out knowing the kind of person she is right from the beginning," I argued. "If she leaves a job she loves to take care of Blake…"

"I continue to believe that is a name without substance and is correctly used as a surname, not a given name."

So, before we could move on, Blake became Robert. But since Max didn't believe in nicknames and wouldn't consider 'Bob' or 'Rob,' we finally settled on Jack, I hoped.

"I still believe a character with a nickname tends to diminish his position as an adult."

"Max, maybe in your day Jack was a nickname, but today it isn't. I like it. It's simple and easy. Besides, he's dead!" I couldn't wait until we tackled what Sarah's new love interest was called. Not!

We finally settled on the prolonged illness rather than the car accident. I convinced Max it was timely and lots of women could relate.

It took another two hours just to rewrite the one and only paragraph I'd been able to decipher. By the end, I felt I'd actually made a contribution to the book. And I liked the way it felt.

When we finished, I read it back to him:

"Sarah Stewart looked around her apartment and, for the first time in as long as she could remember, contemplated her future.

"The whole place screamed of neglect.

"'Well,' she said aloud to herself. 'What do you expect?'

"For the previous six months, she'd spent almost no time there. When Jack first received the cancer diagnosis, she'd continued to work and spent as much time as she could with him at the hospital. But as the disease and grueling treatment quickly robbed her of the man she'd loved and married only five short years before, she realized something had to go. She decided it was her position as account manager with Burns and Steele. It had been her dream job, but Jack was her whole life. That is, until the week before when he simply stopped being.

"Now he was truly gone. The memorial service was probably lovely, but Sarah didn't remember much. She'd just been out on the boat to spread his ashes on the ocean as he'd requested.

"'What happens now, Jack? What do I do without you?'"

"I like it, Max."

His immediate response was silence. Then my grouchy ghost surprised me. "I believe we have vastly improved upon my previous attempt."

Whoa! He thinks it's better! That's a real breakthrough!

I looked at the clock. "Time for bed," I announced. "Come on, Mitzi."

She followed me obediently to the back door and waited while I opened it. Then she ran outside to the small patch of lawn and took care of her needs.

I sat on the porch and listened to the ocean. Lights from the houses along the cove illuminated the sea and the white tips of waves gently broke onto the sand, making them look like showers of silver stars.

The dog returned and sat on the step next to me. I stroked her head. She purred and I realized I liked it—and I liked her. I'd never had a dog, or any other pet, for that matter. Dad had allergies, or so he claimed. Now I wondered if I hadn't missed out on a special childhood relationship.

I took a deep breath and closed my eyes, realizing I was truly content. And relaxed. The pace at work had been hectic and the months leading up to the bank's failure had been filled with more tension than I'd realized until it lifted.

Living with Jeff and trying to please him created its own stress. Losing my job, living with my folks, moving to the cottage, and discovering it was haunted were all trying.

But now I felt settled. I loved living at the beach where I could run on the sand with my dog. Then I realized she was my dog and silently thanked Aunt Netta. She'd known what I needed even better than I did.

"Now, if I just had a little more money, or a new job to earn some," I told Mitzi.

She had no answer.

CHAPTER

Eleven

THE NEXT MORNING, I WOKE EARLY. MAX HAD BEEN SILENT ALL night, and I finally got a good rest. *Will wonders never cease? Maybe we can get along after all. Or not.*

I jumped out of bed, full of energy and ready for a run. When I gazed out the window, I saw a wall of fog, so I threw on my college sweats. Mitzi danced around as if she, too, anticipated our morning ritual. Well, I'm not sure 'ritual' is quite accurate since we'd only been doing it for a few days, but it was clear to me it could easily become a habit.

For the first time since I'd been discarded by the bank unceremoniously, I actually had a sense of accomplishment. Even though we'd only completed a tiny bit of the work on his book, I felt I'd made a real contribution. Apparently Max thought so, too, as much as he hated to admit it.

When we got outside and started to run, I realized that the fog was already lifting. I still felt a light mist on my face, refreshing and cool.

As always, Mitzi kept up with me. I no longer felt I had to slow my pace for her, but I decided to walk the last bit and enjoy the morning. The dog had been so good, I decided to let her off the lead as a reward. Most folks were still sleeping, so I figured she wouldn't bother anyone. Besides, I was sure she knew her way home.

She headed straight for the water. I laughed when she yelped as the incoming foam hit her paws. She raced back up toward me, but then veered away and kept moving in the direction of the houses.

"No, Mitzi," I called trying not to make too much noise.

I ran after her and was horrified as I watched the little black-and-white mop disappear up a set of stairs. Familiar stairs. Stairs that led to the deck of my dream man.

I had no choice but to follow.

"Mitzi, come back," I called quietly as I got to the top.

To my horror, I realized that the slider was open and the tantalizing smells of bacon and coffee assaulted my nose. *No wonder the little mutt came here.*

I knocked on the glass and a male voice said, "Come on in."

Okay, it's now or never. Maybe fate is finally on my side.

I glanced across the wide living room directly into the kitchen, just as the God of the Sea tossed a small piece of bacon to my begging dog.

"No..." I started. But it was too late.

Golden brown eyes met mine. "What's the matter?" As he spoke, I took in the great body in black Speedos that left nothing to my imagination.

"Uh, you see," I stammered. "She's supposed to eat only special food."

"Oh, gee. I'm sorry. Is she sick?" The golden boy—well, man—bent down to pet my wayward pup.

She gazed adoringly at him, then licked his fingers. I was hoping it was just the bacon grease but recognized the look. It was the same one she gave Max. And Steven.

Okay, so the girl's a flirt. But in this case, I can't blame her.

He looked back at me, and I realized I hadn't answered his question.

"No, no. Nothing like that. She belonged to my aunt who spoiled her rotten." I figured he didn't need to know the details about how she came to me.

"Good," he said as he straightened.

"Listen, I'm sorry Mitzi bothered you." I approached, intending to snap her leash back on and drag her out of there.

He chuckled. It wasn't a deep rumble, just a familiar male sound. In fact, the tone was so much like Jeff's, I was a little taken aback.

"She didn't bother me at all," he said. "In fact, I wasn't looking forward to eating alone. Hey, why don't you both join me? There's plenty. I was just about to scramble some eggs. She can have those, can't she?"

He'd seemed so sorry about giving the dog the bacon and besides, the irresistible smells eliminated any hesitation I might have had.

"That would probably be okay," I said. Then I remembered my appearance. I was wearing old, worn and faded sweats with my college logo on the back. Having my hair in the pony tail and wearing no makeup, I was sure he thought I was a kid. A kid with an undisciplined dog. *Great! Just the first impression I intended.*

He pointed to one of the stools at the counter. "Have a seat and watch the master at work."

"Isn't there something I can do?"

"Heck, no. For a few years, I was a short order cook while bumming around the world. I'm pretty good at it, if I do say so myself."

I took the stool he'd indicated. "I guess I should introduce myself. I'm Nan Burton, and this is my dog, Mitzi."

He rinsed his hands, then reached over to shake. "Glad to meet you, Nan." Then he bent down and held the dog's paw. "And you, Mitzi. Bet you're thirsty."

He took a small bowl from the closet, filled it with water and set it on the floor for the dog. She lapped it up. I wasn't sure, but it looked like fine bone china with a gold rim.

Does everyone here in the cove treat their animals as well as Aunt Netta did?

"You were thirsty," he said as he gave her a refill.

Then he scrubbed his hands with soap.

"Where are my manners? I'm Tad Bartholomew. Actually, it's 'Theodore,' but I never use it." He laughed, and again I was struck by how much it sounded like my unlamented ex-boyfriend. "Please don't tell me I look like a 'Theodore.'"

"Oh, no," I said quickly. Too quickly. "Uh, I mean, uh, you look like a Tad." *Okay, now he's convinced I am also a dumb, awkward kid. Wonderful. It gets better and better.*

Tad returned to his cooking, and I had to admit, he seemed to know his way around the kitchen. "Coffee?" he asked as he skillfully cracked eggs into a bowl—one-handed.

"Thanks. I think I can pour a cup for myself." I jumped off the stool, glad to have something to do.

"The mugs are on that rack." He indicated the location with a nod as he gently whisked the eggs.

I prayed I could pour without spilling.

"There's sugar in the bowl, and if you need milk or cream, they're in the fridge."

"No thanks," I said, grateful to have the warm mug in my hands. "I don't love the taste, but the smell's wonderful. And the warmth is great."

"I've seen you guys on the beach." He poured the eggs into the heated pan.

"We've watched you surf a couple of times."

He laughed. "Surfing's my life."

"What do you do for a living? I mean... Well, it's none of my business, really..."

He laughed again. "Actually, I'm currently 'at leisure' as they say. That means I'm just bummin' around. Been doing that for a few years."

"But you live in this gorgeous place." I gestured at the huge living room with the sensational view. I assumed the upstairs was just as impressive. The house looked as though a decorator had planned it. One sofa and a chair were angled to get the best view of the ocean, while another faced the large fireplace and the huge TV on the wall above it. Beige and several shades of turquoise and cream had been used to echo the tones outside the window. I'd been around Aunt Netta long enough to recognize expensive when I saw it.

He glanced around the room and the view, then shrugged. "My folks have a few houses. They hardly ever use this one."

"But you have to eat... Sorry, like I said, it's none of my business."

While we'd been chatting, he'd seasoned and finished the eggs, just the way I like them, set but not browned. He dished up two plates, adding bacon and toast. Then he grabbed another of the obviously-expensive bowls and scraped the last of the eggs into it for Mitzi.

"*Buon apetito*, Mitzi," he said as he set her treat before her. "Or maybe you'd prefer '*bon appetit*' since your name is French."

"Do you speak Italian and French?"

He grabbed a couple of forks and heavy paper napkins, then set our plates on the breakfast bar. I caught a whiff of soap and male as he came near. His muscles were even better up close. After pouring hot coffee into his mug, he joined me.

"I've traveled a lot. But I only learn enough of the language to survive."

I took a bite. "Mmm, delicious." After my few poor attempts at cooking, the simple breakfast was a feast.

I guess he realized he hadn't answered my question.

"My family owned half of Orange County many years ago. Well, my great-grandfather came pretty close." Talking didn't interrupt his eating. "Over time, most of it was sold off, but the family made other real estate investments. I got an inheritance when I turned twenty-one, and there are installments every year. So that keeps me in spending cash."

"Nice." I thought about my inheritance from Aunt Netta. There'd be no cash until I turned thirty. But I'd started to realize the gift of the cottage on the beach was worth more to me than all the money Dad got or I'd eventually receive. I noticed at the little dog lying at Tad's feet. Mitzi was worth more than money, too.

"Yeah, I guess so," he answered. "I enjoy surfing and travel. But there's nothing I'm really passionate about. I'm okay, though." He laughed again. "Guess you think I have a lot of nerve complaining and not appreciating the cushy life I have."

I wasn't going to answer that. "How long will you stay here?"

"Until I feel the urge to move on. Or until the folks decide they need the house. Not likely, though. At the moment, they split their time between Aspen and Lido Isle, with long trips in between. Guess I got the travel bug from them."

We'd finished our breakfast. Tad started to pick up the plates.

"Hey, that's my job," I said. "You cooked. I clean up."

"I can go for that," he said. Then he turned back to the view. "Fog's lifted some, and the surf's up. Think I'll get some rides in before it gets too crowded. You okay here?"

"Sure," I answered, disappointed that he was leaving. "How do I lock up?"

The laugh burst from him again. He laughed a lot. "Just close the slider. I never secure the place. There's an alarm system, but I don't remember the code or how to use it. Guess I shouldn't tell anybody, but it's true. And you're a neighbor, after all."

Without further discussion, he loped to the door and grabbed a pair of baggy trunks off the rail. After he pulled them on, he picked up his board and sprinted toward the sea.

I cleared the dishes but stopped to watch him paddle out. His muscles rippled as his arms propelled him through the water.

I sighed.

Looking at him move reminded me of a beautifully-choreographed ballet, set to the melody and rhythm of the breaking waves. It also reminded me of the handsome lifeguard who'd saved me as a kid. But it also reawakened memories of why I don't go into the ocean.

I finished the last of the coffee as I rinsed and loaded the dishes. Then I scrubbed the pans and left them to dry. The dishwasher was pretty full, so I started it, hoping he'd appreciate finding it done when he returned.

Boy, working in a real kitchen with a dishwasher is far easier than in mine.

I hunted around until I found a mop and used it on the kitchen floor.

Then I watched as Tad worked his way into a wave, stood and owned the sea. Although it was still overcast, his body seemed to capture all the available light. He resembled a golden statue standing straight and tall. Then he bent and moved and the board flew up and down the breaker. Just as I thought he'd get covered up, he pushed the front of his board through the top and over the back.

I didn't know squat about surfing technique, but something told me it was a great ride.

As I anticipated his next wave, I heard the front door open.

"Oh, Tad, honey." It was definitely a feminine voice.

I turned to see a strikingly gorgeous model-type. She moved like a panther as she unwrapped her sarong, revealing the longest legs I'd ever seen. They'd have reached my armpits.

She seemed as startled to find me there as I was to see her. Then she glanced around.

"Looks like Tad finally found a decent cleaning person. Thanks, sugar."

Her southern accent set my teeth on edge. So did her dark, golden brown skin, thick ebony hair and huge black eyes.

"I...uh... was just leaving," I said as I clipped Mitzi's lead on.

The dog had sniffed the newcomer, but hadn't uttered a sound.

Great. My dog loves everyone indiscriminately. And this Amazon thinks I'm the cleaning woman. A dumb one, at that. Another great impression.

Of course, I love people who do domestic work. Arthur and Bertie were like grandparents to me. But somehow her attitude had reduced me to 'the help.' I was simply to be dismissed as unimportant and not worth considering as a rival.

Sure. Only in my wildest dreams.

She sauntered into the kitchen. "No coffee?"

"Sorry, I just finished cleaning up." Of course, I wasn't really sorry.

She sighed dramatically. "I guess I'll just have to wait until my Tad gets back. Where is he?"

I pointed at the waves.

She pouted. "I should have known." Then she settled herself onto one of the sofas—long legs and all. I had the impression she intended to sulk. And I suspected Tad would pay for not being present when she arrived.

"Come on, Mitzi," I said to the dog.

On the short walk back to my house, I replayed the entire incident. It was clear I'd never stand a chance with Tad the Magnificent. But a girl can still dream, can't she?

"WHERE ~ HAVE ~ YOU ~ BEEN?" MAX'S VOICE ASSAILED ME AS I opened the door.

"Eating breakfast," I replied calmly as I took off Mitzi's leash.

"What establishment in this vicinity allows patrons to be accompanied by their dogs?"

"A neighbor invited us, if you must know." I headed into the bedroom. "Right now, I'm going to shower and wash my hair."

"After our accomplishments of yesterday, I expected you to be anxious to continue. Perhaps I overestimated your abilities."

I stopped and watched my dog to see the location of the ghost. She sat before the doorway, looking up adoringly. Then I focused on the same spot. "I can and will finish what I started, but right now, I'm taking a shower, so scram!"

I grabbed underwear, clean shorts and a t-shirt, then entered and slammed the bathroom door, hoping he wouldn't peek.

What a pest! I have no life of my own. Who am I kidding? I haven't had a real life in a long time. Now I'm stuck in this house with a dog and a crabby old grouch. And I can't even see him. This isn't exactly what I'd planned.

The warm water helped to soothe my anger. I think hot showers are one of the greatest inventions ever! You can keep the wheel and the electric light bulb as long as I have hot water at the twist of a faucet.

I really am low-maintenance. Boring, but low-maintenance.

I took as much time in the bathroom as I could, but I couldn't think of anything else to do. When I came out, there was no sign of the dog, which meant that the miserable 'specter' was elsewhere. I headed for the living room where Mitzi sat before the chair near the fireplace. Her topknot moved a little, so I figured Max was petting her.

I ignored both of them and opened my computer. After booting up, I checked my email, hoping for a job lead. But there was only a ton of SPAM. I deleted that. Then I checked the job boards. The outlook was still dismal, as I figured it would be. Here I was, out of college for over five years and my experience was so specialized, no one would be interested, even in a booming economy. Besides, they could hire a recent college graduate for less than I made and train them however they wanted.

Max remained silent during my search. I closed the last window and sighed.

"Are you ready to begin our collaborative effort again?" he asked quietly, but the demand in his tone was unmistakable.

"I guess so," I answered as I took the stack of yellow pads out of the bottom drawer.

I spent about an hour trying to decipher his scrawl and succeeded in typing only a couple of sentences that made sense. And they were as horrible as the original first paragraph.

"What was Helen's last name?" I asked suddenly.

"It was Zeblinsky, but what concern is it of yours?"

I ignored him and typed the name into the search on the White Pages site.

"Where did she live?" I asked.

"Somewhere in this vicinity," he answered. "However, I can't imagine why my former typist is relevant to the task at hand."

"Aha, I found her." I couldn't believe my luck. She only lived a few miles away. There were no others listed, and her information included her phone number. I had to call.

"What are you frittering our valuable time away doing now?" Max asked as I punched in the numbers.

I waved him away.

"Hello," a soft voice answered.

"Uh, hello. Is this the Helen Zeblinsky who used to type manuscripts for Maxine DuBois? I mean Max Murdoch."

"Why yes. But what..."

"Ms. Zeblinsky, I inherited the cottage Max used to live in from my great-great aunt Nanette Burton. In cleaning out the drawers, I found some notes I thought he might have written and wondered if you could identify them. I wouldn't want to throw them away if they were valuable."

Max harrumphed and for a second I wondered if she'd heard him. Then I remembered that I was the only person with that specific ability of highly questionable value.

I wish I didn't have to listen to him. But I seem to be getting pretty good at lying. Not a skill I'm anxious to perfect, but at the moment...

"Oh, my dear. Please don't dispose of anything until I've had a chance to review it. What you discovered could be only old notes, but before he died, Max told me he was working on a new novel. Perhaps that's what you came across."

"When do you think you might be able to come by?" I was hoping she still drove and had her own transportation. And that she could still see!

"I'll have to call and check the bus schedules. It's been quite a while since I made the trip there, you know."

"If you need to take a cab..." I began.

"Oh, no, my dear. I'm very capable of getting around on the bus, and walking is a great pleasure. I'll be more than happy to come to you. I'd love to see the cottage again. Oh, I'm most anxious to review what you discovered. There used to be a bus at around ten-thirty a.m. If it still runs at that time, I could make it. Would that be all right with you?"

"That would be perfect. And thank you."

"No, thank you. I'm thrilled at the possibility of Max's last work. It makes me feel positively young." Then she laughed. She sounded as if she was about to burst with happiness.

"I'll see you soon."

"Well, what mischief have you hatched now?" Max demanded.

"No mischief. Helen is coming over. Maybe she can figure out what you put on these tablets so we can rewrite it."

"I don't believe I appreciate your insinuation that I am a mere collaborator in the endeavor."

"Well, Max, if I'm going to do this at all, it has to be something that modern readers will actually, well, *read*! And that means you need me to work on it with you. Got it?"

I could hear him grumbling quietly, but I got up and walked to the kitchen. I hunted until I found a pitcher in a cabinet. Then I got out a couple of the tea bags Mom insisted I needed. I filled the pitcher with water and popped in the tea bags. It took a minute to locate the plastic wrap and cover the top, and then set it out on the back porch in the sun.

At least I'll be able to offer the lady some sun tea when she gets here.

I puttered around in the kitchen wiping up non-existent spots. But I couldn't hide out forever, so I went back into the living room.

"Aren't you at least going to attempt the appearance of working?" Max asked.

"Nope. I'm taking a break. If Helen can make out your scribbles, the job will go much quicker, and I won't end up with a raging headache."

I tried to work on my resume, but no matter how I spun it, I wasn't very employable. Too long out of school, experience in an application no one wanted, and there were too few IT programming jobs in the financial industry. But I finally put something together and posted it on all the websites.

Then I checked the listings again, hoping something had changed. Nothing had.

I sighed and looked out the window just in time to see Tad on a wave. I was mesmerized by his grace. I imagined a piece of classical music playing as he dipped and glided along.

I was exposed to the arts at an early age. Dad and Mom had season tickets to the symphony, and they love theater. From the time I was a little kid, they took me along.

Going to *The Nutcracker* ballet was a holiday tradition, and I remember hearing show tunes playing during my naps. I learned to enjoy most kinds of music. But I can never remember the exact names for most of the classics, or the composers.

Tad caught several waves along with the other surfers. To my untrained eye, he far outshone the rest.

I was jolted out of my fixation on the God of the Surf when I heard a knock. If Helen had arrived, it was much sooner than I'd expected. Of course, my faithful watchdog was snoozing near the chair by the fireplace.

I shook my head as I walked by her to open the door.

I don't know what I expected. I guess, because I kind of knew her age, based on Max's information, I thought she'd look older. Whatever I'd anticipated, it certainly wasn't the woman facing me.

Rather than being wrinkled and stooped, the lady on my porch was neatly dressed as though ready for tennis. She stood erect, about five-foot six inches, wearing pressed white slacks, a red t-shirt under a crisp white jacket. On her feet, she wore walking shoes. Expensive walking shoes. As a runner, one of my areas of expertise is athletic footwear. Around her neck, she sported a perfectly knotted and draped red-and-white striped scarf.

No matter how I've tried, I can't seem to get the hang of tying scarves so they don't look like old rags. This woman was an expert.

In fact, she could have posed for one of those active seniors ads.

Her blue eyes were the color of my mom's hydrangeas. (She takes a great deal of pride in their color since she works hard to get it.) The eyes that met mine were clear and alert.

Her hair was stylish, reddish-blonde turning silver. To my untrained eyes, it looked natural, not dyed.

"You must be Nan," she said as she offered her hand. "You are the image of your namesake."

"And you must be Helen." I saw her wince as I shook. "I'm sorry. Please come in."

She tried to smile. "A major drawback about aging, dear, is the aches and pains one develops. I'm afraid arthritis caught up with me. I call him 'Arthur,' and I confess, I sometimes swear at him."

She stopped so abruptly in the doorway to the living room that I nearly ran into her.

"Oh, my," she whispered. She looked slowly around the room, then drew a deep breath. "I didn't expect to feel Max's presence so strongly. I assumed after all these years that this place would no longer affect me. I was wrong."

I watched her walk around as Mitzi finally woke up and approached her, tail wagging. Helen didn't notice.

She ran her hand over the fireplace mantle, walked to the desk and touched the top, then looked toward the fireplace again.

"That chair used to be at the desk," she said. "And my typewriter was here." She pointed at my computer.

"Yes," I confirmed. "I heard somewhere that Max died in that chair. It seemed kinda creepy, so I moved it."

"I understand," she said. Then she closed her eyes. "I can almost feel Max here."

"What on earth is she doing? Shouldn't you both get to work?" the gentleman in question demanded and none too pleasantly.

I glared at the fireplace, the direction from which his voice appeared to come.

I decided to get right to the point. I turned to Helen. "I hope you can help me translate Max's scribbling. His publisher is interested in the manuscript, assuming it's a new one."

I retrieved the yellow tablets from the bottom drawer and handed them to her.

She carried them to the sofa where she sank onto the cushions. Then she ran her fingers gently over the top page as if to smooth it or to reassure herself that it actually contained Max's handwriting. When she looked up at me, I saw unshed tears forming in her eyes.

"I'm so sorry," I said. "I didn't mean to upset you."

She shook her head and took a deep breath.

"It's just that seeing his writing again brings back such memories. It's like finding a small piece of him I didn't know existed."

She turned to the page and I gave her time to start reading.

"What infernal plan is this?" Max demanded. "The fewer people who know about this, the better. After all, she could steal my story and sell it to the highest bidder."

Since I was standing behind the sofa, I made the 'zip it' motion across my mouth.

"Would you like something to drink?" I asked Helen.

She looked up as though her mind had been somewhere else entirely. "What was that, dear?"

"I asked if you'd like a drink."

"Not just now, but thank you."

"Can you make it out?" I was anxious to find out if she remembered.

"Of course. I typed his last twenty-two manuscripts. I admit, it was difficult at first, but over time, it became easier. A bit like reading a foreign language."

"How insulting," Max groused.

I ignored him.

"Would you be willing to work with me to get this thing in shape? I don't have much money, but I'll pay you what I can. Or I'll share the royalties or whatever with you."

"What are you talking about? They are *my* royalties. How can you claim them, much less give them away?"

Since Helen was watching me, I couldn't give my annoying ghost the look I'd have liked, but I planned or tell him off as soon as she left.

While Max blustered, Helen took a moment to consider, then frowned. "I don't know just how much help I'd be. With these hands, I can't type any more, or do anything requiring a grip."

"But you could read the words and I could type them on the computer. We could work together."

"I might like that," she said. A smile lit her face. "I've missed doing productive work. But I certainly wouldn't take any money for it. Just seeing his familiar handwriting again is a pleasure. And that is pay enough."

"You have some expenses, like your bus fare. The least I can do is cover that."

She opened her mouth, then closed it. "Very well. Your offer seems fair," she finally said.

"Can you start today?" I asked.

I swear, her face positively glowed. "I'd love to. Max was always a wonderful storyteller. I'd enjoy hearing this tale, especially since it's a new one."

I wondered what she thought of the first paragraph I'd hated. But she'd agreed to work with me. For the moment, that was enough.

Thirteen

HELEN AND I WORKED TOGETHER FOR THE REST OF THE MORN-
ing. When she began on the first paragraph Max and I had tackled the day
before, she shook her head. "Dreadful. Quite dreadful."

"I thought so, too," I said while Max bellowed in the background, "What!"

Then she laughed. "You know, he never read any of my work following
the first couple of books. As time went on, tastes changed, but Max didn't.
So I just made modifications I felt would help. Apparently they did since his
books kept selling."

Max repeated himself, the outrage apparent in his voice. "What? How
dare she take such liberties?"

"Wow! I was sure I was the only one who thought it was junk."

Her laugh was surprisingly rich and deep. "Oh, no, my dear. His writing
was out of style even then. It's even more so now."

I read her the rewrite we'd done the previous day.

"Splendid! You've made a wonderful start! I totally approve."

We moved on quickly. Helen read Max's scrawl, and I typed. When we
had a paragraph or so, we discussed the changes we felt were required. Of
course, Max kibitzed in the background. Helen couldn't hear him, but,
unfortunately, I could. Occasionally he contributed something worthwhile.
But, overall, I was pleased with the changes Helen and I made together.

In the end, even Max's objections diminished.

By one o'clock, we'd actually managed to slog through two whole pages. I'd probably have kept going except that Mitzi started to whine.

"I guess the dog needs to go out. I lost all track of the time."

"I haven't had this much fun in ages," Helen said as she followed me outside.

Mitzi proved her need for the outdoors, but returned right away.

"The least I can do is make us lunch," I said. I picked up the pitcher of sun tea, now a rich golden shade.

"That would be lovely," she replied. "I don't have company for meals often any more. May I help?"

"You've done more than enough work already. I couldn't have struggled through the hieroglyphics on my own."

As we talked, I got out the leftover chicken breast, bread, condiments and fresh lettuce and tomatoes.

Helen laughed. "I had a difficult time as well in the beginning. But after a while, I grew used to it." She paused a minute to glance down at her hands. When she looked up, her eyes glistened. "I've truly missed feeling useful. And I miss Max, more than I can say."

I put our sandwiches on plates and grabbed a bag of chips. "Where would you like to eat?" I asked.

"Why, right here would be delightful. When I worked for Max, we always ate here in the kitchen. Of course, in those days, I usually brought a lunch with me for both of us. Having someone else prepare it is truly a treat."

I poured tall glasses of tea and set out the sugar and spoons. "Well, then, I'll just have to plan lunch on the days you come. By the way, how often are you available? I'm sure you have lots to do."

"Honey, I haven't had anything important to do since 1977 when Max died."

She sounded so sad, I felt sorry for her. I decided to change the subject. "What do you think of the house? Does it look the same?"

"On the surface it does. But when Max was here, the dear man's presence simply filled every inch. He was larger than life, as they say. A huge personality."

"With an ego to match. Uh... I'm sure." *Oops, that was close.*

"I have no idea what you mean," the ghost-in-residence interjected.

"Oh yes, my dear. Most creative people, especially those with his level of talent, are aware of their genius. Max Murdoch was no exception."

"Now, that was an astute observation," the person in question commented.

Helen took another bite of her sandwich. "Delicious." She looked at me as she had several times already. "I simply cannot get over the resemblance between you and your aunt Nanette."

I didn't bother correcting her on the relationship.

"I've heard that all my life," I said.

"Amazing. You look the image of a photo of her that used to be on the mantle. There was another of Nanette, Carole Lombard, and Jean Harlow. All three of them were in fur coats, smiling at the camera. I always wondered if it was taken at a movie premier. Of course, that was before my time. But I envied all the Hollywood excitement."

"I didn't realize Aunt Netta knew either of them. Wow, that's a surprise."

"As I understood it, the three of them were great pals. Such a shame the other two died so tragically young."

I'll have to ask Max about that. I bet he knows the whole scoop.

As we ate the rest of our meal, Helen told me some great stories about Max. Apparently he was very handsome and charming and always had a flock of young beauties circling around him.

Just like Tad, I thought.

As we finished, I threw Mitzi a corner of my bread. She swallowed it whole, then ran to the door again and danced around.

"Ready for a walk, girl?" I asked.

"I'd love to go with you," Helen said as she started to pick up her plate. I could tell from her wince that even the weight of the dish caused her pain.

"Here, I'll do that," I said, taking it from her. "Why don't we both 'powder our noses' first. Then we can take the dog out."

Helen looked as if she was about to cry again. "Max and I always 'stretched our legs' after lunch," she whispered. "It was a nice break after sitting."

"Sounds like a very wise and healthy practice," I replied cheerfully. "You go first while I clean up." I turned to run the dish water, not wanting to embarrass her further.

* * * *

"What a perfectly beautiful day!" Helen observed as we started down the beach.

Mitzi responded quickly when I said, "Heel," once again confirming my suspicion that she'd been well-trained. She trotted along between us with her head held high.

"I love it here," I said. And I meant it.

I glanced at Tad's house and thought I spotted a couple in a heated embrace just inside the door. Very heated.

Of course.

"Did you ever date Max?" I asked.

She laughed heartily. "Oh no. He only went for the 'glamour girls.' I was a mouse. A little brown mouse."

I stopped to stare at the woman next to me. Even at her age, which had to be close to eighty, she was very attractive.

"You've got to be kidding! You're beautiful."

She blushed. "Oh, no, my dear. I've worked hard to stay trim, but I've never been even pretty."

I couldn't believe what she was saying.

"Haven't you ever looked in the mirror?"

Another laugh, but there was no amusement this time.

She began walking again. Mitzi and I followed.

"When I was your age, I had pale red hair, pale blue eyes, and freckles. My parents were quite strict, and I lived at home at the time. I'm afraid I dressed quite unfashionably and wore glasses. So you see, I was nothing at all like the perfect specimens Max dated." There was a slight edge to her voice.

"What happened between then and now? I wasn't just trying to flatter you, or anything. You're a really attractive woman."

She gave me a sad smile. "Thank you, young lady. You've made my day." She sighed. "I guess the years can be kind to some of us 'plain Janes.' I never smoked or drank. Mother and Father didn't approve. And I usually kept a large straw hat here for our beach walks, so I never got too much sun. I've eaten healthy food and gotten exercise." She shrugged. "Maybe those things contributed."

I made a mental note to get a couple of straw hats. I knew I could order those online.

Then she genuinely laughed. "Or maybe it was just a life without the stresses of a husband or children."

I laughed with her. "Is that the real secret?"

She grew serious again. "No, dear. Don't live your life alone, if you have a choice. I can't recommend it. Certainly, being with someone who is demeaning, or violent, or takes advantage of you is not wise. But if you find someone who genuinely cares and wants only what's best for you, grasp his love and hold on tight."

"Yeah, sure." I dismissed her statement. "But it's not easy finding anyone like that."

"It's not as hard as you might imagine."

I realized it was hot, and I didn't want her to burn. "Maybe we'd better turn back. It's the middle of the day, and Mitzi and I are usually out only in the early morning and at sunset." It sounded like a good logical reason to reverse course.

Apparently Helen agreed because she nodded and turned with us.

On the walk back, I told her about Jeff. Self-centered Jeff. Cheap, mooching Jeff.

The more I talked, the clearer our relationship became. I gave. He took. He'd become a habit. Probably a bad habit.

"How long were you involved with him?" she asked.

"We lived together for two years. Two years too long. And we'd dated off and on for about a year before that."

I'd met Jeff when I first started working at the bank. He was cute in a sort of nerdy way, and he knew it. He helped me when I had problems, so I thought he was a really nice guy. I didn't discover the other side of him until it was too late. At least it seemed that way at the time.

"Why did you continue in the relationship?"

I thought about it for a minute. "I guess it was just easier to stay with the familiar than to make a change. Besides, he'd moved in, and getting him out seemed like more of a pain than letting him stay. And sometimes he cooked dinner. It was nice to come home from work and find food on the table. Of course, he usually barbecued steak. The expensive cuts. The ones

I couldn't really afford."

She stopped and looked straight at me. "Was he worth it?"

I hesitated, then shook my head. "No. Honestly, I guess he wasn't. He sat at home all day, watched TV, guzzled beer, and smoked cigarettes I paid for. I only drink wine once in a while at dinner and have never smoked. I'm a runner and know better."

"Were there other women?"

I'd never really allowed myself to ask the question, even in my mind. "Probably. I guess I suspected he had other girls. But as long as I didn't ask, I could avoid dealing with it."

"Did it work?"

"Not really. No. I just wore blinders and stumbled along. But I think I suspected."

She smiled. "We all do that when faced with an uncomfortable truth."

We started walking again.

"Was there ever anyone special in your life?"

She looked down. I was afraid I'd gotten too personal.

"I was deeply in love once. With the wrong man. After that, no one else I met ever measured up."

"Why was he the wrong one? Was he married?" I realized I was really prying. "You don't have to answer if you don't want to. I mean, it's really none of my business."

She smiled. "It's quite all right. Many years have passed, and what's done is done. I've never spoken about this to another soul. But perhaps it's time. And you might learn something from my mistakes." She hesitated and I could tell she wanted to say more. "Or maybe not..."

"I'd really like to hear about it. That is, if you want to tell me."

She took a deep breath. "Actually, the man in question was a bit like your Jeff. Oh, he was self-supporting. Quite well, at that. But he was selfish and self-centered, egotistical, and very taken with himself. He was handsome and charming. And he knew it."

"Well, Jeff was kinda cute, but he'd never be mistaken for Prince Charming."

She smiled. "Well, this man was movie-star handsome. I watched him give some young lovely his undivided attention, flatter her, woo her. Then, the moment she left the room, he did the same to the next beauty who came along. I guess 'fickle' should have been his middle name."

"Did any of the women find out?"

"Oh, they all knew it. But he wined and dined and bedded them. Then they went their way. Most were models or aspiring actresses, and he introduced them to influential people. He had all the necessary connections. He was a rung on the ladder to the top. They slept their way up."

I'd heard the term, but hadn't really thought what it meant. Now I was starting to get the picture, and it wasn't a pretty one.

"But if you saw all this and knew about him, why were you attracted to him? I mean, why didn't you try to find someone else?"

"That's a very good question and the one I didn't allow myself to ask."

She looked at me as we neared the cottage.

"I guess I believed that someday he'd look away from the fawning women, who grew younger and younger through the years, and see that I'd been there all along. Faithfully caring for him and waiting. It was a foolish fantasy, but I sincerely believed there was more to him than he let on. He revealed his caring side around me enough that I hoped I saw the real person. And I continued that hope until the day he died."

There was such sadness on her face, I wanted to stop the conversation, but I had one more question.

"Wasn't there ever anyone else in your life who genuinely cared about you?"

"Actually there was for several years. His wife was institutionalized with Alzheimer's disease and no longer knew him. He loved me deeply. And he also loved her. We made a life together."

She stopped, but I wanted to hear more.

"What happened?" I asked softly.

"He grew ill, and I nursed him as best I could. Then his wife died, and two months later, so did he. It was as though he stayed alive only long enough to see that she passed."

I felt tears forming. "How sad for you."

"No, my dear," she said softly as we reached the back steps. "He was a wonderful man and made those few years worth living."

"But you never stopped loving the other man." Don't ask how I knew, but I did.

She shook her head, then looked at the cottage. "No. I never did."

Sometimes I'm really dense. The truth suddenly hit me like a punch between the eyes.

"You were in love with Max."

She smiled weakly. "Of course, I was."

Fourteen

AFTER OUR WALK, I SUGGESTED WE STOP FOR THE DAY, BUT Helen insisted we continue. She said she hadn't had as much fun in years.

We reached the end of the chapter at around three o'clock, with Max's counterpoint to our own discussion. (I probably wouldn't have come up with the word 'counterpoint,' but that's how Max described it later, and I liked it.)

I was very happy with the finished product. "You know, I think this just might work!"

"Oh, I know it will," she replied. "It's far better than any of his previous books."

"How dare she?" Max blustered.

As Helen left, she hugged me. "Thank you, my dear. I felt useful for the first time in years. I didn't realize how much I needed something productive to do."

"When can you come again?" I asked.

"Would tomorrow be too soon?"

"Tomorrow would be perfect."

It might just have been the afternoon sun, but I swear, her face glowed. "Tomorrow at ten-thirty again it is."

As she started down the street, I yelled, "Are you sure I can't call you a cab?"

She dismissed my question with a wave of her hand.

I shut the door, and immediately Max exploded, "How dare the two of you compromise my creativity?"

"And how dare you take advantage of that sweet woman all those years?"

"What on earth are you implying? I paid her quite well for her services and assumed she was recording my words precisely. Instead, I discover the vixen was taking liberties! It was she who took advantage of me!"

There's nothing more annoying than outraged ghost, especially when he's loud, but I wasn't through, either.

"She changed your books to make them commercial successes. And you were too self-centered to bother even reading them or doing your own editing or—or anything!"

"Very articulate," he remarked, his voice so patronizing I would have slapped him if I'd known where his face was.

Instead, I took advantage of his comment to continue. "And she stayed with you all those years, even though you never saw her as the lovely woman she was. Is."

"Helen was an employee and I believed she was a good one. That is, until today."

"How blind can you be? The woman was in love with you, you fool!"

"I'm quite certain you are mistaken."

Ooh, men! They're so dense! I thought about Tad. I could be madly in love with him, but he'd never notice, even if I took off all my clothes and danced in front of him. And Max was the same.

"I am not mistaken! She told me so herself. She still loves you, although I can't figure out why."

I heard his chair creak. Then he sighed.

In the silence, I continued. "You were always looking for the next young girl who thought you'd connect her with the right people to make her famous. But you didn't see the real woman right in front of you. She adored you! And you ignored her."

I dropped onto the sofa and glared at the spot next to the fireplace where I thought his head should be.

"I had no idea," he said softly.

"That's the problem," I said, my outrage dissipating.

"She never gave any indication of her infatuation."

"Max, she was always there for you. All you had to do was notice. But you were too self-absorbed."

I heard another sigh. I had the feeling Max was seldom at a loss for words.

"I shall have to give this revelation some thought," he finally said.

"I should hope so," I answered. "Oh and when we're working, would you please shut your trap? I felt like a neighbor's radio was playing so loud I couldn't concentrate."

"My dear girl, you and your newfound friend, my *former* secretary, are dissecting and destroying the product of *my* imagination—my creativity. I refuse to remain silent when I observe my hard work being adulterated."

"Then hold the complaints until after Helen leaves. We can discuss your issues then."

"I shall attempt to withhold my advice. However, if you negatively impact the arc of the story, or of the character, or violate the spirit of a character, I shall be forced to speak up."

"What the heck are you talking about?"

Max began to describe the basics of plot and story and character. He told me the overall story has a beginning, middle and ending. He'd written the beginning and some of the middle and he'd told me the end. I had to remember at all times that the story was moving toward the end and not get lost in the plot.

Then he described how each character had to change during the course of the story and how each chapter had to follow the same beginning-middle-ending pattern as the story. And it was the same with each scene in a chapter.

He was surprisingly patient, considering we were working on his 'baby.'

"Wow! I didn't know there were scenes, and I didn't know writing was so hard. Or complicated."

"The secret of great writing is to make it look effortless. If your reader senses the mechanics, you haven't done your job as an author."

I'd have to think about what he'd told me. It was a lot to take in.

I changed the subject. "Helen said there used to be a picture here of Aunt

Netta with Carole Lombard and Jean Harlow. I never knew they were friends."

"Oh yes. Carole and your aunt traveled in the same social circle when they were younger. Nanette dated several prominent matinee idols. She was very beautiful, you know."

"So I'm told." I wondered how anyone could think I looked like my glamorous great-great aunt. But there's no accounting for people's opinions.

"When Jean Harlow arrived in Hollywood, they befriended her. Nanette kept the photo to which you refer here at the cottage. She was devastated when Jean died. That was before I knew her, of course, but she disclosed her feelings of grief to me."

"I can't imagine how shocked she must have been. I guess the whole world was."

"I recall hearing the news in London. Women wept in the streets."

"Did she and Carole stay friends?"

He paused, and I wondered why. Then he said, "They were bosom chums until Miss Lombard's untimely death. At that juncture, I had taken up residence here. Nanette came to me. She was shattered. She repeated, 'First Jean, then Rod, now Carole.'"

"Who's Rod?"

"Your aunt was engaged to a young flier named Rodney Oliver when I first met her. I saw him once. Dashing young man. He joined the RAF shortly after Nanette and I became acquainted."

"I never knew she was engaged." I sat forward, as if I could hear better being closer.

"I'm quite certain she would not have disclosed the information. It was frightfully painful for her."

"Why?"

"Rodney was killed during a bombing raid in 1941. Many pilots died in those years."

"Oh, no." I sank back into the cushions and felt a lump forming in my throat.

"Nanette lost her dear friend Jean Harlow. Four years afterward, her fiancé. Carole Lombard's death less than a year later seemed more than she could bear. Nanette was also close to Miss Lombard's mother who perished in the same flight disaster. The woman had treated her like a second daughter."

I felt myself choking up just thinking about losing the people I loved. "What did she do?"

"She came here. She never explained her reasons. The cottage was the first property she purchased. She may have wanted to return to a familiar location. I also suspect she found the ocean soothing. Or at least hoped to."

"And did she?"

He hesitated again. "When Nanette arrived, she was in a terrible state— unresponsive, uncommunicative. I recall speculating about how she had managed navigate her fancy sports car from her home in the Hollywood Hills to the beach without doing herself in. Or, perhaps, that had been her intention. Nevertheless, she arrived on my doorstep."

By now, I could feel tears forming. It was hard to think about my sweet little aunt dealing with anything like this.

"What did you do?" I whispered.

"I offered to contact a doctor, but she refused. Instead, she ignored me and made her way directly onto the sand where she sat, staring at the ocean. I feared for her health. As I recall, it was rather chilly, and she was garbed only in a sweater."

"Was she okay?" She'd obviously survived. After all, I knew her growing up. But I wondered how.

"When it grew dark, I brought her inside, undressed her and put her to bed. I prepared a strong cuppa, but she refused it. I recall her appearance to be that of a small child rather than a grown woman. She pleaded with me to stay. So I slipped beneath the counterpane and held her through the night."

"Were you lovers?" I heard myself ask, even though it was none of my business.

"Not then," he answered simply. "I merely remained with my arms surrounding her. The following morning, I managed to get her to accept a bit of porridge and weak tea. She lingered in my bed for nearly a week, during which time, I held her hand, insisted she take nourishment and cosseted her at night. She rarely spoke, other than to beg me not to leave.

From time to time, she roused to use the facilities and make her ablutions."

I could almost picture Aunt Netta curled into fetal position, perhaps in the very same bed I now used. I sensed her overwhelming grief.

"So, how did she recover?"

"One day, she roused herself, bathed, dressed, and emerged. She was wan and extremely thin, but mobile. I boiled an egg and prepared a piece of toast. To my surprise, she consumed both. Then she opened the rear door and stepped outside. I watched her meander along the beach. She did not ask me to accompany her."

"Weren't you afraid she'd just walk into the ocean and drown?"

"The thought did not occur to me until much later. At the time, I was pleased to see her ambulatory. After nearly an hour, during which time I occasionally peeped out, she returned. As long as she was in my sight, I refrained from concern. And when she arrived, she behaved more rationally. Over the next two days, she regained her strength and *joie de vie*."

"Did she ever tell you what was going on during that week when she was in bed? Inside her head, I mean."

"By tacit agreement, we never spoke of that period again. Even later."

"When you became lovers, you mean."

He sighed. "Your aunt required physical comfort and turned to me. Her beauty and vulnerability were a heady combination, especially for a young man with few friends of the female persuasion. However, our love affair did not last long. We both realized our friendship was more valuable than a liaison, however pleasant."

"Did you ever talk about marriage?"

"Both of us knew we were too independent for a permanent relationship. It would never have survived. As it was, we remained lifelong cherished friends."

I know Max was too selfish, and Aunt Netta was one of the most independent people I ever met. But she managed to keep Max as a friend all those years. Maybe Helen's observation of the soft side of him isn't as far off as I thought.

I suddenly remembered the photo.

"Max, what happened to the picture? The one of Aunt Netta and Jean and Carole. It wasn't in her stuff when we went through her house."

"Nanette retained that photograph and several others, keeping them where they had always been, even following my own demise. In fact, nothing in the cottage was altered. Prior to your arrival, however, several ladies arrived. I presume they were employed as charwomen. However, they performed their duties poorly. They also removed the decorations. Perhaps they secured them in storage."

I agreed with his assessment of the cleaning crew. They'd done a lousy job. I just hoped they hadn't taken all of Aunt Netta's and Max's personal stuff. Then I remembered.

"There's a stack of boxes at the back of the garage," I said. "Come on, Mitzi. Let's take a look."

The dog followed along obediently.

I opened the door off the entry and realized it was nearly black in the back corner. I felt for a switch, but there wasn't one. The house was old, and I suspected the garage may have been added later. At the time, they probably didn't think about a light.

"Guess we need to see, huh girl?" Mitzi wagged her tail.

I went out front and lifted. The wooden door was heavy. When I moved in, Dad had opened it, so I had assumed since it was only one-car-wide, it would be easy. It wasn't. Using muscles I didn't know I had, I finally managed to hoist it up.

"Hi ya, Mitzi," I said as she emerged from the darkness. "Let's see what we can find."

I headed for the pile in the corner. The first box contained old bedding. Worn blankets and sheets.

"Looks like I'll have to call for a charity pick-up," I told the dog. She was sniffing all around, her tail stirring up dust. I sneezed. "Glad you're happy, Mitz."

The next one contained towels in the same sorry state. "Maybe the trash is a better idea, don't you think?"

The dog had found an interesting spot between the stacks and seemed intent on digging.

Finally, in the third carton, I hit pay dirt. "Pictures, Mitzi. Here they are!"

The first was of a distinguished-looking man with a small moustache, posed seated in a chair, holding a pipe. "I'll bet this was a publicity picture of Max." Even though the man in the photo was probably at least fifty, he had a movie-star quality. If it was Max, I could understand how all the ladies flocked to him.

Next was a much younger photo of the same guy with Aunt Netta. The glamorous Hollywood Aunt Netta I remembered from her parties. But here she was, not much older than I. And, for once, even I couldn't deny the resemblance. Although my hair has never been that blonde and I don't wear that much make-up, it was like looking in a very, very flattering mirror. It took my breath away.

Beneath that one, was the picture I was looking for. There they were: Jean, Carole, and Aunt Netta. How young and carefree they looked. All in fur, made up, and grinning at the camera. I guessed they had their arms around each other. Even though it wasn't a posed photo, it could have been used as an ad for friendship.

Seeing the picture, my tears fell at last. The love between these three girls was so evident, and for Aunt Netta to have lost both of them somehow seemed an even greater blow than when Max told the story.

I clutched the picture to me and rocked and cried softly. I swear, I only was distracted for a few seconds. Then I realized the dog wasn't digging at the box any more.

"Mitzi," I called softly.

No answer. No dog.

"Mitzi, where are you?" I put the picture down carefully and started to hunt.

No sign remained in the garage. From the front of the house, I could hear the traffic on busy Pacific Coast Highway in the distance.

"Mitzi, Mitzi, come here," I yelled, frantically running to the door and looking down the street. My dog was gone.

"Oh, no," I cried, all thoughts of Aunt Netta and the photo and even of Max, replaced by fear. "What have I done?" Then I cried for real.

It didn't occur to me until later that I might have put my inheritance on the line. My only thought was to find the little pooch I'd come to love.

Fifteen

"MITZI! MITZI!" I SCREAMED AS I SPRINTED UP OUR LITTLE CUL-de-sac, Looking around and between the houses along the way.

No answer. No sign of the little black-and-white fur ball.

Most places, mine included, didn't have fenced yards, so the dog might have headed toward the beach. Or busy Pacific Coast Highway a couple of blocks away.

I won't even think about that possibility.

Even though I was in good shape and ran all the time, my heart pounded, and my throat constricted.

"Mitzi, where are you? Come! Now!"

I reached the end of Seashell Cove where it met the cross-street leading to the highway. I couldn't bring myself to make the turn, afraid of what I might find.

No sound of squealing brakes. That should be a good sign. Maybe she decided to take a run on the sand.

I headed back down the street, still calling her name. Then I spotted Tad coming out of his garage with a familiar black-and-white mop at his side.

"Mitzi!" I cried.

I've never run faster. I swooped down, grabbed her, and clutched her to my chest.

"Don't ever, ever do that to me again!" I kissed the top of her head. She responded by bathing my face in sloppy kisses. I thought all the salt from the tears on my cheeks might have appealed to her. But I hoped it was because she was as glad to see me as I was to see her.

Then I took a good look at Tad. Most men appear awkward and uncomfortable in a tuxedo. Not Tad. He should have been featured in the *People Magazine* "50 Most Beautiful People" issue.

"What happened?" he asked.

"I was in the garage and glanced away for a second. She just disappeared."

Tad laughed. "I was upstairs dressing, and she came to visit. Maybe she remembered I fed her forbidden food. Heck, even I'd remember bacon." He flashed a megawatt grin. I'd have sworn the sun glinted off his teeth.

Just when I didn't think he could look any better, he did.

"How'd she get in?"

He shrugged. "I rarely close the slider."

"Makes sense. The little beggar. I'm sorry if she bothered you."

He reached over and scratched her head. She licked his hand.

"She's a great dog. She can visit anytime."

I noticed he didn't include me in his invitation. I also saw not one dog hair on his perfectly-pressed jacket and pants. If I'd gotten within a foot, I'd have been covered.

"You headed out? You clean up really well."

Stupid! Stupid comment. Every time I open my mouth I sound like a geeky kid.

He laughed again. "Command performance at the club. The folks have a new debutant they want me to meet. It's a pain, but the music's usually pretty good. Oh and dinner. It'll be nice not to have to fend for myself."

When he fixed us breakfast, he seemed pretty competent in the kitchen. Better than I was. But I didn't bother to mention it.

"You know the club," he continued. "Everyone always trying to impress the same old people. Kind of a snooze. But, hey, the parents are paying."

"Actually, I've never been there." I knew there were a few country clubs in the area and assumed he referred to one of those. I also figured it was the super-expensive one since he'd said his folks lived on Lido Isle, at least some of the time. That takes big money. Mostly old money.

"You should go sometime. The young crowd's kind of fun, I guess. I don't hang out with them."

There it was again. He thought I was a kid. "I may look like a teenager, but I'm actually twenty-seven."

"Really? I thought you were about eighteen. You're lucky."

"How?"

What's lucky about being treated like a child?

"All the women I date would kill to look younger. And some of them are. Younger than you, I mean."

"Hmmm. How old are you?"

"I'll be thirty in a couple of months, but I sure don't feel like it."

You don't act it, either.

"Well, thanks for finding my dog." At the word 'dog,' Mitzi slurped my face again. I laughed. "Hey, I already had a shower." I felt so relieved to have her safe in my arms, I decided she could clean my face with her tongue any time she wanted.

"See ya," he said as he folded himself into his sports car. When he pulled out, I noticed it was a red Lamborghini. It looked a little like the Batmobile—only red. And it took off just like the proverbial bat, as well.

In high school, one of my guy friends, as opposed to 'boyfriends,' was obsessed with sports cars, particularly that Italian brand. He wore the logo on all his clothes and had pictures on his notebooks.

Wonder if he ever got one, I thought as I carried my little pup home.

I set her in the entry, and she ran to the back of the house.

She's probably thirsty. Come to think of it, so am I.

I returned to the garage, picked up the carton of treasures, and set it in the entry. Then I walked back out front and closed the big door. I had to just let it go since I wasn't strong enough to ease it down. It hit with a *'clunk,'* followed by a loud *'thwang'* and a crash.

What the heck? I got the important stuff out and there isn't much left. I'll find out what happened later. Right now I want to finish looking at Max and Aunt Netta's keepsakes.

"Were you able to locate the photograph you sought?" Max asked when I carted the box into the living room and set it carefully on the floor.

"Yep," I answered.

I left and returned quickly with a tall glass of sun tea.

About time to replenish my supply.

Then I reached into the carton and brought out the picture in question.

"They were happy and beautiful. It's hard to believe two of them died so young. But Aunt Netta made up for them!" The last thought made me smile. I was grateful to have had that wonderful, if eccentric, lady in my life.

I placed the frame on the mantle and then brought out the one of Max.

"This must have been a publicity shot of you," I said.

"Indeed. It was used in an advertisement for a series of lectures and author panels in which I participated. Deuced bother. Traveling about the country stole time from creating my masterpieces."

"You wrote in longhand. Couldn't you take your yellow tablets with you?"

"The muse refused to cooperate. I required the solitude and routine of this location for optimal inspiration."

I wondered if he'd been a bit agoraphobic since it seemed as though he'd rarely left the cottage once he settled in.

I placed Max's image on the mantle, then brought out the one of him with Aunt Netta.

"You both look like you're having fun here."

"Ah, yes. That was taken at one of Nanette's famous New Year's Eve soirees. I believe it was the year she purchased that enormous estate with the outlandish converted barn."

I closed my eyes and was transported back in time.

A long, tree-lined drive had led to the semi-circle at the Tara-like entrance of what had been the Caldwell Estate before Aunt Netta bought it. A dozen or more luxury cars could park in front of the house and still leave room for easy passing. The driveway then meandered back to the eight-car garage, Olympic-size pool with pool house, rose garden, tennis courts, and converted barn. It was a sprawling property with lots of privacy near Brentwood, home of the stars.

Aunt Netta held lavish soirees in 'the barn.' That's how she referred to the huge high-ceilinged building with a stage at one end and a large loft.

Even though we were not at all in her social circle, my family was invited each year to her New Year's Eve parties. They were legendary. I remember the crystal chandeliers, silver and gold streamers, guests in dazzling clothing, dancing to the music of a live band, and the fabulous buffet with the fantastic ice sculptures. Oh and the delicious desserts. I always ate too much and ended up with a stomach ache the following day. It was worth it.

Even as a little kid, I recognized the latest movie and TV stars, popular singers, and other famous people.

"I went to some of her parties growing up," I told Max. "I never got over all the celebrities. It always seemed very glamorous. Still does." I set that picture with the others.

"Glamorous, yes. Intellectually stimulating? Hardly."

I pointed to the picture. "You look contented at this moment." I had to call him on his snobbish remark.

"Perhaps that was the year Noel Coward graced us with his presence. Now, there was a true wit. Cutting, rude, outrageous, but very clever."

"Max, I can't believe you actually met so many famous people."

I turned to see what else remained in the box.

Several other frames held photos of Aunt Netta. Some were of her alone, others with a group. The last one struck me. In it, she posed with a slender young man in uniform. I don't know much about the military, but I thought I recognized his as RAF from old movies I'd seen on TV.

"Is this Rod?" I asked.

"Ah, yes. I haven't seen that particular image since..." He paused, as if in thought. "Perhaps it was when Miss Lombard died. Nanette must have packed it away."

My great-great aunt was a young girl gazing adoringly at the handsome man. He looked back with equal affection.

"I believe that was their engagement photo. It might have appeared in the local rotogravure."

For some reason, it was important for me to add this to the collection on the mantle.

At the bottom of the box were a gorgeous crystal vase and matching candle holders, wrapped carefully in towels. I knew they were expensive just by looking at them. They joined the photos.

"Nanette always liked having her 'rogues' gallery' as I referred to it, in view. I would have preferred simpler surroundings. But it was her house, after all."

"Isn't a rogues' gallery a police line-up?"

He chuckled. "Indeed. That was the joke."

"Oh."

I tweaked the placement a little more, then stepped back to see the overall effect. It made the room look homey, and I liked it.

For the first time, I really took notice of the oil painting hung next to the chimney. It looked similar to the view from the front window. I stepped closer to see the signature.

"This looks like 'Hills'," I said, squinting to make it out.

"I believe the artist was called Anna Hills. Nanette once said Miss Hills visited the cottage often and painted here. Nanette purchased the piece from the former owner."

"That would explain why this looks so much like the waves breaking outside. But it could probably use a good cleaning."

I started to lift the frame to take it off the wall. But it didn't budge.

"What the heck?"

"Many years ago, I reframed the seascape and anchored it to the wall in order to prevent its coming loose during an earthquake. With Nanette's permission, of course." Max explained.

"Oh, I guess that makes sense. But it still needs cleaning. I really like it."

"It was my understanding that Miss Hills's work had appreciated considerably during my lifetime."

"Well I can find out."

"How will you accomplish that feat?"

"You'll see."

I fired up the laptop and Googled: *"Anna Hills" art price*, then hit *Enter*. I clicked on the first site.

"Whoa! One of her seascapes just sold for over eighty-thousand dollars!" I clicked through a few more. "Some of her prints are going for hundreds."

I looked back at the one on my wall.

"Nice to know there's a goldmine in that frame."

"Nanette insisted that particular piece of art remain in the cottage. She would not be pleased if it were to be sold."

"But, Max, if I needed cash, I *could* sell it. It's just nice to know it's there."

He was uncharacteristically silent.

I glanced at the fireplace wall again.

"I'll have to get blue candles and fresh flowers next time I'm at the store."

Some of my other supplies were starting to run low. I'd have to cook for Mitzi again before long, and I'd said I'd fix lunch for Helen. That brought to mind my last trip to the store. And that reminded me of Steve.

"I should tell Steve we finished the first chapter. He said he wanted to see it."

"Why have you been shilly-shallying about? Contact the man, by all means." Max had returned to his demanding, bossy self. But I had the distinct impression something had changed in him. There was no hint of a difference in his tone, but I knew I'd made him think—and feel—perhaps for the first time in years. Maybe forever.

I picked up my phone and hit Steve's number. I was surprised when he answered himself.

"Oh, hi. It's Nan Burton."

"Hi, Nan. Nice to hear from you."

"You said you wanted to see the first chapter of the manuscript when I got it translated. Well, it's done. Do you want me to email it to you?"

"I was planning on heading down that way tomorrow. Why don't I take you to lunch again, and I can look at it then. Besides, I've been thinking how much I enjoyed my run with you." His voice sounded warm. I could just picture the unruly lock of hair falling onto his forehead and could see him push his glasses back up his nose.

"I enjoyed having human company, too, for a change."

"I thought figuring out Max's handwriting was a challenge."

"It was until I enlisted a secret weapon. I found Max's old secretary, Helen Zeblinsky. She and I worked most of the day, but we managed to get through it."

I heard Max harrumph as his chair squeaked.

"Oh, I almost forgot. Helen's coming to work with me again tomorrow morning. I guess I won't be able to make lunch."

"I'd love to take you both. I'll just bring the other car so there'll be room."

Of course, he has another car. Doesn't everyone? Everyone but me.

"Uh, okay. That would be great."

"I'll get there around twelve-thirty, if that's okay with you. I have an eleven o'clock appointment."

"Sounds good to me."

We hung up and I realized lunch out with him and Helen sounded like fun.

Then I remembered the earlier crash in the garage. I picked up the packing material, put it back in the box, and opened the door off the entry.

Daylight streamed through a rather large hole in the roof. A heavy spring sat on the floor in a pile of glass. Apparently I'd missed some bottles sitting on a shelf to the side. The spring hadn't.

"Oh, God. What next?"

Sixteen

I STOMPED BACK INTO THE LIVING ROOM AND PLOPPED DOWN on the sofa. "Damn, double damn!"

"Is it absolutely necessary to use vulgar language? Surely you can find a more creative manner to express your dissatisfaction."

"Stuff a sock in it, Max. The spring just came loose and blew a huge hole in the garage roof. How the heck am I going to get that fixed?" There was that money question again. Then I got up and walked over to the Anna Hills painting. "Maybe it wasn't an accident that I discovered what this is worth today."

"No!" roared Max.

"Hey, what's the use of having a valuable piece of art if your house is falling apart?"

"Would it not make better sense to have a professional evaluation of the situation before overreacting?"

"Oh, that's easy for you to say. You don't have to deal with it."

I stomped over to the computer and booted it up. Several roofers were listed as well as a couple of garage door companies in the area. I called several. Even though it was getting late, a few agreed to come that day, so I made appointments.

* * * *

"Oh, Max. I don't think there's any way around it. I have to find some money and fast," I told him when the last of the 'professionals' left. "Even the lowest estimates are much, much more than I can begin to afford."

Just then the phone rang. "Oh, darling, you won't believe what's happened," my Mom gushed.

I was so depressed, even her excitement failed to improve my mood. I slumped back in the chair and watched the waves break, hoping they'd bring some peace. They didn't. "What?" I tried to match her enthusiasm but failed miserably. Even that one word was strained.

She didn't notice. "Your dad and I are leaving next week on an around-the world trip. You know how I've always wanted to travel? Well, now we can do it! We put the house on the market, and it sold in one day. Isn't that exciting?"

Exciting? Exciting! Heck no! If I have to move out, there's nowhere to go. And what about all the furniture? And the cars?

"Uh, isn't this rather sudden?" I was buying time to get my emotions together. I felt completely abandoned in the cottage, which was falling apart around me, with nowhere to run.

"Oh, no. Not really. You know, we've talked about doing it for years. Since even before we were married. Then you came along and, well, life happened. But your Aunt Netta gave us the chance to fulfill our dream while we still can."

"Aren't you still working?"

"Oh, we both decided to retire early and enjoy life. We have this amazing opportunity, and we don't want to waste it."

"But what about the house?" *The house I could have moved back into. The house that didn't have a hole in the garage roof.* "Where will you live?"

"We talked it over and decided when we get back, we'd rather have a nice condo with an ocean view so there'll be no upkeep. We might find somewhere else in our travels to buy a vacation home. Meanwhile, we won't have to worry about anything while we're away. We only put the house on the market to test the waters, so to speak. We didn't expect it to sell so quickly."

Of course, nothing else in the world is selling. Only my parents' house. Figures.

"What about your furniture and cars?"

"That's the best part! The church was looking for a couple of used but dependable transportation cars for members who need them for job hunting, so we're donating them. We'll get a tax deduction, too. And we'll buy new ones when we get back. We'd intended to do so anyway since they're both old."

Great. Don't bother thinking about your only daughter who's out of work, whose car died, who's stuck in her tumbledown hovel waiting for the next disaster. No, have a great trip. Don't worry about me.

She didn't wait for my reply. "As for the furniture, we selected the special pieces, you know, the ones we wanted to keep and we're giving the rest to the church for the rummage sale. We'll also be able to deduct the value of it. Our tax advisor thought it was a great idea. And we knew you didn't need anything since your little place is already furnished."

"Uh, great, Mom."

"What's the matter, darling? We thought you'd be happy for us."

Okay, Nan, quit acting like a spoiled brat. Mom and Dad tried gave you everything when you were growing up. And they have talked about traveling for years.

"I am, Mom, really. It's just that one of the garage springs broke and punched a big hole in the roof. The roofers said the whole thing has to be replaced. It's so old, it probably leaked already. It'll just get worse. And the garage door guys all said the old one is too waterlogged and termite-ridden to be safe. One even said I was lucky to have opened it without hurting myself. So it has to be replaced, too."

"Oh, sweetie, I'm so sorry. Do you want your dad to come over and have a look?"

"Thanks, Mom, but I can take care of it."

I really don't want to spoil this trip for them. After all, it's their lifelong dream. So I'll manage somehow, even if it means selling the painting.

"How long will you and Dad be gone?"

"We're not completely sure. Our tickets are open-ended. We leave California and cruise to Hawaii. We can take land tours and stay somewhere for a few days or a week if we want. Then we'll fly to Tahiti..." She went on to tell me about all the great-sounding places on their itinerary.

"Sounds like at least a couple of months," I said.

"Oh, at least, unless we get homesick. But I don't think that will happen.

We'll try to email when we can, and we'll send postcards. Oh, I can hardly wait!"

"I'm glad you're finally getting to do this." I meant it. They'd both worked hard all my life and deserved to enjoy life now. "You've earned it."

"Thanks, honey. We'd like to take you to dinner on Sunday night before we leave. Okay?"

"Sure, Mom." We made the arrangements, and then I hung up.

"Great. Just what I needed." I stared at the phone.

"Have you received unpleasant news?" Max actually sounded concerned.

"Yeah. No. Well kinda. Mom and Dad have sold their house and are taking off on a 'round-the-world trip, just when I could have used a place to stay for a while."

"You can't possibly mean you would abandon me and the book. Not at this juncture."

"Max, your little sanctuary is falling apart. I can't afford to make the repairs on my unemployment checks. The attorney won't part with a dime of Mitzi's trust or mine. And without a car, I couldn't get to a job, even if there were any to be had. What the heck am I going to do?" Then I did the one thing I never did, not even when Jeff left. I started to cry.

Max didn't say a word.

"I'm sorry, Max. It's just all so overwhelming."

When he spoke, his voice was gentle. "For a moment there, you resembled Nanette when she arrived after her friend died. I wanted to comfort her, but could only observe her pain." He hesitated, then continued, "However, in this instance, I believe I may have a solution to your immediate dilemma."

I sniffled and grabbed a tissue to blow my nose. "Oh, Max, what can *you* do?"

"I might be able to resolve your current economic crisis."

I'd forgotten about his 'missing' fortune, but suddenly remembered. "Is there a secret stash here somewhere I can use?"

"Um, perhaps."

"Max, 'perhaps' won't replace the roof or repair the garage door. And unless I can sell the painting fast..."

He sighed. "Very well. I suppose sooner or later someone will discover it. And since you are currently engaged in assisting me to complete my terminus opus..."

"Yes?"

He sighed again. I was afraid he was reconsidering, but I heard his chair creak. Then Mitzi headed toward the bedroom.

"Are you coming?" I heard Max ask.

I followed the dog.

"I don't see anything valuable, Max. Besides, the cleaning people went through here. Wouldn't they have found the money?" Then I remembered the ceramic strawberry.

"As we previously discussed, the charwomen employed to absterge this domicile were less than efficient."

"You're right, Max." He was. Besides, I didn't want to irritate him now that he seemed willing to help.

"If you would be so kind as to reposition the bedstead so that the head is accessible..."

I began to laugh. "Oh, Max, it's not under the mattress."

"Of course not!" There was the pompous Max I'd come to know. "That particular location is a bit of a cliché, don't you think?"

"Yeah," I said as I muscled the heavy old wooden frame away from the wall. It was one of the few pieces in the house that wasn't wicker. "I knew you wouldn't do anything that obvious. This thing weighs a ton. You're sure it's here?"

"You have heard the phrase, 'hidden in plain sight,' I presume. And in my day, furniture was sturdy and meant to last."

"Sure," I answered, panting with the exertion.

No wonder the cleaning people didn't try this. The darn thing's massive.

"Are you sure you don't have lead weights somewhere in here, Max?"

At last there was room for me to walk around the bed.

"Okay, what now?" I asked.

"I believe you will find a gap below the solid section of the headboard."

I walked to the head and, sure enough, there was a small space above the mattress. The pillows had covered the gap.

"Loosen the bed linens."

I did as he commanded.

"You will find a tear in the covering between the padding on the top and the wooden frame."

I felt around and found it. "Here it is."

This is starting to get interesting!

"If you place your hand in the opening, you should feel a zippered bag."

I felt around, then put more of my arm into the space. It connected with something metal. It felt like a zipper.

"I've got it!"

I grasped the zipper-thing and pulled. To my surprise, I withdrew a canvas bag about a foot long and eight inches wide. It looked kinda like the bags I'd seen the armored car drivers use when transferring money at the bank.

"No wonder the bed felt so lumpy. I've wonder why Aunt Netta never replaced it."

"I believe she had a certain fondness for that particular item," Max said.

I remembered his story about Aunt Netta staying here for days in mourning.

He may be right. This could have represented security for her.

"I guess I can see why she didn't want to get rid of it." I looked closely at the bag. "Max, I hate to mention it, but there's a lock on this thing. Do I have to tear or cut it open?"

"In the same manner you smashed the crockery berry?"

"Yeah. That was kind of the same idea."

"In this particular case, there is no need for theatrics."

"Then where's the key?"

"In the desk, of course."

"Of course," I replied.

Sure. Doesn't everyone hide their keys in their desk? And where the heck is it? And why didn't anyone else find it before now?

I grabbed the bag and returned to the living room.

"Okay, Maxie, where's the key?"

"I believe if you remove the second drawer on the left, you may locate it."

I set the bag on the desk and opened the drawer. Inside, I saw file cards and a stapler, paper clips and various other office supplies. But there didn't appear to be anything like a key. "It's not here, Max."

"I believe I said 'remove the drawer.'"

"Oh, yeah."

I pulled it out and turned it around. No key. But I'm not altogether stupid. I lifted it over my head and spotted an envelope taped to the bottom.

"Eureka!"

I pulled the tape loose and opened the flap. It was easy since the old glue no longer created a seal.

Out plopped a small key.

I picked up the canvas bag and tried the lock. It opened!

"Hey, Max, it worked!"

"Of course it did."

I reached in and pulled out a stack of bills. Green bills. Green bills with the number '100' on them. Lots of green bills.

"Max, did you rob a bank?"

"I never had faith in banks. I told you that during the great worldwide collapse of the 1930s, my parents lost everything they had worked for and saved over their lifetime. Fortunately, I began making a decent living and was able to help support them until they died. But my father, in particular, was never quite the same. Losing his entire savings crushed the man. I swore then I would never entrust my hard-earned resources to a stock market or any other financial institution."

"But, Max, if you'd invested this, it would be worth a whole lot more."

"Perhaps, but at what cost to my personal peace of mind?"

I didn't have an answer to that. "The article on the Internet said they hadn't found your fortune when you died. Is this why?"

"Um, partially."

"Then where's the rest?"

"I don't recall saying there was any 'rest.'"

His tone of voice indicated the subject was closed. Period.

I started counting. There wasn't as much as I'd first thought, but more than enough for the house repairs. Probably not enough to get a car, too, even a used one, but at least I could salvage the house.

"Thanks, Max. This will get everything fixed."

He didn't say anything more.

I called the roofer and the door guys who'd given me the best quotes and arranged for the repairs.

Just as I hung up, the phone rang. It was my dad.

"Kitten, your mom just told me about your roof. I'll come right over and see what I can do about it."

Good old Dad to the rescue.

"It's okay, Daddy. I figured out a way to get it fixed. As a matter of fact, it should be done tomorrow."

"Are you sure?"

"Just go and enjoy your trip."

"Okay, but if you need me, just call."

"I will. I promise. And thanks."

"Love you, kitten."

"Love you, too, Daddy."

It felt good to know that he was concerned and even better to know that I'd solved my own problem—with a little help from Max, of course.

My ghost was uncharacteristically quiet, so I decided to read a book I'd downloaded onto my computer. I figured I should be exposed to at least one of 'Maxine's' later books to get a feel for her... his style.

I looked forward to seeing Helen again and to lunch with Steve and felt optimistic that everything was going to work out just fine.

I just hoped fate didn't have another bad joke in store. But I wasn't counting on it.

Seventeen

THE NEXT MORNING, FOLLOWING MY RUN ON THE BEACH WITH Mitzi, my phone rang. I'd charged it the night before, but it was in the living room and I had to race to get to it in time.

"Hello," I said, out of breath.

"Ms. Burton?" said a female voice.

"Yes," I answered in a more natural tone.

"This is Mrs. Owens, Mr. Spencer's secretary."

"Oh, yes. Thank you for calling." *I sure hope she has some good news for a change.*

"Mr. Spencer asked me to locate a mobile groomer, a grocery with delivery service, and cab company in your area. The arrangements have been made and the office will be billed directly."

"Thanks. Let me get something to write on." I fumbled around in the desk drawers looking for paper and a pen or pencil, swearing softly under my breath and hoping she hadn't heard. I finally located a few pens in the center desk drawer, but no paper. I grabbed the bottom tablet in Max's stack and tore off the last sheet.

"How dare you deface my property?" he bellowed.

I waved him away and tried the pens. Of course, the first three were dried out. When I got the fourth to work, I started taking down the information Mrs. Owens provided. When she mentioned grooming, I looked at the little ball of fluff sitting near the Max chair. She certainly didn't look like the spoiled pooch I'd inherited. I hadn't brushed her since I moved in, and with all the time we'd spent outdoors, she was in need.

Note to self: Brush the dog before the groomers come.

"I've arranged appointments for them every other Tuesday morning. I hope that will be convenient for you."

"It should be as long as I'm not working."

"I've given you their phone number in case you need to change the schedule. Now, as for the groceries..."

I dutifully recorded all the information about the market as well as the account number. Same with the taxi company.

"Will there be anything else?" Mrs. Owens asked.

"I think that's about it for now."

"Please let us know if you need anything further for that sweet little dog."

"I will. Thank you."

I hung up. "Well, Mitz, at least you're taken care of. And I might be able to add a couple of my own items to your grocery order." Then I remembered that Mrs. Owens knew precisely what should be on that order. She'd cared for the dog before I got her. "Oh, rats. I guess I'll have to figure out another way. But at least I can keep you in the manner you're accustomed to or learn to like dog food." Actually, the dog was probably eating better than I was.

She cocked her head and raised one ear as if trying to figure out what I was talking about.

"Will you please concentrate on completing your assignment?" Max was getting testy, but I couldn't allow him to bully me.

"Sure thing—after I take my shower and dress and after Helen gets here." I headed for the bathroom, ignoring his huffing and puffing as I left. Of course, the traitorous dog stayed with her 'boyfriend.'

A hot shower and clean hair improved my mood considerably. This time I remembered our lunch date with Steve, so I actually located a pair of newer jeans and a clean yellow t-shirt. I left my hair down since I knew we wouldn't be driving in the convertible. For once, it sort-of cooperated, although I had to use an iron on it.

I slapped on some lip gloss and mascara after slathering my body with sunscreen.

One last glance in the mirror and I was ready for the day. "Not bad, Nan. Not bad at all."

"And what, pray tell, are your plans?" Max asked. He tried for a friendly tone, but failed.

"Until Helen gets here, I intend to check my email and look for jobs. My check arrived yesterday, so I need to show I'm seriously searching."

With that, I booted up the computer. Of course, the results were the same as they'd been since I was let go. The only consoling factor was that I wasn't alone. Several of my former colleagues were on LinkedIn, so I checked to see how they were doing. A couple had found other positions, but most were still in the same situation I was.

Then I created an account on Facebook. The gal from EDD mentioned using social media as a good place to network but warned me to be very businesslike in all my postings. I hunted and found a couple of people I knew, including the guy I went to high school with who loved Lamborghinis.

"Small world," I said as I invited him to be a friend.

My former boss was there, too, so I invited her. She was also on LinkedIn and had offered to recommend me if I needed it. And boy, did I! All I had to do was find at least one position I was qualified for.

The time passed quickly, and before long I heard a knock on the door.

There stood Helen in a cheery apple green ensemble, looking like the fashion plate I expected. She carried a tin, which she handed to me.

"Just a little something for after lunch," she said. "I baked them myself this morning."

"Mmm, cookies. They smell great. Oh, I forgot to tell you," I said as I took the can and closed the door. "We've been invited out for lunch."

"By whom?"

I laughed at her startled expression. "Max's publisher. He's coming around noon to see the first chapter and asked if we'd like to join him. I hope that's okay with you."

"Why, that would be delightful," she said. "I haven't seen John in years."

"Oh, this isn't John Peterson," I explained. "It's his son, Steven."

"My, my. So John has a grown-up son. I look forward to meeting him."

She opened the bottom drawer and extracted the tablets, then seated herself on the chair we'd moved next to the desk the day before.

We got right to work on the second chapter, and the words flowed into the computer smoothly. Each of us made suggestions with only a few comments from the 'author' along the way. Most made sense, so I passed them along or asked Helen's opinion. We managed to get several pages of the manuscript completed before we heard a car pull up in front.

"That's probably Steve now," I said. I couldn't believe two hours had gone by. I was starting to enjoy the project.

I opened the door even before Steve knocked.

"Hi," I said as he reached the porch.

"You must be starving," he replied. "I'm sorry my meeting took longer than expected."

"No problem. Helen and I were just working on the manuscript."

I led him into the living room.

"My goodness. You look so like your father," said Helen.

"Steve, this is Helen Zablinsky, Max's secretary. Although I've discovered she did far more than that for him."

"The strumpet," Max muttered.

I ignored him. I was actually getting pretty good at it.

"Glad to meet you, Helen. You knew my dad?"

"Oh, my, yes. I worked on the last twenty-two Maxine du Bois novels, and I was the liaison between the publishing house and Max. I spoke with your father often and met him on several occasions."

"Only because I invited you to accompany me," my un-silent ghost grumbled. I figured he was sulking, but I didn't care. I knew his books were successful in great part to the changes Helen had made and that she'd received no credit for her contributions.

"Are you ladies ready to eat? I'm famished," Steve said.

"I'll just run Mitzi outside while you get settled," I said.

"What a lovely treat," I heard Helen reply as Steve offered his arm. "What a gentleman. Your parents raised you well."

I could tell she was flattered at the attention.

After a quick trip to the yard, I grabbed my wallet and lip gloss and stuck them in my pocket. Then I locked the door.

I had expected Helen to be in the front seat, but she was happily settled in the rear.

Steve held the door open for me. "I thought I could sit in back," I offered.

"Oh, heavens, no," came the voice from behind. "You young people make conversation while I enjoy all the lovely scenery. I usually only glimpse the same routes from the bus. Now I'll see something different."

"I thought we could go to the Montage. Their food's pretty good," Steve said as he started the car. The black SUV was quite a change from the Jag, but all three of us were comfortable in it. And I was grateful for his thoughtfulness.

"I suppose you have reservations," I said.

He looked a little sheepish. "Well..."

Then I laughed, and so did he.

"You're pretty sure of yourself, aren't you?"

"I guess so. It's just that I do a lot of business entertaining and know quite a few good spots in this area."

"Well I, for one, have no complaints about your choices so far," I replied with a grin.

Okay, so I hadn't actually been to the Montage, although quite a few people had raved about it. I knew where it was, of course. You can't miss it driving on the coast near my place. The craftsman-style buildings are really appealing, and the location and view are fabulous. But I'd heard it was very expensive. I was excited to see it at last.

The meal and the resort lived up to all the hype. It was gorgeous, but not in the over-the-top formal way the Ritz was. This was class and charm with great service and excellent food. We ate in the Loft at a table with an awesome view of the ocean.

Each of us ordered a different meal, and we sampled each other's. Steve insisted on dessert again.

"I'm going to get really fat eating with you," I said.

"No you won't," he answered. "You promised me a run on the beach this afternoon, remember?" When our waiter arrived, he ordered three different selections, and we all tasted them.

"I believe I'm ready for my afternoon nap after that delicious meal," Helen said. "Would you young folks mind dropping me off at the bus stop?"

"Not at all. Where do you live?" asked Steve.

"In Corona del Mar," she replied. "I've owned the house for years and it belonged to my parents before that."

"It's a lovely little town," Steve said, helping her out of her chair. "I have a client there. I'll be happy to drive you home."

"Oh, no. That's not necessary," she started to protest.

"Oh, yes it is," Steve answered as we waited for the valet to bring the car.

Steve was right. I'd never spent much time in Corona Del Mar, but I found the older homes charming. Helen lived on a quiet street with an ocean view. Her home was about three times the size of my cottage.

"Thank you both so much. I've had a lovely day," she said as Steve opened the door for her and helped her out.

"Will I see you tomorrow?" I asked.

"Unless you don't want me to come."

"Of course, I do."

"Then I'll be there. I haven't enjoyed myself this much in years."

With that, she headed up the walk.

Steve closed his door. "She's really sweet," he said.

"Yes, she is," I agreed. "And she's the only one who can decipher Max's scrawl. I'm just lucky she's still around."

Steve started toward Pacific Coast Highway.

I looked at him. "Could I ask you a favor?"

"Sure."

"Could we stop by the bank and the store? See, I don't have a car and..."

"Of course we can. Just say where."

I gave him the name of my bank. While he waited in the car, I hopped out and used the ATM to deposit my unemployment check and Max's cash. It felt good to have a nice balance in the account, at least until I paid the repair bills.

Then we went to the store where I stocked up on all the basics. I also got a few items for dinner, including some pasta and a couple of jars of sauce. I figured if he was staying again, I'd be prepared.

This time, he picked up a few things that didn't require refrigeration for himself.

When we got back, he helped me carry my bags in.

"I'll print out the chapter and you can read while I put these away," I offered.

"Sounds good to me," he answered.

The night before, I'd finally gotten around to hooking up my printer. I figured we might need it.

I handed the pages to Steve and then went back to the kitchen.

"This is brilliant," I heard him say.

"Well, of course it is," replied Max, although no one could hear him but me.

"So you like it?" I asked as I entered the room.

"It's terrific. Although it doesn't exactly sound like the old Maxine du Bois books."

I felt myself blush. "Well, Helen and I thought the original was a little too old fashioned. We tried to make it sound more contemporary."

"Well, whatever you did, keep it up. If the whole book is this good, we have a winner on our hands."

I could feel the grin spread across my face. Not only was I having fun working with Helen, but I was beginning to really enjoy the whole writing thing.

Maybe I can do words, after all.

Eighteen

AFTER A NICE LONG RUN ON THE BEACH WITH STEVE AND MITZI, I fixed dinner. Spaghetti, a simple green salad, and warm bread looked and smelled good. I even broke out some wine.

I don't drink much, but I'd brought a few bottles with me when I moved in. They were the ones left after Jeff either drank up or stole the good stuff.

"I can't believe I'm hungry after that great lunch," I said. I was glad that Max had some nice glasses. They sure beat the mismatched tumblers in my old apartment.

"Me either," Steve replied. "But a good run and the beach air always perk up my appetite."

We enjoyed our meal and the conversation flowed easily. I couldn't believe how late it was by the time we finished and cleaned up.

"I better get going." Steve looked at his watch.

"Since I've been down here, I don't pay much attention to the time."

Of course, I don't wear a watch. Most of my friends don't either. We depend on our phones. They're more accurate and we always carry them with us.

He's a little old-fashioned. But I kinda like it.

We said good night, and I promised to email him the chapter so he could start looking at marketing the book. I also told him I'd send a summary of the plot. It would be Max's plot but a little updated. Okay, a lot updated.

After sending the chapter, I checked my email.

A couple of friends confirmed and requested friendship on Facebook. I was actually glad to hear from them.

There was also a notice that the coffee pot had been shipped, but that the microwave was backordered.

"Just as well," I muttered. "I'd like save a little more before it gets here."

"What are you mumbling about?"

"Nothing, Max. My microwave is on back order. Figures."

"And why would you require one of those dangerous experimental contraptions? Aren't they prohibitively expensive?"

I laughed. "Max, every kitchen has one. And they're really cheap. I nearly singed my eyebrows off on that ancient stove of yours. Besides, a microwave cooks easier and much quicker."

"What has the world come to when women no longer prepare meals using proper appliances?"

I sighed. "In the first place, both men and women cook. In the second, nearly all women work outside their homes. It's a necessity if you want to live in this area. The cost of living is really high, so both need jobs. It's important to be able to throw something in the microwave when you get home from work. Whoever is cooking can have dinner on the table in no time."

"I still do not see what is wrong with preparing food in the correct manner."

"Please define 'correct'. I think your definition and mine are worlds—and years—apart."

"My dear young woman, meals should be prepared with consideration for the eye, nose, and palate. Meat and produce should be selected from only the finest available and handled with the utmost care, cooked properly, and served at the correct temperature."

"And what makes you such an expert? Don't tell me you were a gourmet cook."

"Well..."

"Aha! Just as I thought. You never made a meal in your life. Did you, Max?"

"Uh, the truth is..." he blustered.

"Yeah. I'll bet you always had a cook or had your food delivered."

"I'll have you know that many excellent meals were prepared in that kitchen you so disdain."

"By whom?" I knew I had him on that one.

"Is this line of conversation necessary? I enjoyed the taste and smell of well-prepared cuisine and had the resources to secure it." He was back to being pompous again.

"Yes, this conversation is necessary. If we're going to update your darn book, you need to understand how things work now! So who prepared your perfect meals?"

He was silent for a moment, then he answered quietly, "Helen."

"Helen? You mean to tell me that after working for you all day, you expected her to cook, too?"

"It was not precisely expected. She—she offered and I obliged her."

"You make it sound as though you did her a big favor."

"Precisely. She insisted on sharing her luncheon and evening meals with me. I couldn't very well deny her, now could I?"

Arrogant jerk!

"Please tell me that you at least paid for the fixings."

"I certainly offered, at first."

"Do you mean to tell me that Max Murdoch, wealthy author of dozens of books, allowed his secretary to buy and cook his meals?"

"I suppose if you put it that way..."

"Ooh! You really are—were... No, you *are* a pompous, arrogant, inconsiderate, insufferable, self-centered, obnoxious idiot!"

I stomped out of the room with Mitzi at my heels and slammed the bedroom door as soon as her tail cleared the opening. I paced around calling Max every nasty name I could think of.

"I can hear you, you know," came a voice from behind me.

"Get out of here, Max," I growled.

"I shall be happy to oblige as long as you keep your voice down."

"Ooh!" I picked up a small silver box from the dresser and threw it at the door. It left a dent. Unfortunately, my rings and earrings scattered over the carpet.

"Temper, temper," Max scolded.

"Get out!"

I didn't hear any more from him as I picked up my jewelry. Well, except for his laughter.

* * * *

The next few days were busy. With all the activity and noise from the roofers, working with Helen was more difficult than it had been. She brought a couple of large straw hats with her, and we wore them on our after-lunch walks. I enjoyed our conversations and the escape from all the pounding.

I asked her about cooking for Max.

"Oh, the dear man would have forgotten to stop for meals if I hadn't been there," she said. "I was more than happy to care for both of us."

"Did he pay you extra for this service?" I already knew he hadn't, but I hoped I was wrong.

"Oh, no, dear. You see, Max lived for his art. It was his driving motivation. I loved being in his company and would have done anything to prolong our time together."

"Yes, but he was rich. I'm sure he didn't pay you enough to justify buying his groceries, much less acting as his chef."

"What makes you assume that he did not provide the foodstuffs?"

"Well, from what you've told me, he rarely left the house." I hoped that would be enough to cover my slip.

She looked at me. I guess she decided my logic made sense since she continued. "If I'd left it up to Max, who knows what he'd have purchased. You see, this way I could make my own selection."

"You brought them on the bus?"

"Of course. When you go to the market daily, the quantity isn't terribly great or heavy. In my day, many women did the same."

"But could you afford to feed him?"

She laughed. "Oh, darling girl, I was quite comfortable. My parents were wealthy. Following their deaths, I inherited their home as well as a great deal of other funds. My brother also received a large bequest, but there was more than enough for both of us. Since I never married or had children, my needs were few. It was my pleasure to provide a bit of comfort for Max."

She hadn't said, 'the man I loved,' but it was implied.

I nodded. I didn't really understand and I sure didn't excuse Max's attitude or behavior. But I think I got Helen's reasoning. Even if I thought she was wrong.

* * * *

I had a nice dinner with my folks on Sunday. I suggested going to the Montage, but Mom had already decided on the Harbor Grill in Dana Point. It was her favorite. One of mine, too.

The evening's conversation was all about their trip.

"We're having a limousine pick us up early tomorrow to go to the ship," Mom said, her excitement evident.

"I don't know if there'll be room for your mother's luggage," Dad said with a smile.

"Now, Craig, you know that one of the suitcases is empty." She turned to me. "I plan on buying new clothes during the trip, even if I have to send some home to Nan ahead of time. You wouldn't mind, would you, dear?"

"Of course not."

Dad just shook his head, but then he grinned.

"I'm really happy for both of you," I said. I meant it. "This is something you've dreamed about for a long time."

Dad reached across the table and took my hand. "I can't tell you how grateful we are to your Aunt Netta for making all this possible. And we're so happy you have that sweet little house to live in and a watchdog to protect you."

Some watchdog! As usual, she didn't bark when they came to the door.

"What about your car?" I asked since they'd driven it to get me. I was hoping they'd remembered I didn't have one, but they didn't.

"Mr. Morgan from the church will pick it up tomorrow. We gave him the spare key when we took Dad's car over last week," Mom said.

"You know, it feels really good to be able to do something nice for other people. I think that may be the best part of having a little extra. Sharing with those in need." Dad sat back with a contented sigh.

"We were so lucky with the house." Mom practically glowed. "Escrow closed on Thursday. It helped that the buyers paid cash. They were downsizing."

"Where are you staying now?" I asked.

"Well, we've always wanted to stay at the Ritz," Mom said. "So we are!"

They were both so full of the details of the trip, they couldn't talk about anything else.

After dinner, they dropped me off with a folder full of contact information.

"We'll write every few days and call when we can," Mom said as she kissed me goodbye.

Dad gave me a big hug and kissed me on the forehead, like he did when I was little. "Take care, kitten."

I saw tears in his eyes and tried not to cry myself. "Have a great time, both of you. I'll be sharing your adventure vicariously. And make notes of all the places I should go when my time comes."

If my time comes. If I can ever afford to go anywhere.

I waved goodbye and watched until the car turned the corner. Then I cried.

* * * *

On Monday morning, Mom called before they boarded the ship. After saying *bon voyage* to both of them, I had another small pity party. They were going on an adventure while I was trying to salvage a house that was falling apart around me.

By late morning, the new roof was completed. It felt good to write the check. It was Max's money, but I was sorry it wasn't my own. In the afternoon, the new garage door was installed.

I loved the idea of having a remote control for the car—whenever I got one—and a button next to the door off the entry.

My writing routine with Helen continued in a comfortable pattern. She arrived at ten-thirty every morning. She usually brought some food with her for lunch. I guess she'd gotten into the habit with Max. But I insisted we at least take turns.

Did I mention her cookies were delicious? Well they were! Every few days, even in the heat of summer, she baked a different variety. Each time I'd say, "Mmm. I think these are my favorites." Then she'd make a different kind.

Max got better about not kibitzing as Helen and I worked. When we finished the draft of each chapter, I sent it to Steve. He managed to get down our way once or twice each week. When he did, he took us to lunch, each time to a new and special place. And he also insisted on driving Helen home. He still looked like a scruffy and nerdy Clark Kent, but his consideration for the older woman won him points.

After Helen left each day, Max continued teaching me the basics of writing.

I still saw Tad nearly every day on my early-morning runs with Mitzi. We'd occasionally stop at his house where he always spoiled the dog. But his bevy of beautiful girlfriends kept him from even acknowledging my presence. I noticed the same one never came more than about three times.

The mobile groomers arrived as scheduled every Tuesday and gave me back a different dog than the one they picked up. I received lots of critical looks, even though I always tried to brush through her coat before they came.

I wasn't too happy about the pink bow they stuck in her topknot, but it kept the fur out of her eyes. At least for a day or two.

I cooked for Mitzi every couple of weeks and froze her meals. I was glad Mom had suggested it since I got it done in one marathon session.

My parents sent postcards from exotic locations, all with the news that they were having a wonderful time. They called once a week or so. It was terrific to hear their voices, and I never let on how much I missed them.

The job boards continued to be frustrating. The positions advertised either required software experience I didn't have or other skills I didn't possess. I applied anyway to keep the people at the unemployment office happy. But I knew employers wouldn't call back.

The coffee pot arrived, but the microwave continued on backorder. The first time I tried to make coffee, a fuse went. Max told me where the box was and I was surprised that most of the spots had pennies in them.

"Hey, Max. Aren't you supposed to replace the fuses?"

"Why go to all that trouble when a penny will do as well?"

Was Max cheap? Wouldn't he pay someone else to do it or did he avoid going out to get the fuse? And if he was that cheap, then where the heck was his fortune? But I guessed he knew what he was talking about since he'd lived there all those years without mishap.

He told me how to put the new penny in.

"You might consider plugging that contraption in a different receptacle," he suggested.

Since there was an empty one in the living room right around the corner from the kitchen, I tried it. And it worked.

That first cup of brewed coffee was like pure heaven. The smell. The taste. I felt as though my life was starting to fall back into place, at least a little.

I became contented with the sameness of the days, with Helen's company and with Steve's lunches and trips to the grocery.

I like routine. And I had one. At least until Steve broke the news about the marketing campaign for the book. Then my whole world turned upside down again.

"YOU WANT ME TO DO WHAT?" I SHOUTED INTO THE PHONE.

"Start making public appearances for the book," Steve explained again.

"But I don't do that stuff. And why me?"

"Because Max is dead. Besides, from what I've read so far, you've made quite a few changes in the manuscript. Don't forget, I know Max's work. Don't get me wrong. Everything you did made the book better. But most of them are no longer Max's original words, are they?"

He had me there. "No," I confessed.

"We can publish it under the name 'Maxine de Bois,' but we'll introduce you as the actual writer."

"Can you do that? Use Maxine's name, I mean."

"Use Maxine's name for what purpose?" asked Max in my ear.

I shooed him away and turned my attention back to the phone.

Steve answered. "It's been done many times in the past. The name 'Carolyn Keene' was used for a number of authors who wrote the Nancy Drew books. That's probably the most famous instance, but there are others where the original writer died and someone else picked up the pseudonym."

"I don't know..."

"Look at it this way. We still have an account in Max's name. We deposit his royalties in it. But since he had no heirs, it will just sit there unless our lawyers think of a creative way of dispersing it. It would be silly to continue for the new book. Besides, you've done the bulk of the work. We want you to be the author of record."

"Helen helped."

"I'm sure you'll pay her well for her services or make some other arrangement once you begin receiving royalties. But we need to start telling the media the story of how this book came about."

"Just what do you mean by 'media'?"

"Radio, TV, newspapers, wherever we can get placement."

"But shouldn't we wait until the book is published before we start doing that?" I was hoping to delay as long as possible and even considered dragging out the completion.

"I talked to our marketing people in New York, and they want to build interest well ahead of publication."

"Like when?"

"In the next month or two, as soon as it's finished. That was your last estimate. You should have visibility soon."

"But..."

"No buts." He was getting almost as bossy as the 'famous author.'

"Steve, I'm really not comfortable with this whole idea. You've seen my wardrobe. I don't think jeans and t-shirts would give the impression you want. And I haven't had a haircut in a long time. Besides, I don't wear make-up, and I don't photograph well, and I've never been a public speaker and..."

"That's why I asked Brooke Davidson, my assistant, to come with me next week. She's pretty savvy when it comes to fashion and photography."

I wanted to say, "Great. Did she style you?" But I didn't. Instead I asked, "So what will she do?"

"Help you pick out some clothes and get you camera-ready. Oh and she'll work with you on the points you can make and answers to questions you'll probably get."

"I still don't think..."

"You'll be fine. You'll see. So what day works best for you?"

We settled on Wednesday of the following week.

My stomach was doing flips when I hung up the phone.

"What grand scheme were you and your love interest hatching regarding my nom de plume?" Max demanded.

"Steve is not my love interest, and we weren't hatching anything. He wants to publish the new book as Maxine du Bois, since it started out as your story."

"Quite sensible, dear girl. Perhaps your young man has possibilities after all."

"He is not my young man, especially since he wants me to do some publicity."

"And why, pray tell, did he select you for this particular activity?"

"Because he knows I—well, Helen and I—modified your original manuscript. He wants me to be the identified as, I think he called it, the author of record."

"How dare he make such an outlandish suggestion?" Max bellowed.

"Because, Maxie dear, you're dead. It's that simple."

"It seems terribly inappropriate."

"They have to pay someone the royalties, and I'm afraid you're not eligible. Since you died, they've accumulated a lot for your other books, according to Steve. They can't pay them to anyone because you have no heirs."

"I suppose paying them to you makes business sense to the publisher, but it seems somewhat dishonest."

"Since you were listening, you might remember I tried to tell him that."

"I suppose you did."

"Believe me, buddy, talking about this book in public was not what I signed on for. Especially when he's thinking of radio and TV. Oh, God, how the heck am I going to do that?"

I sank into the sofa.

"As we previously discussed, I only attempted to tout the virtues of my work one time. I found it quite exhausting, and it detracted from my ability to produce any worthwhile material."

"At least you understand."

"I most certainly do."

"Hey, Max. Do you realize, this may be the first thing we've ever agreed on?"

He laughed and I joined him.

If I had to be totally honest, I'd come to like the idea of having someone around to talk to. Even if he was a ghost.

Otherwise, I led a pretty solitary existence in my new life. Just me and Mitzi and our routine. Helen and Steve added some variety to my days, as well as the neighbors I greeted on our runs.

And then there was Tad. I was content just to look at him. Good thing, since he still barely acknowledged my existence except as Mitzi's owner.

Our shared laughter was interrupted by a knock.

"Who the heck could that be?"

It was a Saturday morning, and I didn't expect Helen or Steve or Tad or anyone else, for that matter.

To my surprise, Mitzi started barking and growling as I opened the door. Jeff stood on the porch.

"What do you want?" I asked as my little dog placed herself between us and continued to growl. She seemed to be trying to sound menacing, but because she was so little, it was almost comical. I didn't try to silence her.

"Oh, baby, I made a big mistake," he started, taking a step forward.

"You sure did," I countered before he could go any further.

"I know I hurt you and I'm sorry. I've missed you so much. I still need you."

The 'need' part was no surprise. It was the 'sorry' part I questioned.

"Why are you here?"

"I just need a place to crash for a little while. Until I get a job." He pushed forward and both the dog and I backed into the house.

"What happened? Your new girlfriend discover what a lazy bum you are?" I was in no mood to be nice or forgiving. My conversations with Helen had finally shown me what a colossal jerk Jeff was.

"Well..."

"My answer is no. Not now. Not ever. Never again. Besides, how did you find me?"

"I saw your name and city on Facebook, babe. But I really had to ask around to figure out exactly where you lived."

"Well, now that you know, get out."

"Oh, baby..."

"Don't start. I'm not your baby and I never was. You're a loser and a user. Well, you're not using me ever again." I placed my hand firmly on his chest and shoved him back out the door.

"Okay, okay. I'll come back when you're in a better mood." He turned to leave, then shot back over his shoulder, "You know you need me."

"Ooh!" I slammed the door and locked it. "That guy just doesn't learn! This time I meant it." I looked down at my little black-and-white defender. "Good job. I guess you might make a decent watchdog after all."

It seemed Mitzi had pretty good instincts about people. After all, she liked the same people I did. And then it occurred to me, she liked Max.

I wonder if Helen's right. Maybe Max isn't quite as self-centered and selfish as I thought. Then again, she said she was in love with him. Maybe she wasn't exactly objective.

I decided to wait a little longer to make my final judgment.

* * * *

The following Wednesday, Steve and Brooke arrived. I was surprised when he introduced her. She didn't look at all like I'd expected.

Well, I don't exactly know what I expected, but it wasn't at all what showed up.

Brooke was about my age and had short spiked shoe-polish-black hair with red streaks, a pierced eyebrow, and rather Goth makeup. She was dressed all in black leather with a few chains. I noticed a butterfly tattooed on her neck and wondered if there were others hidden by her long sleeves and pants.

I hope Steve doesn't have her make me over to look like her!

"Wow! Cool place," she said looking around.

"Thanks," I replied.

Steve offered to give her a tour while I took Mitzi out.

"You don't have to take me with you. You youngsters should be able to enjoy yourselves without dragging an old lady along," Helen said as we got ready to leave. "I'll just walk to the bus stop."

"Oh, no you won't," Steve insisted. "I need someone to keep me company while they do their girlie stuff. Besides, if you get tired, I'm sure I'll have more than enough time to drive you home before I go back for them."

"Well, if you insist..." Helen said.

"I do." Steve opened the back door for her.

He'd brought the SUV again so there'd be room for everyone. I was surprised when Brooke went around and got in next to Helen. Steve opened the passenger door for me.

I must confess, when she arrived, I was a little uncomfortable when I thought about them working together. I didn't think she was exactly his type. But then I didn't really know what his type was. And after all, I wasn't really interested in him.

"Cool music," Brooke said from the backseat.

"Thanks," Steve replied. "It's the Missiles of October. They're a local group."

It was one of their more upbeat songs.

Brooke started snapping her fingers.

I'd thought the group's sound was probably a little tame for her usual taste. She surprised me. It wasn't the first and wouldn't be the last time that day.

Steve headed to South Coast Plaza. After looking at the list of restaurants, we all agreed on California Pizza Kitchen. Brooke was a vegetarian and said she could get things she liked there.

As we finished our meal, Brooke said, "I have a couple of stores in mind to start with." She looked me over.

I felt like I was being stripped naked.

"I think we'll start with sportswear separates. Classic mix-and-match pieces. Blue would probably look good with your eyes, but we'll try some lavender and maybe some deep jewel tones. Then you'll need a couple of dresses and maybe one cocktail number."

"Hey, wait a minute," I said. "I don't have that kind of budget."

Actually, I didn't have *any* budget for clothing. I barely had enough for the basics. Nothing for extras.

"Oh, this is a business expense," Steve said. "Brooke has the corporate card, and I've told her to charge whatever she thinks you'll need. Consider it part of your advance."

She turned her head away from him and winked at me. "I think with some of the media appearances you've been thinking of, Nan's gonna need plenty of outfits. You also mentioned a book tour after publication. Whatever we get today should work for that, too."

Steve looked thoughtful. "I guess you're right. Okay, Brooke, lead the way."

The next few hours were spent trying on clothes. At least I tried them on. Brooke ran around bringing me more and more items, looking at them, approving or rejecting. When she found a look she liked, she paraded me out to wherever Steve and Helen were sitting. In each store, he announced that he was looking for a couple of 'man chairs' for them to wait in. I figured these upscale places expected rich husbands or boyfriends to wait while their significant others shopped. Convenient seating was always close at hand.

When Steve, Brooke, and Helen all agreed on an outfit, Brooke charged it. I was only asked if I liked it, once they had reached consensus.

What wasn't to like? I'd never owned such great stuff in my life! For someone who looked like a fugitive from a motorcycle gang, Brooke really had pretty nice taste.

After each store, Steve took the bags to the car. Brooke insisted we include underwear, shoes, accessories, and everything else required to put together complete outfits.

At three-thirty, Brooke's phone played a strange ringtone.

"Oh, that's my reminder. We have an appointment to get your hair done in half an hour. We'll have to wrap this up for now and get going."

I looked at Helen. She seemed to be fading a bit, although her enthusiasm and encouragement had been a real boost for me throughout the afternoon.

I guess Steve realized she was tired, too, because he turned to her. "I think that's our clue to disappear for a while. I'll take you home. That way I won't have to hang around with nothing to do."

Helen smiled.

I love the way he made something that might have been a chore sound like a reprieve. Unless it really was...

Brooke led me to the old Crystal Court building and into a really classy salon. She gave her name, and we were introduced to Jacques. He and Brooke began to whisper together while staring at me.

"Hey, guys. I'm here. Can I take part in this discussion?"

"Oh, oui. Meez Brooke, she suggested a glamorous old-time movie star look and I agree. *Magnifique!*"

"Well, I..."

"But Jacques, he will make you gorgeous. All zee other women weel envy you. Trust Jacques," he assured me.

Brooke nodded.

"Uh, okay, I guess." I mean, what else could I say?

My hair was washed, cut, colored, and styled. Then my nails—all of them—were soaked, shaped, and polished. The make-up artist steamed my face, applied a masque, and then moisturized, plucked, dabbed, drew, brushed, and painted. When I was finally turned toward the mirror to see the result, I couldn't believe my eyes. My huge blue eyes.

I looked just like Aunt Netta!

"But how..." I started.

"Steve showed me the picture on the mantle and said he thought it would be a good look for you." She tipped her head. "He was right."

When we emerged, Steve was waiting.

"Wow," he said. The look on his face told me he thought we'd done a good job.

#

"NANETTE?" MAX ASKED QUIETLY AS I OPENED THE DOOR. I couldn't answer him because Steve was right behind me carrying a load of bags. Those were in addition to the ones in my hands. Brooke followed with more sacks and boxes.

"Hi, Mitzi," said Steve as we entered the bedroom, where I dumped my load on the bed.

Once he dropped everything he carried next to mine, Steve reached down and petted my dog.

Brooke made the pile even higher, then focused on Mitzi. "Wow, it sounds like she's purring. I never heard a dog do that."

I laughed. "Thanks. I thought I was imagining it."

"Nope," Brooke answered, then laughed with me. "That's a purr if I ever heard one."

We both stared at the mountain we'd created.

"Whew," I said. "I've never had this many clothes before—especially new ones all at once." To be honest, I was a little overwhelmed.

Brooke laughed. "We didn't completely buy out the mall, but we sure tried."

Steve looked a little stunned. He shook his head. "I just hope this will get you through."

Brook looked at him seriously. "Well, we may need to fill in with a few more pieces."

At the shock on his face, she laughed again. "Steve, you look like you just swallowed a goldfish! I was kidding."

She turned to me. "I wanted to get everything you might need in one shopping spree."

"Well, looks like we did that," I said.

Steve glanced at his watch. "I guess we should head back. It'll be a long trip."

"It shouldn't be too bad at this time of night," Brooke reassured him.

After shopping, we'd enjoyed a long, relaxed and delicious dinner and lost track of the time. It was after ten when we returned to my place.

"I wish we had time for a run. After that day, I could use one," I said. Then I added, "But I'm afraid I'm worn out."

Steve nodded. "I wish it was earlier, too. I'll come down one day soon, if you'll give me a rain check. Tonight, Brooke and I need to get home."

Somehow the thought of them going home together didn't feel too good, and I couldn't figure out why.

"Sure. Come back anytime. You, too, Brooke."

"Thanks. I'll do that," she said. "This is a way cool place."

I walked them to the door and said good night. Then I closed it.

"Is that you, Nanette?" Max asked.

"It's just me," I answered as I entered the living room.

"For a moment, I hoped your aunt had returned and that perhaps I had finally been released from this bizarre confinement."

"Sorry to disappoint you, pal, but it's still just me. Do I really look that much like her?" In the salon, my own eyes had told me I did, but he'd actually known her when she was about my age.

"The absolute image," he said.

I walked to the mantle and picked up the photo of the three friends. I could finally see the resemblance everyone had mentioned since I was little. I was a lot taller and my face was thinner, but it didn't take much imagination to see we were related. I ran a finger over her face as if trying to feel her through the glass.

Jacques had cut my hair to just above shoulder length and changed the color back to blonde with lighter highlights. It now looked a lot like hers in the picture. He showed me how to put gel into it and then 'scoorunch,' as he said, to get the curl to stay. He said I could blow it dry and straighten it and showed me how.

I'd never liked my curls. Part of the reason I wore a pony tail was to keep my hair straighter and out of my face. But I knew I could manage it easier the way it was cut now. And even I had to admit it looked pretty good.

Of course, the makeup helped, too. With my eyebrows plucked and darkened a little, my eyes showed up. Then the subtle shadow, liner, and mascara Yvette had added made them look even bluer. She showed me what she'd done, and it didn't look too hard. Of course, I'd need some practice, but I thought I could do it myself.

Max sighed and I heard his chair creak. "Since you have nearly reached completion of my portion of the manuscript, I anticipated freedom. But I now assume the entire story must reach fruition."

"Hey, Max, are you getting tired of me so soon?"

"No, my dear girl. Just the endless incarceration. I am unable to travel beyond the walls of this abode." He sighed, then added. "I must admit, I find my current situation more bearable with someone to talk to."

I sat on the sofa facing his chair. "I know what you mean. Just having you here has helped me, too. Since I can't go many places without a car, I appreciate your company and Helen's. I must be going crazy, but I think I'd miss you if you weren't around."

"And I you, as difficult as I find it to make such an admission."

We sat in comfortable silence until Mitzi headed for the back door.

* * * *

The next morning, I heard pounding as I returned from my morning run.

"Just a sec. I'm coming," I yelled.

I threw open the door and Mitzi started to bark frantically.

There stood Jeff with his duffle bag.

"I told you, you aren't welcome," I said as firmly as I could.

"Oh, babe, you know you need someone to take care of you." He looked at Mitzi. "And that little *fru-fru* dog isn't going to be much help. I only need a place to stay for a while, and you have this nice little house all to yourself."

Mitzi'd settled next to me, growling.

Jeff tried to step past, but I blocked his way.

"I said, get out," I screamed. I knew he was stronger than I was. So did he. "You better leave, or I'll call the cops," I shouted as loudly as I could, and I prayed he'd get the message. I wasn't sure exactly what I'd do if he didn't.

I heard footsteps running my direction just as Jeff put his hand on my shoulder to push me out of the way.

"Take your hands off her." It was Tad, acting like the hero of my dreams. "The lady told you to leave. I suggest you do so immediately."

He called me a lady and sounds serious enough to be intimidating. He's also a lot bigger and stronger than Jeff. Even that idiot should notice Tad's muscles. His trunks and tank top hide nothing.

Jeff backed off. "Hey, man. I wasn't going to hurt her."

"See that you don't or you'll have me to deal with."

Oh that voice!

"Come on. I just need a place to crash. After all, Nannie, we were together a long time." He looked at me. "You know we made a good team."

"Team? Jeff, the entire time you lived with me, you contributed zip. And the minute I lost my job, you bailed. I didn't need you then. And I don't need you now. So leave."

"You heard the lady. Now, beat it."

There's that 'lady' thing again. Wow! I guess Tad doesn't see me as a kid any more. And I'm glad Jeff reminded me of how much I hate being called 'Nannie'! I'm not a goat!

"I'll walk you to the corner." Tad took Jeff by the arm and led him away. Jeff didn't look back.

A couple of minutes later, Tad returned. "Are you okay?"

"Yeah. I think so."

"The guy's a real jerk."

"You can say that again. He only hung around as long as I paid the bills and cooked and cleaned up after him. When things got tough, he left me for someone else. Oh, and he wiped out my savings, too."

"I hope I didn't mess up anything, but you sounded like you need help."

"I did. Thanks for coming to my rescue."

"I was just about to leave when I heard you and decided to check the situation. When I came up, it looked like he was manhandling you. I don't go for that."

"He probably wouldn't have hurt me, but I wasn't sure how I was going to get rid of him. I'm glad you stepped in."

"So am I. By the way, he asked if we were an item, and I didn't tell him no. I hope that was okay."

"Maybe he'll stay away if he thinks we're together. Thanks."

"I was afraid he'd come back otherwise. Now it's probably safe for me to go. But holler if he shows up again."

He loped off, and I heard his sports car start up and roar away.

"Now, that's a great guy," I told Mitzi as we went back in.

* * * *

The next few weeks passed quickly. It was the end of September when we finished Max's tablets.

"Well, dear, it looks like you won't need me anymore," Helen said with a sigh after I typed Max's last words.

"Oh, no you don't. You're not getting out of completing this book that easily! I need you, Helen. I can't imagine finishing this thing without your help. After all, you know how Max wrote much better than I do."

She looked thoughtful. I realized she'd seemed tired as we neared the end. After all, she was getting older.

"I mean, I'd really love your help if you feel up to it," I said.

Her face brightened. "Why, of course, I'll help if you think I can make a contribution."

I hugged her gently, careful not to put too much pressure on her joints. I knew she was in constant pain from 'Arthur.'

"I've been meaning to talk to you about something," I said.

She looked at me with interest.

"Steve told me he wanted me to be the author of record for this book."

She nodded and Max snorted, but I ignored him and continued. "I told him it was okay, but I really think we should share the royalties. After all, I wouldn't have been able to do this without you."

"Oh, yes you would have. You'd already completed the first paragraph when I arrived."

"Yeah. And it took two days just to get that little bit done. You were able to do several pages a day. Oh, and we also rewrote everything, too. There's no way I could have done that by myself."

I heard Max mumble. But it was quiet, so I knew his heart really wasn't in the complaint. In the end, he'd admitted our rewrite was better than his original.

Helen put her hand on my arm. "Darling girl, I thank you for the thought, but as I told you before, I have no need for any more money at this stage of my life. Just being here with you and seeing Max's words again made me feel younger than I have for years."

"But..."

"Hush. We'll not discuss it again. If you think I can still be of use, I'd love to help you finish the book."

"There must be something I can do for you."

"Just allowing me to be here with you, sharing a meal, taking walks is more than enough. Oh." She looked at me. "And being my friend."

I felt tears forming.

"I haven't had a real friend in a very long time," she continued. "And despite the difference in our ages, I consider you a very dear one. I had hoped you'd felt the same."

I could sense the dampness spill onto my cheeks. "Of course. But I didn't think you saw me as anything other than a kind of—well—young pain-in-the-neck."

She laughed. "No, darling. You've become the granddaughter I never had. I'm happy it wasn't too late for me to know how precious that relationship could be."

"I love you, Helen," I whispered, my eyes blurring.

"And I love you, too, Nan dear." Her smile was so beautiful, I knew she meant it.

"Let's call it a day and start in again tomorrow. I know where there are some delicious-looking apples to go with our lunch," I said.

Twenty-one

THE NEXT PHASE OF THE BOOK WENT DIFFERENTLY THAN THE first part since we no longer had Max's words to work from.

The first day, Helen and I sat in silence trying to find the right beginning for the next chapter.

Finally, I heard Max in my ear. "As the holidays approached, Sarah found herself contemplating the new man in her life."

I nearly said, "Great." But I stopped myself just in time. Then I turned to Helen. "How about this?" And I repeated Max's suggestion.

"Oh, my," she said. "You sounded just like Max."

I had to think quickly. "It must be from hearing you read his words all these months."

We made a couple of changes so it sounded more like something a girl my age would say.

"Wonderful," she said when we'd finished.

Our process became one of writing until we needed words. Then we'd pause. Helen probably assumed I was thinking, but I was really waiting for Max to come up with the next ones. Then I'd suggest them to Helen. About half the time, however, I'd change his suggestions to make them more contemporary. And the longer we wrote, the less I depended on Max.

When the modifications to his suggestions were substantial or when he disagreed with something I proposed, Max would sometimes harrumph, but he mostly remained silent. He seemed to be a little less grumpy. Maybe it was because we were getting near the end of the book or because he had nothing to complain about.

Once in a while he'd bluster, "No, no you have it all wrong again."

Then I'd ask Helen if she'd reread what we'd written. Most of the time, when I heard the words aloud, I understood what he meant.

After Helen left each day, Max continued his master class on the finer points of creativity.

"Wow, Max. I didn't know writing was this hard. I mean, I thought all you had to do was put down the words. I never realized there were so many rules!"

"Dear child, the trick is to make the process appear effortless. And that requires a great deal more attention to detail than, as you described it 'putting down the words.' A story which is truly worthwhile should be crafted in such a way as to draw readers in and entice them to continue." His voice moved around as if he was pacing. "The very best ones are compelling. Readers won't be able to stop until they have reached the conclusion. At which point, they should feel the same satisfaction one achieves following a delicious meal."

"So, tell me how to do it." I suddenly felt overwhelmed.

"Each chapter must begin with what is sometimes called a 'hook'. A sentence to set the action in motion is required in order to keep the energy flowing toward the climax. The final sentence in the chapter, likewise, should pose a question, quandary, or problem."

"I get it! You want people to continue—to keep turning the pages."

"Precisely."

"But isn't that sort of... I don't know. Manipulative?"

"My dear, when you have been thoroughly entertained by a great book or a play, do you feel manipulated?"

"Of course not."

"Ah, but in a way, you were."

"Really?"

"Indeed. Someone wrote the words. They were intended to draw upon common human emotions. All great tales evoke a response."

"Hmmm, I never thought about it that way."

"And the author must create a range of moods. If there are no lows, there can be no highs. And the deeper and more profound the sensations evoked, the more effective the work becomes."

I had to think about that one a little. I remembered stories I'd read and plays and movies I'd seen. "So what you're saying is that crying and laughing are both important."

"Ah. I believe you are beginning to comprehend."

"And I should try to get my readers to feel both."

"Yes, but a writer must always guard against appearing blatant or obvious. The situations must be the source of the characters' reactions. Hence, the reader's. Otherwise it will become awkward and stilted, or seem as though the author is taking unfair advantage. Then it becomes the dreaded manipulation you fear."

"This is all a little too much to take in."

Max was on a roll and continued. "Furthermore, all well-crafted pieces are mysteries."

I was confused again. Just about the time I sort-of got what he was talking about, he came up with something new. "But you didn't write mysteries. You wrote romance novels."

"Women's literature," he corrected. "But each one asked the same questions: 'What happens next?' and 'How will it end?'"

I'd never really thought of it like that before. But I realized he was right. "So how do you do it?"

"Ah, that is a most difficult challenge. Some people are blessed with the required instincts and intuition. Others are not."

I was afraid to ask the next question, but I had to know. "What about me?" If he answered wrong, I knew I'd never get the book finished, even with his help.

He seemed to consider for a moment. "I do believe you may possess the qualities required. Of course, you must learn to apply them with a critical eye and ear. Nevertheless, it is my considered opinion that I just might be able to mold you into a passable writer."

"So you're my Svengali? My Professor Higgins?"

"Quite so. And you are my Galatea. My Eliza. My Trilby."

"So you're saying you created me, that I was nothing when you discovered me?" I sure didn't like the idea one little bit.

"My dear child, if you had not possessed some inherent talent, I would be unable to mold you into anything remotely resembling a competent novelist."

"Okay... I guess." I still wasn't sure whether he was taking most of the credit or giving me a left-handed compliment. But it did sound as though he thought I had promise. Knowing how impatient my resident ghost was, I had little doubt he'd have given up on me long before if he hadn't thought I stood a chance.

Then I had another thought. "What about Helen?"

"What about her?" he asked dismissively.

"Does she have the right instincts, or whatever?"

Again he hesitated. "Well, I suppose she has some innate intelligence. However, I believe she acquired whatever knowledge of the creation of literature she possesses from her years under my tutelage."

Okay, now I was mad again. "Max, you know as well as I do that your later books would have flopped without her changes. Steve said it and so did Helen. You owe her a huge debt of gratitude. And she only did it because she was in love with you."

"You continue to insinuate that Helen had undying *amour* for me."

"She did, and she still does. She considers you the one great love of her life. And you were too blind and stupid to see it." Now I was on a roll. I'd told him all this before, but he was still in denial. Just like he'd been in life. "Furthermore, she spent her own money to get here and feed you and..."

"Absurd."

"Not! You are without a doubt the most selfish, vain, stupid, blind man I've ever known!"

He sighed, then surprised me by saying, "Perhaps you are correct. During my lifetime on terra firma, I suppose I never thought to examine the emotions of those near at hand."

"Now there's an understatement!"

"You must realize the information you are conveying is enlightening, if incomprehensible. You see..." I heard his chair creak. "I was an only child, born when my parents were aging and had not expected to have progeny. In my youth, they promptly fulfilled my every desire. It seemed my due. Once I became somewhat well-known in the literary world, the adulation seemed natural and deserved."

"And you never bothered to think about how you treated the young ladies you—uh—entertained, either. Oh, except how to jerk them around and get them into your bed."

"I suppose if I were to appear before the magistrate in a court of law, I should have to plead guilty to your accusations." He sounded weary. "However, you are also oblivious to the suffering of others."

"What the heck do you mean?"

"Have you not noticed that Helen seems quite exhausted? She appears to have a dearth of energy. As I recall, she had an abundance until quite recently."

He was right. She was slowing down. But at her age, I guess I'd just expected it. "You're right, Max. I did notice, but she seems so eager to complete the book. I guess I should've made her get some rest."

"Then it appears we were both somewhat remiss regarding that particular lady."

"I hate to admit it, but when you're right, you're right. I think I'll suggest we only work half days. We can share lunch and our 'daily constitutional' as she calls it. Then in the afternoons, maybe you can teach me more about writing."

"It would give me a great deal of pleasure to pass along my years of wisdom and experience."

"And I probably should spend more time working on my job search. Although to tell you the truth, I don't have as much enthusiasm for programming as I used to."

He had no response to that, probably because he had no clue as to what programming was.

* * * *

My life settled into a new pattern. Helen still arrived at ten-thirty each weekday. We set to work and kept at it until around noon or one. Then we stopped for lunch.

I had few cooking skills... Okay, I had zero cooking skills. So I asked

Helen to teach me a few simple dishes.

"Oh, Nan dear, I would love to pass on some of my favorite recipes."

Steve came down once or twice a week to get new chapters and took us out to eat and then to the store. (He said he wanted to see the words in print the first time before I emailed them. I wasn't sure whether or not I believed him.)

I got enough money from my unemployment check for groceries and my basic needs. Ahead of each shopping trip, Helen prepared a list for our next cooking project, and then I bought the ingredients.

After we worked on the manuscript the next day, I carefully followed her directions. I can't say I'd actually conquered the old stove, but I managed a truce.

"I always found this oven to be more accurate than the one I have at home," Helen said as I placed the meatloaf pan on the rack and closed the door.

"How is that possible? I mean, I thought all stoves were the same."

Helen laughed. "Oh, no. Some are much better than others. I remember one my niece had that never worked right. The oven was consistently at least fifty degrees off. The more she used it, the less accurate the temperature. But Max's oven always held nice and steady. Whatever you set the control to is precisely the temperature you get. You can depend on it. And the burners are easy to adjust as well."

"Helen, with you around, I learn something new every day!"

"At my age, it gives me a bit of satisfaction to pass on what little knowledge I may have."

I tried a slice when it came out. It was even better than Mom's. And I made it!

I fixed cold meatloaf sandwiches for our lunch the next day and told Helen how good her recipe was.

She blushed. "I'm so glad you enjoyed it. But, after all, you're the one who prepared it."

"I did, didn't I? You may make a real cook out of me yet!"

A couple of weeks later, I made the same recipe for Steve. We ate it with baked potatoes and green salad after our evening run.

"Wow. This was great," he said as he pushed his chair away from the table after finishing his second helping. "Mom always worked long hours, so we ate a lot of fast food and prepared meals when I was a kid. A real dinner from scratch is a treat."

"Thanks. It's Helen's recipe."

"Then she must be a great cook."

"She is, and she's teaching me. Mom always wanted to, but I couldn't be bothered when I lived at home."

I suddenly missed my parents so much I was afraid I'd burst into tears. Steve must have seen the sadness on my face.

"What's the matter? Did I say something wrong?"

I shook my head, not quite trusting my voice. After a deep breath, I whispered," I just miss my folks, especially with the holidays coming."

"Oh, yeah. I forgot. Where are they now?"

"Headed for Fiji. From their latest postcard, it sounds as though they're having a great time. But it feels like they're on the other side of the planet."

"I kind of get it. Dad and Mom are in New York, and I don't see them too often. I usually try to get home for Thanksgiving and Christmas, though."

"Do you have any brothers or sisters?"

"One sister. She's a few years older, married with three kids. We didn't have anything in common growing up, but now that we're adults, we're pretty close. How about you?"

I looked down at my hands. "There's just me. Maybe that's why I miss my parents so much. This trip was Mom's lifelong dream, and I want them to have a wonderful time. But..."

"But you miss them." I looked up and was struck by the tenderness in Steve's eyes.

"Yeah."

"I guess we all have to make new traditions when we get older. You're welcome to come to New York with me for Thanksgiving."

"You mean it?"

"Sure. Mom wouldn't care. She always likes a big crowd."

"I'd love to, but what about Mitzi? I can't leave her, and I'm not sure how she'd handle a flight. I don't think Aunt Netta's lawyer would be very happy anyway. I guess I'll just celebrate Thanksgiving alone." But I wasn't thrilled with the idea.

"By the way, how much longer before you finish the book?" He'd asked this a lot lately.

"We should have it done by Christmas." Since it was already the week before Halloween, I figured we could wrap it up by then. But I have to confess, I wasn't sure I wanted to. I was enjoying the process and didn't want it to end.

"Great. We'll schedule your first publicity interview right after Thanksgiving."

"That soon?" I panicked.

"Don't worry. I'll bring Brooke next week. She can start running you through some practice sessions. You'll be ready."

"I don't think so..."

"Well I do."

We left it at that, but I shook just thinking about standing in front of lots of people. *How the heck can I do it?* It seemed like another good reason to put off finishing for as long as possible.

Besides, I was content with things just the way they were.

I got to see Tad nearly every day on my early morning runs, although he was usually with one of his long-limbed beauties, as Max would have said. Sometimes he asked us for breakfast. Well, to be honest, he asked Mitzi. But he seemed to care a little about me because he always made sure Jeff wasn't bothering me.

Yep, life was pretty sweet. Well, except for the email notices that arrived weekly saying the microwave was still on backorder. Oh and for missing my folks. And anticipating the public appearances Steve was going to make me do. And worrying about Helen. But, like Scarlet O'Hara, I decided to put those concerns off until later.

CHAPTER

Twenty-two

THE FOLLOWING WEEK, STEVE CAME TO TAKE US TO LUNCH AND brought Brooke, as promised.

While we ate, we started talking about the holidays, and I felt really sad again.

"I hear you'll be alone for Thanksgiving," Brooke said.

"How'd you know?"

"Oh, a little bird told me." She raised her eyebrow and looked at Steve. He blushed.

"Don't feel too bad," she added. "I'm by myself this year, too. The folks are headed to Ohio to be with my brother and his new baby. And my mean old boss won't let me take the time off."

"Hey, wait a minute..." Steve began.

She laughed. "No, the truth is, I'm not too close to my brother, Jay. And his wife, Heather, doesn't like me. I'll bet they wouldn't let me get anywhere near that kid Mom and Dad want to drool all over. So... whatever." She shrugged.

"I get the impression you're not big on babies," I said.

"Oh, I like them okay. But Jay's so fussy. He's probably boiling the kid after anyone breathes on her. And Heather... Oh, don't get me started."

"You really should try to mend fences while you can." Helen said softly. "Life is far too short not to insist on having the relationships you want and deserve. It's too late, once the other person is gone." She looked at me.

I knew she meant Max. I sensed she regretted not telling him how she felt while she could.

None of the rest of us had a response to that and returned to our meals.

Helen said she was tired, so we dropped her off as soon as we finished.

"I'm worried about her," I said when Steve got back in the car after walking her to her door. "She seems so listless. And that's just not like her."

"I know," he said as he pulled into traffic. "I've noticed it too. It's almost as though she's just hanging on long enough to get this book finished."

"Oh, I can't even think like that," I replied. "I love her too much. She's like the grandmother I always wanted. I want her to live... well... forever."

Steve smiled. "You know that's not possible. But it's easy to see you've brought a lot of happiness to her over the last few months."

"Thanks. I hope so. She's certainly made a difference in my life."

"Quit avoiding the whole reason for my being here," Brooke said. "We need to concentrate on your appearances."

I groaned. "Must we?"

She shook her head firmly. "We must."

When we got home, she made me put on my makeup and then gave me tips until she was satisfied I could do it right.

"Remember, you're going to be photographed. You need to use more than usual. The camera shows every little flaw."

"I hate this junk," I grumbled as I tried once more.

"Well, live with it." She wasn't at all sympathetic.

She'd brought the initial schedule of appearances, and we selected outfits for the first three.

Then she styled my hair a couple of different ways.

"This is for daytime," she announced as she fluffed my curls into what she called a 'halo.' I thought of it as my Aunt Netta look.

Then she slicked back the sides and slid in pretty combs. "And this will work for evening. See, you can do it in just a couple of minutes."

"I can probably manage that. It's the talking I don't think I can do."

"Sure you can. That's why I have these scripts." She withdrew some cards from her seemingly-bottomless bag and handed them to me.

While we'd been working in the bedroom, Steve had been reading the latest chapters. He brought a flash drive with him whenever he came to download the latest.

When we emerged, he looked me over, smiled and nodded his approval. Then he asked, "So, when will you be done with the yellow pads? I mean, I know the book wasn't complete when Max died, but I figured you must be getting close to the end."

I laughed. "We finished with his stuff about four chapters ago."

Max groaned, but quietly.

"You're kidding! It reads so smoothly, I thought..."

"Having Helen really made a difference. Remember, she knows Max's style and helped write his later books."

This time Max harrumphed louder, but by now I'd become really good at ignoring him.

"Okay, okay. You've put off practicing long enough," Brooke interrupted. "Now stand over there." She pointed to the fireplace. "Steve and I'll pretend to be your interviewers. That way, you'll get the feel of what to expect. You have some notes and scripted answers, but try to go with your own. We'll let you know if you screw up."

"Gee, thanks."

"No problem." Brooke sat next to Steve, facing me.

When they started firing questions, I was totally flummoxed! Tongue-tied doesn't begin to describe my reaction. I panicked.

"Okay, hold it," Steve said. "When you hear a question, take a beat to think about your answer. You don't have to rush. Then look at only one person and talk to whoever you've picked. Don't try to address the whole crowd."

"That's easy for you to say. What if I don't know anyone? What if they're all strangers? What if..."

"I'll be there," he said calmly. "Talk to me."

"You promise? You'll be there every time?"

"I promise." He nodded, then smiled.

"What about you?" I asked Brooke.

She shrugged. "Maybe."

I took a deep breath, then said, "Okay. I'll try."

It got better when I followed Steve's suggestion. It helped to talk to him alone. He nodded encouragement to keep me going.

"Good job," Steve said when they decided we'd done enough.

"Not bad," Broke added. "But you'll need more practice before you're confident."

"That's why we'll be back in a couple of days," Steve added.

And, true to his word, they were.

* * * *

The day before Thanksgiving, Mom called. "Hi, sweetheart. We're in Bora Bora! Can you imagine? We're having a wonderful time, but we wish you could be here for Thanksgiving with us. The ship has a real feast planned."

"I wish I was there too, but you know I have to take care of Mitzi. And I'm still trying to find a new job."

Okay, so I wasn't trying too hard. I hadn't told my folks about the book. I was afraid they'd think I was crazy. Maybe I was.

"Well, darling, your dad and I've decided to make a trip back to California for Christmas. We love the Ritz, especially when it's decorated for the holidays. Maybe you can bring Mitzi and stay with us for a few days."

"I'll check to see what their policy is on pets." I wasn't too optimistic. After all, this was a top-rated resort hotel. But it was worth a shot.

"Here's your dad. He wants to talk to you."

After spending some time on the phone, I missed them even more. But I was excited about seeing them at Christmas.

I fired up my search engine and found the hotel. I was amazed to read that they welcomed pets! There would be a $150 cleaning fee plus $50 a night. So Mitzi could come with me! I just hoped Mom and Dad would cover her as well.

"Hey, girl," I said to her. "You get to spend a few days in the style you used to be accustomed to."

She tipped her head as if she didn't quite understand.

"Now, don't tell me you've forgotten already."

She jumped up next to where I sat on the loveseat and licked my cheek. I ruffled her fur. "I know. I love you, too." And I meant it.

Steve had helped me pick out a small turkey breast at the grocery store earlier in the week and Helen suggested I put it in the Crock-Pot we'd found in a cabinet.

"But it won't have crispy skin," I objected.

She laughed. "About an hour or so before you're ready to eat, just pop it into a hot oven. It should brown up nicely. And the house will still smell wonderful."

She told me what spices and vegetables to put with it.

"You'd better be hungry for turkey for a few days, because I can't possibly make a dent in this thing by myself," I told her.

"I'll just have to teach you some of my favorite recipes for leftover turkey. Max always loved my Mulligatawny soup." She got that far-away look she always had when she mentioned Max.

"What's that?" I asked.

"Just the most delicious soup you've ever eaten," she replied.

"What's in it?"

"That's my secret—for now." She smiled.

"Okay," I groused. "But I'm going to have to know pretty soon so I can get the ingredients."

"I'll bring the recipe the day after Thanksgiving."

"You're coming then?"

"I'd planned on it, if that's all right with you."

"It's always okay with me," I replied. It was true. I wanted to spend as much time with her as I could. While I still could.

* * * *

My heart really wasn't into it, but early on Thanksgiving morning, I started the turkey breast.

"Well, at least you and I will enjoy this," I said to Mitzi as I put on the lid and turned the dial.

"I remember some wonderful meals in this kitchen," Max said. He sounded almost wistful. I didn't know he had that tone of voice in his repertoire.

"Helen always cooked a small chicken or turkey, and we ate right here at this table," he added. "The next day, she cooked down the bones and made that delicious soup."

"What's so special about it?"

"She never revealed her secret and, of course, I never participated in the preparation. But it was hearty and savory and very different from anything else I'd ever eaten."

"You think I'll like it?" I asked.

"I doubt that you have a terribly sophisticated palate, but I suspect you will enjoy the flavor."

"Great." I was going to cook something I'd never tried. I wondered if I should practice making one of those happy faces in case I didn't like it.

At about eleven-thirty, I heard a knock on the door. Mitzi ran with her whole bottom moving from side to side.

I was surprised to see Brooke and Helen on the doorstep.

"Surprise!" they both said at the same time.

"But..." I started.

Brooke barged in before I could say anything else. Helen followed. Brooke carried a bag, and Helen held a box.

"I thought you were having dinner with your niece," I told Helen.

She smiled and shook her head. "Too much confusion. Besides it's a tiring drive and a long day. Brooke suggested we join you instead. I hope it's all right."

My heart was dancing. "It's more than all right." I hugged her. "This is the best present I've had in a long time."

"Hey, I've got yams and potatoes in here and they're heavy," Brooke complained.

"Sorry. Right this way."

I showed her to the kitchen.

"That should be really good with the green beans and dressing. I didn't bother with potatoes just for me, but I planned on making dressing in a casserole like Helen said."

"Well, I have the pumpkin pie," Helen added, placing the box on the table. "I wish my hands were strong enough to make my own, but some of the restaurants have excellent ones. Good thing I ordered early. Brooke took me by to pick it up on our way over."

"Wow! Sounds great."

"And I got the whipped cream," Brooke announced as she finished emptying the bag. She held up an aerosol can. "Helen objected, but I like the stuff and it's quick."

"Sounds perfect," I said.

Helen sat and directed operations as Brooke and I put the potatoes on to boil.

"I'm a great masher," Brooke announced. "That was always my job at home."

Who knew?

We'd just started getting out the dishes to set the table, when there was another knock. Mitzi was dancing impatiently in front of the door when I got there.

"Who is it, girl?" I asked as I opened it.

There stood Steve, looking a little embarrassed.

"Why aren't you with your family?" I asked.

"I talked to Mom, and she said she thought they could manage without me this year. I wanted to be with you."

"Did you bring the rolls and butter?" Brooke yelled from the kitchen.

"That's all they'd trust me with," he confessed sheepishly.

As he walked in, he gave me a kiss on the cheek, like it was the most natural thing in the world.

"Happy Thanksgiving, Nan," he said.

"Hurry up. The potatoes are ready for that butter," Brook shouted.

"Coming, coming," he said as he hurried into the kitchen.

Yes, it was shaping up to be a very happy Thanksgiving indeed.

Twenty-three

DINNER WAS PERFECT! I COULDN'T BELIEVE IT. WE ALL ATE FAR too much, but then, isn't that part of the Thanksgiving tradition?

Helen was fading as the afternoon wore on, so Brooke volunteered to drive her home. "That means you're stuck with the cleanup," she said to Steve with a grin as she dashed out.

He grimaced, but it looked half-hearted.

"I'll see you tomorrow," Helen said as Steve helped her through the door on the way to Brooke's waiting car.

"Maybe you want to take it easy and not work," I suggested.

"Oh, no, dear. A little rest and I'll be right as rain." She waved her dismissal.

"I'm really concerned about her," I said to Steve as he closed the door.

"Nan, she's old and frail. She also has some pretty serious health issues."

"Such as? And how do you know?"

He looked down. "Because she talks to me. She doesn't want to worry you, but she tells me things when I drive her home."

"Like what?" I asked even though I was sure I wouldn't like what was coming next.

He took my hand and led me to the love seat.

"Now you're scaring me," I said as we sat down.

"Helen has some serious heart issues. She takes medication, but it can only help so much and for so long."

"Surely something can be done. They make new discoveries every day. There must be..."

He shook his head.

The thought of losing Helen after all the other losses I'd been through was just too much. To my embarrassment, I burst into tears.

Steve put his arms around me and let me sob. He didn't say a word. When my crying slowed, he finally said, "I know how you feel. She's a special friend, and we've both been fortunate to know her."

"I remember you said you thought she was hanging on just to finish the book."

He nodded.

I took a deep breath. "You may be right. Maybe if I stall..."

But he shook his head. "Don't rob her of the joy of seeing Max's last book finished. It's her final act of love for him."

"How did you know about her and Max?"

"I told you. She talks to me."

I didn't know what to say. But then, I didn't have to say anything. And I liked that.

He kissed me on the forehead. "Now, enough stalling. We have a huge mess in the kitchen to clean up. And I expect a big reward for my help."

"Like what?" I asked skeptically.

He chuckled. "Like a run on the beach to work off that great meal."

I held out my hand. "Deal."

We shook, then got up to finish the work.

* * * *

The air was brisk and the sky was clear and filled with stars as we headed out. Mitzi acted as though she needed a good run as much as we did. After the turkey I'd seen Brooke and Steve slipping to her, I didn't doubt it.

I looked at Tad's house as we passed, but it was dark. I figured he was probably at a holiday party or off somewhere with a gorgeous companion. Even though I'd have liked to have been with him, I couldn't have asked for a better Thanksgiving—that is, unless Mom and Dad were here with me.

"Guess I'd better get on the road," Steve said when we got back. "Traffic will be a bear."

I nodded. "You have a long drive ahead of you."

He seemed to hesitate for a moment.

"Oh, wait!" I said. "I nearly let you go without a little sustenance for the road."

"Sustenance? That doesn't sound like you."

"Well, I—uh—guess I've read too much of Max." I nearly said, "I've been hanging around Max too much." And that would have required a whole lot more explaining than I was ready for!

He chuckled. "I guess the old boy rubbed off on you."

"You have no idea," I whispered under my breath, my back to Steve as I filled some containers.

"What?"

"Uh, yeah. I guess he has." I slipped the food into a bag and handed it to him. "Need anything else to survive the long journey?"

"Nope. Guess not."

He still seemed reluctant to go.

"Well, have a safe trip." I walked to the door and opened it for him.

As he left, he said, "Thanks again for dinner. You're getting to be quite a cook." Then he gave me a quick hug and kiss and was gone before I could decide whether it meant anything.

I closed the door as Max said, "A very gallant young man."

"Huh?"

"He sacrificed his own holiday plans to be with you. I believe he's quite smitten."

"Come on, Max. This is just Steve we're talking about. Steve, the nerd. Steve the runner. Steve the editor. Steve..."

"Steven who cares deeply about you."

"Oh and when did you become an expert on the affairs of the heart? Seems to me you missed an awful lot of cues during your own lifetime."

"I have recently had an opportunity to observe those around me in a manner unavailable to me during my mortal incarnation. You and Helen have been instrumental in my education on the ways of amour. In addition, I once was a young man like your Steven myself. I recognize the look of one too timid to confess his passion. But I suspect beneath that mild exterior beats the heart of a noble man."

"Don't go all poetic on me, Max. Steve's a simple guy. He's pretty much what you see on the surface: just a nice person who likes to run on the beach and took pity on the three of us because we were all alone this year. Now, if you don't mind, I'm exhausted. All that cooking wore me out."

I flipped off the light. "Happy Thanksgiving, Max."

"And a very happy one to you also, my dear."

* * * *

I half expected Helen to be a no-show the next morning, despite her commitment to come. But she arrived at her usual time. She seemed a bit winded as she came in.

"Helen, you have to let me at least call you a cab when you leave. As soon as I get a car, I'll pick you up."

"No, no, dear. The walk is invigorating."

But she didn't look as though the hike from the bus stop had done her any good.

"I would like a cool glass of water, if you don't mind," she said.

I helped her sit at the table and got her drink.

"I brought the soup recipe with me," she said as she pulled a slip of paper from her windbreaker pocket. She wore it over a sweater. I hoped she was warm enough, but she'd let me know from the beginning that she could take care of herself, so I didn't pursue it.

"Steve won't be coming today. Do we have everything?"

She smiled knowingly. "I added all the ingredients we'd need to my list for Thanksgiving."

I looked at the recipe and she was right. I had bought every item. A couple of them surprised me. "Are you sure this is good?"

She laughed heartily. Well, as heartily as an elderly woman with a serious heart condition can laugh.

"I promise you'll love it," she replied.

She was right. We ate the soup for lunch with left-over rolls and dessert from the day before. Yummy!

"Helen, this is really good."

"Perhaps you'll trust me next time."

"I'll never doubt you again."

"Good because if you'll get my purse, I brought some more recipes for you."

I got her bag. She removed a small stack of old three-by-five cards and handed them to me.

"But, Helen, these look like your originals."

She smiled sweetly. "They are, but I don't plan on making any of them again."

"What about your niece? Doesn't she cook?"

Helen laughed. "Susan has a very good cook. I don't think she even knows how to use her stove."

"But..."

"No buts. I want you to have them and to enjoy them." She sighed. "I used to make these things for Max. I recall sharing them with him, and I hope you will make new memories with them."

I kissed her cheek. "Helen, I owe you so much. You taught me how to write and cook. But more than that, you've become my friend."

"My dear, you'll never know how much our friendship means to me. You've made an old lady very happy. You've given my life new meaning. For that, I'm very grateful."

I hugged her, then noticed how tired she looked.

"What if we play hooky today and I call you a cab."

"That sounds like a very good idea. Perhaps yesterday was a bit too much excitement for me."

"Not to mention the walk here today," I added as I grabbed my cell phone and looked up the number for the local cab company Mrs. Owens had given me.

I heard the horn honk much sooner than I expected.

"Here's your ride."

"Thank you, dear, for everything."

I walked her out and made sure she got in okay. Then I saw her wave and drive off. For some reason, I stood there watching until the car rounded the corner and was gone.

"How I wish I'd been able to share your repast," Max said quietly when I entered the living room. "The flavor of that delicious soup is a very fond memory. And I never realized until now how much I enjoyed that woman's company."

"Finally."

"Whatever do you mean?"

"They say, 'better late than never.' This is really late, but at least you finally got it! She loved you!"

He sighed, and I heard his chair squeak. "I would like you to know I have regrets where she is concerned. I wish there were some way to make amends, but alas, it is too late for that."

"Well, when you see her in heaven—if you get there—maybe you can tell her. I know that's where she'll end up."

"No doubt of that, my dear. None at all."

We sat in silence. I thought about Helen and how I'd miss her when she was gone. And I was very afraid that day was coming much faster than I wanted it to.

Twenty-four

I TOOK AN AFTERNOON RUN WITH MITZI AND THEN DECIDED TO get some work done. We were near the end of the book, and I wanted to finish the story.

Amazingly, the words started to flow, and suddenly the plot headed in a direction I hadn't expected. I decided to trust that it would end up where it needed to go and kept on writing.

It was quite dark when I finally stopped. I'd completed more than a chapter by myself. And I liked it.

"How about that, Mitz?"

"How about what?" asked Max.

"I wrote a whole chapter myself," I answered. "Would you like to hear it?"

"I certainly would." He sniffed as if he didn't expect it to be very good.

However, when I finished, he grunted and said, "Excellent. I must be an extraordinary teacher. That small plot twist was unexpected but very effective. And it made good use of what otherwise would have been a very minor character."

"You're not mad because I didn't stick completely to your original plot?"

He laughed. "The mark of a great writer, as opposed to a hack, is being flexible. I'm afraid I was a bit too controlling. That unfortunate personality characteristic is the element Helen identified, which made my characters perhaps a little stiff."

"Max, are you saying what I think you are? That I could be a great writer?"

"If I hadn't thought you had potential, I'd never have wasted my efforts on you."

"Max, I wish I could hug you!"

"Why on earth would you consider doing such a thing?"

He was trying to sound like the curmudgeon he loved to pretend he was, but I'd learned better.

"Maxie, you think I have talent! You really do!" I danced around the room. "And I love writing more than anything else I've ever done. Maybe I could make a career of it. Wouldn't that be cool?"

"Don't get your knickers in a bunch, dear girl. It takes many years to make a name in publishing. Perhaps you should temper your enthusiasm."

"I know you're right, but it's like a whole new window has opened up for me. Oh, Max, I just love you!"

He chuckled. "And I've grown quite fond of you as well."

"Seriously, Max, thank you for everything. If you hadn't made me finish your dumb book, I'd never have known how much fun writing could be. And I like having someone here to talk to. I just wish I could see you like Mitzi can."

"Perhaps it is best as it is. You can still picture me as young and dashing instead of as an old man."

"I picture you as Helen described you. And, because she loved you, her description was of a very sweet and charming guy."

"Ah, dear heart, your tender spirit and limitless imagination are the very qualities that will allow you to become a fine writer."

I sat on the loveseat. "I know this is going to sound crazy, but it's as if Sarah is telling me her own story."

I was surprised to hear Max laugh. "Ah, young lady, you truly have the makings of an author. Trust your characters. I fear I did not allow mine enough voice, and my work suffered for it. If Sarah is speaking, capture her words on the page. You shall not regret the decision to do so. Many of the great *auteurs* of my acquaintance mentioned writing the stories of their creations as if they were individuals apart from their imaginations." Max sighed. "Perhaps Helen's ministrations would have been required to a lesser degree had I followed that practice."

"You really think I should try it?"

"Most certainly, child."

So I did. I sat at the computer and listened to Sarah. Then I typed like crazy. I didn't look up until about eleven when Mitzi began dancing around the room, wanting to go out.

I decided to go to bed, but woke at four in the morning with Sarah demanding I complete her story. So I got up and began again. Some of her changes required revisions to earlier sections of the book. I typed until Mitzi bugged me. Then I took her for a quick run or ate with her or let her relieve herself. But I returned as soon as I could because Sarah wouldn't leave me alone.

After another restless night, Sunday passed in the same manner as Saturday. Late in the evening, I finished. What surprised me was that I knew it was done. And it was a good story. Heck, it was a great story.

"Max, let me read this to you!" I shouted.

"There is no need to bellow. I am confined to this small domicile. And my hearing is quite acute."

"Well, do you want to hear it?"

"Certainly."

I filled him in on the changes I'd made in the beginning. Then I began reading the last third of the book.

It was very late when I finished.

Max was silent.

"Well?" I said.

I thought I heard him sniff, but I couldn't imagine stiff-upper-lip, serious Max being touched. Of course, I was crying as I read it, even though I already knew the ending.

"You will not become a great writer, dear."

My heart sank. He hated it.

"You have already become one," he whispered.

"Oh, Max..." But I couldn't continue for my sobs of joy. And I really wanted to hug him and be held. Instead, I wrapped my arms around myself.

Max cleared his throat. "You have put in a very long and productive weekend. Now the time for sleep and restoration has come."

It wasn't until he said the words that I realized I was exhausted.

"Come on, Mitz. Time for bed."

* * * *

I didn't wake until the sun was well up the next morning. Mitzi and I took our usual run and ate breakfast. Then I sat back down at the computer and reread the end of the book again. I looked with a critical eye as Helen had taught me and found a few minor changes. But I was still buoyed up with excitement and couldn't wait to share it with her when she came.

But she didn't arrive at her usual time. At first, I wasn't too concerned. I figured Thanksgiving and the day after had probably worn her out. But when one o'clock rolled around and she hadn't called or come, I began to worry.

I phoned her house, but no one answered.

Then I called Steve.

"Helen's not here and I can't reach her," I blurted breathlessly as soon as he answered.

"Calm down, Nan. She may have gone to the doctor. Or her niece might have taken her somewhere."

"But she'd have called or something..."

"Listen, if you don't hear by two, call me back and I'll come down."

But at one-thirty the phone rang. It was Helen's niece, Susan.

"I worried when I couldn't reach Aunt Helen this morning," she said. "She fell and couldn't get to the phone."

"Is she okay?"

"She will be, but she cracked a rib and won't be going anywhere for a few weeks. We've arranged for a caregiver."

"Could Steve and I come to visit?"

Susan hesitated and I wondered why. "Perhaps it would be better if you phoned first to make sure she's alert. We're keeping her somewhat sedated to control the pain."

"Okay. I understand. Thanks for calling."

My heart dropped. My grand and glorious day had just clouded over. I called Steve and told him what had happened.

When I got off the phone, Max asked, "Will she recover?"

"I certainly hope so. Maybe Steve and I can get by to see her this week."

I was glad I'd finished the book, but without Helen to share it, my elation had dissipated.

"Come on, Mitzi," I said as I headed for the back door.

We took a long run and I felt a little better as I neared the house. There was no sign of life at Tad's. I didn't really expect to see any.

However, someone was sitting on my back steps as I approached. I was stunned as I got closer and realized it was Mr. Spencer, neatly dressed in his suit.

Then I looked at the little fur ball prancing at my side.

Uh oh...

He stood and smiled.

"Uh, hi," I said, still a little breathless.

"Hello."

Mitzi ran up to him and the lawyer patted her on the head.

"The groomers are coming tomorrow," I started to explain.

Then he surprised me by grinning. "She appears to be happy. And she's obviously in good shape. In fact, she acts much younger. I think you've done wonders for this little pup."

What? Really?

"Would you like a glass of iced tea?" I asked.

"I'd love one," he answered.

He asked about the house, and I told him how much I loved living there. "Of course, sometimes, I feel a little trapped without a car, but we manage just fine."

"I owe you an apology," he said, setting his glass on the kitchen table. "I was afraid you were just a young, careless kid who wouldn't appreciate the gifts you'd received."

"I probably was," I confessed.

He looked surprised.

"I didn't want the dog. In fact, she's the last thing I thought I needed. But Aunt Netta knew better." I reached down to pet Mitzi, and she licked my hand. "Now I don't know what I'd do without her."

He smiled.

"And I've always loved this house, even if only from a distance. But there have been a few problems."

"Problems?"

"Oh, the garage spring broke and put a hole in the roof. I had to replace the whole thing as well as the door."

"How did you manage that? Did you have enough funds?"

I laughed. "Right now, all I get is my unemployment insurance, and that doesn't go very far."

I saw a questioning look cross his face, so I jumped in to explain. "Of course, I'm on line job hunting every day, but there just isn't much demand for my computer skills right now."

"Then how did you survive your emergency situation? Were you able to borrow enough or get a loan?"

"You won't believe this, but Max had some money hidden in the house. And I found it just when I needed it." Then I had a horrible thought. "It was okay, wasn't it?"

"Well, according to your aunt's will, you inherited the house and all its contents. That would include any money you discovered."

He picked up his glass and drained it. "I'm very happy I came down here today. I've felt guilty about being so protective of your aunt's intentions. But I can see I had nothing to worry about. You and Mitzi are doing very well. I'm sure Nanette would be pleased."

I was hoping he'd offer to buy me a car, or give me an advance, or something, but he didn't. He shook my hand, patted Mitzi on the head.

As he left, he said, "Be sure to call if you need anything. I'd be more than happy to see what we can do to help."

"That was strange, Mitz. Very strange," I said as I closed the door. "He didn't sound too encouraging about actually giving us any more money. But I'm glad he didn't want to take you away from me." I scratched her behind her ears and she purred. That made me laugh. "I'm so glad I have you, you silly pooch."

And I meant it.

Twenty-five

STEVE MUST HAVE BEEN AS WORRIED ABOUT HELEN AS I WAS, because he showed up at my door the next morning.

"Hi. I didn't expect to see you today," I said as I let him in.

"I thought we might call and see how Helen is. If she's up to it, maybe we could visit her."

I felt my eyes filling. "Oh, Steve, that would be wonderful."

He noticed my emotional state and knew just what to say. "Then get on the phone and call."

Susan said her aunt was just waking and would love to see us.

I grabbed my laptop on the way out the door.

"Why are you bringing that?" Steve asked.

"I finished the book!" I said in triumph. "I want you and Helen to hear the end."

He smiled as he pulled out onto PCH. "I didn't know you were that close to finishing."

"Neither did I. But it just seemed to write itself, and I couldn't stop until it was done."

Steve nodded as he concentrated on changing lanes.

"This may sound a little crazy, but I felt like Sarah was actually telling me what happened next. And she wouldn't leave me alone until her story was completed."

He laughed. "You have no idea how often my authors tell me the same sort of thing. They're always fighting with their characters because they want them to do one thing, and their creations refuse."

"Wow. Really? I mean, I thought I was a little nuts."

"Well, most authors are a little nuts. But that's what makes them good at their craft. I was in a restaurant once with a couple of mystery writers we publish. They were discussing how to commit a murder so it would be completely undetectable. The conversation grew quite heated until the waiter whispered to me, 'Are you sure they're okay? Should I get help?'"

Steve laughed, and I joined him. "What did you say?" I asked.

"I thanked the poor guy and said I thought I could handle it. When he left, I told the others what he'd said. They enjoyed his discomfort. Of course, we explained when he returned."

"So I'm not crazy?" I asked as we turned onto Helen's street.

"No more so than the rest of the loonies I work with."

I arched an eyebrow. But then he laughed again.

"Just kidding," he said. "You're perfectly normal."

As he came around to open my door, I realized that I liked the sound of his laughter. In fact I liked being with him. I didn't tingle with the electricity or excitement I felt when I was with Tad, but Steve always managed to make me feel good. He was a comfortable guy to hang out with. And he'd become a good friend.

Helen was sitting up in bed waiting for us when we arrived. She looked pale and quite frail, but her eyes were bright. And her smile was most welcoming.

"Well, if it isn't two of my favorite people," she said as each of us kissed her cheek. Then she spied my computer. "I hope you aren't going to put me to work today."

"No, she brought you a surprise," Steve answered quickly.

Helen looked at me in anticipation.

"I finished the book," I announced proudly.

"How wonderful! Why, you must have worked all weekend."

"I did," I said. "I got started and just couldn't stop. Would you like me to read it to you?"

"I haven't heard it either. She made me wait until we were with you,"

Steve said.

I could see how pleased Helen was.

"Then let's get started," she answered.

"Tell me if you get tired," I said as I booted up.

"Would it be okay if I listened, too?" Susan asked. "Aunt Helen has told me so much about the book, I feel as though I've already read most of it."

"Sure, if it's okay with Steve and Helen," I said.

They both nodded.

I explained quickly how the plot had changed and then began reading where we'd left off. As I reached the places where I'd had to rewrite earlier sections in order for the current plot to work, I described the modifications. We stopped for a couple of breaks, including lunch, which Susan insisted on making for us.

"We all have to eat anyway," she said.

I continued to read as we ate. I watched to be sure we weren't tiring her, but Helen appeared alert and engrossed. I should have been exhausted but was so excited about their hearing my story, I felt energized instead.

When I paused to ask Helen if she'd like us to come back another day to finish, she replied, "Oh, no, dear. You can't stop now. I want to know what happens to Sarah."

Steve and Susan agreed, so I kept on through to the end.

I looked up, and Susan and Helen were both crying. Steve looked as though he was trying not to.

"Oh, my dear, it's wonderful!" Helen said as she sobbed. "I loved it. What a glorious and bittersweet ending. It's just perfect."

"You really think so?" I asked. I wasn't fishing for complements, but their opinions counted more than anyone else's. Except for Max, and I already had his.

"It's better than anything Max ever wrote. With his name on the cover, you should have a best seller in no time," Helen added.

"I think we should give you primary authorship with 'based on an unpublished manuscript by Maxine Du Bois' below," Steve said.

"Oh, no. It was Max's book. I just finished it."

"You did much more than that, dear," Helen added. "You brought the old, dead words on Max's yellow tablets to life. You made them sing."

"But I couldn't have done it without you. We should probably share authorship."

"Absolutely not," she said firmly. "All I did was translate Max's chicken scratching. You did the rest."

"Well I..."

"Then it's settled," Steve interrupted firmly. He looked at me. "You have the talent and potential to become a truly great writer, and as your publisher, I intend to see that it happens."

"Really?"

"Well if my opinion counts for anything," Susan said, "I think you are one already. That was the best story I've heard in years. It would make a great movie."

The others nodded.

"You mean it?"

They all said, "Yes," at once.

I chuckled, overwhelmed by their enthusiasm.

"Well, as Max once said, I've had an emeritus class in literary fiction."

I realized too late what I'd blurted out. Three pairs of eyes were locked on me. All appeared to be in shock.

"Uh, I guess I should explain."

"I guess you should." Helen spoke first.

"Well, see, Max is still in the cottage. At least, his ghost is. I mean, I can hear him, but I can't see him. And Mitzi can see him, but I don't think she can hear him." The words rushed out.

"That explains it," Helen said softly.

"What?" Steve asked.

She smiled at us. "I've felt his spirit each time I was there. That's why I loved coming every day. Oh, I've enjoyed our time together, dear, but I think I sensed his presence. And that made me feel young again."

"So Max really ghost wrote this book?" Steve asked.

"Well, yes. I mean no, not really. We did start with his original notes, but then Helen and I began making changes. Sometimes he'd grumble or shout about them. I finally got him to wait until you'd left before he vented," I said to Helen. "But as time went on, he began to trust our instincts. He also taught me about voice and motive and character and plot development and, oh, lots of other stuff."

"So Aunt Helen's Max is still there?" Susan was slower than the others to catch on.

"Uh huh."

"And you two talk?" She was having a hard time even accepting the concept.

"Well, at first he bellowed and shouted. He was a real old grump. And bossy! He even rattled the windows and interrupted my sleep trying to get me to leave. But I had nowhere else to go. He made me take on his dumb book. But once I started, it wasn't so dumb."

Helen chuckled. "The old grump part sounds like my Max. He loved playing the curmudgeon."

"Oh, yeah. It took me a long time to figure out it was an act. He's really a softie if you can break through that crusty exterior."

"I truly do believe you have been in touch with Max. Please tell him—well—give him my best."

"Helen, I'm afraid he heard everything we talked about."

Her cheeks grew pink. "Oh my."

"But he's finally come to realize how much you meant to him. Too bad it took this long."

"He said that? He told you he cared about me?"

"Yes. In fact, after we ate your special soup the other day, he grew positively poetic about the lovely meals he'd enjoyed in that kitchen and what a comfort you had been. He said he was sorry he didn't recognize what a lovely woman you were during his lifetime."

She began weeping softly.

"Let me get this straight," Steve interrupted. "Max Murdoch's ghost lives, or whatever he does, in your house?"

"Yep. And you know what? Now that we've become—well, sort-of friends—I kind of like having him there to talk to. I've grown very fond of him, as he says."

"So that's why you sometimes use the big words. I thought it was just from reading his writing."

"Not entirely. I've had to stop myself from copying his British accent. It's amazing that he never lost it."

"Oh, he cultivated it. He said he thought it made him sound more urbane, erudite, sophisticated, and intelligent," Helen explained.

I smiled. "Well, I have to confess, it did that for me. But his funny old-fashioned words sometimes make me laugh."

"So what does he think about all the modern gadgets?" Susan was now getting into the spirit of the discussion.

"At first he hated the computer and my cell phone. I don't have a TV, but I occasionally stream media. He's usually disdainful. But I think he'd have liked having a cell phone. Well, on second thought, he probably wouldn't have had one. After all, he never had a phone before."

"He didn't?" Steve asked.

"Oh, no," Helen answered. "Your father and his agent always called me or Nanette. We relayed his messages. And if he needed to contact someone, he used a pay phone."

"Pay phone? He didn't drive, did he? Where the heck would he have found a pay phone in his area?"

I jumped in. "He told me there was one at the convenience store about three blocks away on PCH. Of course, the store and the phone are long gone."

"That's correct, my dear. You truly have been talking to Max." Helen seemed quite pleased at the idea.

"I don't know, Aunt Helen. This is a lot for me to accept."

Helen smiled. "If I hadn't been there and felt Max's presence, I'd be skeptical, too. But I knew he was around. He sits in the chair by the fireplace, doesn't he?"

"Yep. How did you know?"

She chuckled. "I thought I heard it squeak. And, come to think about it, your little dog often sits next to the chair and looks up at a spot on the wall. I wondered if her eyes were following shadows or bugs or something."

"Nope, just Max. Good thing she can see him. It helps me figure out where he is. He still sneaks up behind me once in a while, but I've pretty well trained him not to just speak in my ear without warning."

"I think we've kept Helen and Susan quite long enough," Steve said.

"Oh, yes. I'm so sorry. You must be exhausted."

"Quite the contrary, Nan dear. You've given me a great gift. I can't remember ever being quite so happy. Tell Max I love him."

I packed up the laptop. "I'll be sure to tell him, but he knows it already." I kissed her cheek.

Steve did, too. "Good night, Helen. We'll come to see you again soon."

"See that you do. I love you both." She waved as we walked out the door.

"I'm really sorry we stayed so long," I told Susan as we left.

She smiled. "It obviously wasn't long enough for Aunt Helen. Thank you both for giving her such a lovely memory. You may not have noticed, but she didn't ask for any medication all day, and her rib has been quite painful. I'd better get back and give her a pill. She'll be feeling it soon."

Steve didn't say a word on the drive to my place.

Twenty-six

WHEN WE GOT BACK, STEVE LOOKED AROUND CAUTIOUSLY AS HE entered. Mitzi was sitting in her usual spot next to the chair by the fireplace. Her topknot moved slightly, so I figured her buddy was scratching her head.

"So..." said Steve.

"So, what?" I answered.

"Uh, is he here?" he asked in a stage whisper.

"Max, are you here?" I asked loudly.

Mitzi looked over and cocked her head.

"Why this sudden curiosity regarding my whereabouts?" came the familiar voice.

"I made the unfortunate mistake of mentioning that you're still around to Steve and Helen. Now he's questioning my sanity."

Steve stared at me.

"And how did dear Helen receive the information?"

I chuckled. "She'd been sure you were here all along. I just confirmed it for her."

"Are you talking to him now?" Steve asked.

"Well, I'm not talking to you," I answered.

"In that case, ask him where all his money went."

"I've wondered about that, but I figured he'd tell me when he was ready. I doubt he'll reveal his secrets to you, especially when you ask that way."

"Then ask him what street my grandfather lived on when he first took Max as a client."

"Thank you, my dear, for respecting my right to privacy. As to the young man's question, his grandfather lived on Satinwood in Briarcliff, New York. Later, he moved to the city. I always preferred his residence in that quaint little village to his lavish townhouse."

I repeated what Max had said.

"But—but how did you know? Did you see some mail or papers with that address on it?"

"No way, buster." I was starting to get angry. He thought I was making all this up. "Why on earth would I want to pretend Max was here if he wasn't?"

My resident ghost chuckled.

"This isn't funny, Max."

"Ah, but I find it quite amusing."

"I'm so glad to have provided the comic relief," I said. Now I was ticked off at both of them.

"Come on, Mitzi. We're going outside." I figured she had to go anyway, and I needed to get away from both of the aggravating males in my house.

Steve followed. "Are you going for a run?" he asked. "Because if you are, I'd like to join you."

"I don't know if I want your company," I responded.

"Listen, I'm sorry if I find your talking with a ghost a little hard to swallow. I've never known anyone who actually knew one—a ghost, that is. Let me get used to the idea. Okay?"

"I guess so," I said as I took off my shoes.

The sand still felt warm even though the air was cool. We were at the end of an Indian summer. Winters here at the beach tend to be mild with cooler temperatures and rain.

"Guess we'd better enjoy this weather while we can," I said, already over my pique. I went inside and returned with Mitzi's leash.

Steve removed his shoes. "The sand feels good."

"Then let's go."

We headed off at a fast pace and kept it up until we nearly reached the end of the cove.

I slowed and reversed direction. "Time to turn back."

The return was a little slower. As we passed Tad's house, I noticed lights on and figured he was back.

"Want something for dinner?" I asked.

"No thanks. I should get home. I'm expecting an early call from the East Coast first thing in the morning. But I'll come back in the afternoon to take you to the first radio interview."

"Is that tomorrow?" Panic overwhelmed me

"Yeah. But don't worry. You'll do fine. It's just a local radio show during evening drive time. I know the hostess. She'll be easy on you. I've already told her the story, and she's anxious to find out about the book. But—uh— it might be better not to mention living with Max, if you know what I mean."

"Don't worry. I've learned that lesson. In fact, I had no intention of mentioning it at all. It just slipped out."

"Oh and you might think about the dedication and acknowledgments for the book. While you're at it, we need bios of both you and Max. Why don't you work on those in the morning? They'll keep your mind occupied."

"Okay. You're sure I have to do these interviews?"

"Positive."

I followed him to the door. He turned and kissed me so quickly he caught me off guard. He didn't grab or touch me, just pressed his lips to mine. It must have been static from the carpet which caused the spark—except the entry was tile. I was so stunned, I just stood there as he walked to his car.

What the heck was that?

* * * *

I worked all morning on the dedication and other things Steve had asked me to do. As I expected, Max had very definite ideas about everything.

"Keep your dedication to one sentence and make every word count," he'd instructed.

We finally settled on: *Dedicated to Helen Zeblinsky, the finest secretary and friend in the world.*

"I still think she's far more than a secretary," I muttered.

"That was her chosen profession and she was justifiably proud of the appellation. A secretary she was, and a secretary she remains."

"I guess so, but I'm going to mention her again in the acknowledgments."

"My dear, sometimes too much is precisely that—too much."

"Then let's start on your biography. I'm sure you've had many written over the years." I switched to the Internet and Googled his name. Several pages of references came up, including a Wikipedia listing.

"Hey, Max, you've made the big time."

"Whatever do you mean?"

"You're listed in Wikipedia."

"And what, pray tell, is a Wikipedia?"

"It's an online encyclopedia that everyone can contribute to."

"The entire concept smacks of amateurism and misinformation." Then he added, "What does this glossary of the masses have to say about me?"

"It says your birthday was April 2nd, 1902 and that you were born in the heart of London."

"Nonsense. My birth occurred in the waning moments of April 1st in the suburb of Tooting. However, within days, my parents relocated to London where I spent my childhood."

"Then I guess we should set the record straight."

"And by what method would one perform such a correction?"

"Watch me." I'd already clicked the 'Improve this article' link and was entering the information he'd just given to me.

"When did you become Maxine DuBois?" I asked. "This doesn't say."

"The first tome published under that nom de plume was in 1933, *A Kiss at Midnight*. Of course, I had no intention of continuing to write as Maxine, but the response was overwhelming and lucrative. Her persona allowed me a great deal of anonymity. In the end, it became quite comfortable."

I added this information and finished.

"Now, where did you get your education? When did you come to the U.S.?"

We spent the next hour or so putting together a couple of paragraphs.

"At least you have a life," I moaned when it was time to do my biography. "What can I say? 'Girl failure at programming dusts off old manuscript and finishes it.' Great."

"Never belittle yourself or your life experiences." Max sounded like he was scolding me. "Begin with, 'A happy accident brought Nan Burton together with the final incomplete manuscript of Max Murdoch.' Or some such verbiage. Tell the story of inheriting Nanette's house and discovering the tablets. Convey the adventure and the serendipitous discovery of your talent as an author. But never, never apologize!"

"Okay, Max. Thanks. I guess I still can't believe this is something I could do again. I mean, it seems like this was just a fluke, a one-shot deal. What I'm trying to say is, I wish I believed I could do it by myself without you."

"You are certainly capable of producing memorable work independently."

"I guess I really don't want to," I confessed. "I'd love to start again and work with you, despite our disagreements. You pushed me into doing my very best, but I don't know if I could do it on my own."

"I have complete confidence in you, my dear. I wouldn't have wasted your time or my own if I harbored any doubt regarding your ability."

I sighed. "Thanks, Max. I think this appearance tonight really has me freaked."

"You have my sympathies. I avoided all such situations unless they were absolutely imperative. And I scurried back to this haven of sanity as quickly as possible afterward."

I understood what he meant about the cottage. There was something comforting and nurturing within its walls. I can't explain it, but the place had felt like home even before I walked through the door.

"I understand, Max. I truly do."

We kept at it until we'd finished everything Steve had asked for. We were so busy, I hardly noticed the day pass. But before I knew it, Steve was there.

He whisked me to the radio station before I had time to get flustered. Once we arrived, he introduced me to Autumn Brown, the host of the show. I liked her immediately.

I was fitted with a headset and seated before a microphone. No one had told me it was a call-in show. Good thing or I'd have been panicked! But, as he promised, Steve sat across from us throughout the whole thirty-minute segment.

Brooke and Steve had practiced with me, so many of the questions came as no surprise. Autumn asked me some different ones, though. Before I could freeze up, I looked at Steve. He nodded and smiled or winked, and I managed to come up with the answers. Once I actually made her laugh. It felt like a huge triumph.

The time passed quickly, and I was surprised when Autumn said, "I'd like to thank my special guest Nan Burton, the author of *Finding Sarah*, based on the final manuscript of Maxine DuBois, coming soon from Masterworks Press. It's been a pleasure speaking with you."

"Thank you, Autumn. The pleasure was all mine."

And then it was over. We said our goodbyes and walked out into the cool evening.

Steve stopped and hugged me. "You were wonderful."

"I couldn't have done it without you."

He kissed me, and there were those sparks again.

Man, there must be a lot of static in the air.

"Oh yes you could have, but I'm glad I didn't miss this. Let's go somewhere to celebrate. How about the Salt Creek Grille?"

"Sounds good to me." I realized I hadn't eaten all day. I'd been too nervous. Suddenly, I was famished.

During dinner, we rehashed the interview. "The next one is Friday with a reporter from the Orange County Register. He's scheduled to be at your place at eleven in the morning. I'll get there around nine to make sure you're set."

"I can fix breakfast, if you'd like," I volunteered.

"Great. We'll stop at the store on the way back."

And we did.

When he dropped me off, I gave him a flash drive with the material we'd written that morning.

"Max told me some of the information about him is wrong. He wanted to set the record straight," I told him. "And I updated Wikipedia. That amused him."

"I'll bet it was a real paradigm shift. He must be overwhelmed with the changes since his day."

"It's taken me quite a bit of time and energy, but I think he just might be convinced that this current world isn't so bad after all. You know, I used to think he avoided people because he didn't like them. But I'm starting to suspect he really suffered from agoraphobia. He was afraid to leave the house."

"You think so?"

"Yeah. Today he was talking about hating to go out and rushing back to the safety of his home. I think that's why he didn't want a phone. He was afraid someone would call and make him leave. He made it really difficult for people to be his friends."

"Did he have any? I never heard about him hanging out with anyone."

"Only Aunt Netta and Helen. Oh, and your grandfather and father. But they were business contacts. So was Helen, I guess, but she was different. I guess that's because she was in love with him. It's hard for me to think of her as his employee."

"I know. After she told me how she felt about him, I saw their relationship differently." He turned to leave. "Don't forget, I'll be here for you on Friday and for every appearance. You won't be alone."

"Thanks, Steve. It really helped tonight."

He kissed me again. There it was, the familiar jolt. But it had started to feel right. "Good night. Sleep well," he said as he left.

But I lay awake for a long time. It wasn't until he'd gone that I realized he'd asked me about Max as if he believed me. But did he? And how did he really feel about me? Was Max right? Did he really care? And how did I feel about him?

Twenty-seven

TIME SEEMED TO ACCELERATE TO WARP SPEED AS I GOT READY to spend the holidays with my folks. I was anxious to see them since we'd never been apart for so long in my whole life. I cleaned and polished everything. I wanted my little cottage to shine.

There were also my appearances. Steve and Brooke had lined up a local cable program on the arts, another from a nearby college, and several additional radio and newspaper interviews. I couldn't figure out how they'd managed to get so many people interested, but I guessed the last work of a famous dead author could be the reason. I printed the online pages for my folks and Steve brought by copies of the print ones. He also said he'd recorded the TV shows and would play them for me sometime. True to his word, he was right by my side for each one. He held my hand or put his arm around me whenever we were walking. And he always kissed me good-bye.

We visited Helen a couple of times each week, but she seemed frailer with each visit. Still, her excitement about the book remained vibrant. She wanted to know all about my adventures. And she always had messages and questions about 'dear Max' for me.

At last, I received the phone call I'd been waiting for. "Honey, we just landed at LAX. We've arranged for a car and driver. We'll be at your place in about an hour or so, depending on traffic."

"Woo hoo! Mitzi, they're on their way!" I practically danced around the

room. My bag had been packed for most of the week. Of course, my old
duffle bag really didn't qualify as luggage, nor did it hold very much. But I
had everything I needed for myself and the dog. Mitzi had been groomed
the day before, so she hadn't had a chance to get too messy.

"You even look like a ritzy dog," I told her, retying the pink bow on her
topknot. "Actually, you look more like you belong in that expensive hotel
than I do."

I was wearing a clean pair of khaki slacks, a navy t-shirt and nice warm
khaki jacket. The clothes were some of the ones Brooke helped me pick
out, and they looked nice. I'd also packed some of the other new outfits.

"Thanks to Brooke, I have decent clothes," I continued my conversation
with my pet.

Mitzi just cocked her head, and I could tell she knew something was up.

"You look quite lovely, my dear," my resident ghost said.

"Thanks, Max. I wish I could see you." There were times when I envied
Mitzi.

He chuckled. "It is probably fortuitous for me that you are unable to
behold my visage. The current situation allows you to imagine me as the
dashing man-about-town instead of an elderly old reprobate."

"I doubt you were ever an old reprobate, Max."

He chuckled again. "I should well have become one had I lived longer.
Perhaps fate allowed me to make a graceful exit before being subjected to
illness and suffering."

"What did it feel like? I mean, did you know when you died? Did you
feel it? I don't mean to pry, but, well, I'm curious."

"I recall sitting at my desk. I'd been quite weary for several days, but
hadn't given much thought to the cause. I glanced at the ocean beyond the
window. That is my last conscious memory. I regained awareness observing
my body slumped over my notes. It was most curious."

"How long were you there before someone found you?"

"Your aunt Nanette arrived later that same day, I believe. You see, time
no longer had much relevance to my existence."

"Did you try to leave?"

There was silence for a minute, then he answered. "To be completely
truthful, it never occurred to me to remove myself from this locale. It is my

home unlike any other I previously inhabited. I suppose that is the reason I have been so protective of this abode."

"Max, were you ever lonely here?" I'd had times when, even with Max and Helen and Steve and Mitzi, oh, and Tad around, I'd felt isolated and alone.

"I suppose I preferred my own company to that of any other human being. Oh, and I always had the companionship of my characters. Unlike living beings, they performed precisely as I desired."

"But isn't it the unpredictability of real people that makes them so interesting?" I'd discovered that spark of truth when Sarah had begun telling me her own story. She didn't behave as I'd have thought she would. And she was much more fascinating than she'd have been otherwise.

"Perhaps, my dear. But I grew accustomed to manipulating my stories so that the actions and outcomes were predictable. As I've recounted to you, I feel now that I should have given them their heads more often. Perhaps that is the great talent you have uncovered: the ability to listen to the stories your characters have to convey."

Just then I heard a knock. Mitzi ran toward it, her whole body wagging.

I was surprised when I opened the door to find not my parents but a delivery person standing on the porch. "Package for Ms. Nan Burton," he said.

"I'm Nan," I answered.

"Then sign here." He handed me a clipboard and pointed to the correct line. "Here's your package," he said, stepping back.

I spotted the large box next to him. The microwave, at last!

He'd already turned to go back to his truck.

"Hey, can you carry this in for me?" I asked.

"Sorry, lady. We just deliver to the porch. Besides, it's the holidays. Lots of deliveries." And with that, he got in and drove away.

I was still standing there wondering how I'd get the big box into the house when Mom and Dad pulled up. Mom jumped out even before the driver came around to open the door for her.

Tears blinded me as I hugged her tightly. Then Dad was there and he took his turn.

"I've missed you so much," I got out between sobs.

"I've missed you too, baby," Mom said, but she was crying, too.

"Come on, girls. This is a time to be happy," Dad said. I wasn't sure whether he was embarrassed because the driver was watching or because we were in the street and he was afraid the neighbors might see. Dad's not big on displays of emotion, especially public ones.

I turned to walk back into the house, my arm around Mom.

"What's this?" Dad asked.

"It's the microwave. I've been waiting for months for it. Actually, I'd practically forgotten about it. But it arrived just before you did."

Without my asking, Dad bent down and picked up the carton. "Where do you want it?" he asked.

I remembered the problem with the fuse and the coffee maker. "Just set it on that table." I cleared a spot and he set it down.

"Do you want some help unpacking this?" Dad asked. He sounded like he really wanted to do it for me.

But Mom interrupted. "Craig, we need to get checked in at the hotel soon and I could use a nap and then some food, in that order. It was a long trip."

"Okay. Nan, I'll help you set this thing up when we bring you home."

Good old Dad. I was still his little girl.

"I like what you've done with the cottage, Nan," Mom said while Dad grabbed my duffle bag.

"There wasn't much to do," I replied. "Aunt Netta left it completely furnished. I've cleaned, and there's still some painting I'd like to do. But I love the place."

"I can see why. You have a wonderful location and a great view. Perhaps someday, you can tear down this little place and build a larger house like your neighbors have."

It had never occurred to me to do something like that. In fact, just the thought of losing my little cottage nearly made me cry. "Yeah, well, I'll see," I said. But I couldn't ever imagine doing anything to destroy the place.

Mom finally turned from the window. "Do you have everything?"

"Oh, I'd better get Mitzi's bag from the kitchen. I have a couple of things to add from the freezer."

"Well, hurry along." I heard the click of her shoes as she walked along the short hall and out onto the porch.

"You aren't seriously considering razing this domicile," Max said. It was not a question, more of a command.

"No, Max. I'm not," I answered as I stuffed a few of Mitzi's meals into the grocery bag. I still made her a few things, but she had become used to canned and dry food and seemed to enjoy it for a change.

"I should hope not," he harrumphed.

"It wasn't my idea," I shot back. "I couldn't do anything that extensive in my current financial position, anyway. I'm barely able to hold it together now. So don't worry, Max. Your precious house is safe from the wrecking ball, at least for now."

I don't really know why I baited him. Maybe we'd been getting along too well, and it scared me to think of losing him. That thought disturbed me even more than the thought of losing my home.

"Bye, Max," I said quietly. Then I grabbed the bag and followed Mom through the front door.

* * * *

I loved every minute of the next two weeks. Mom and Dad and I went everywhere. We drove to San Diego one day and enjoyed the city and a great dinner before arriving back at the hotel late.

While we were gone, Mitzi was one pampered pooch.

"Don't get too used to the posh life, girl," I warned her. "When Mom and Dad are gone, it's back to morning runs on the beach for both of us."

Mom and Dad hit all their favorite spots, including Disneyland, and we dined in restaurants we remembered fondly.

"We've eaten so well on this trip that I need to lose some weight," Mom complained.

"You look terrific," I told her. "I've never seen you so rested."

It was true. Both my parents looked younger and less harried than they had in years.

"We've certainly enjoyed all the wonderful places we've seen."

"Well, your mother has," Dad groused. Then he smiled and I saw that special look pass between them.

"Oh, Craig," Mom said. They both laughed and it was obvious they were still having fun as a couple. But then, they always had. No matter what they were doing, they enjoyed just being together. I wondered if I'd ever find someone I'd enjoy that much.

"What's next?" I asked. "After California, I mean."

"We're taking a tramp steamer through the Cook Islands," Mom said. "We'll be completely out of touch for ten days."

She went on and on about the primitive conditions and pristine locales. Dad looked over her head and raised his eyebrows. I could tell that roughing it wasn't exactly his idea of a good time. But Mom wanted the adventure, so he'd go along.

Christmas morning was magical. Mom had arranged for a tree for our suite, and there were packages piled beneath it.

"But how did you get all these here?" I asked.

"As soon as we made reservations, we sent some of our gifts ahead," Mom said. "The hotel did the rest."

Mom had picked out beautiful fabrics, clothing, jewels, and other trinkets from the places they'd stopped. As I unwrapped them, my parents told me the complete story of what country they were in and what they were doing when they found each one.

Brooke had helped me pick out a small digital camera for Dad and a charm bracelet for Mom. Of course, the last of Max's money paid for them.

"Dad, you can take pictures, then download them at an Internet Café. That way, I'll be able to follow your journey."

"Are you sure I can get the hang of this thing?"

"I'll give you lessons before you leave," I promised.

"And, Mom, there's only one charm on your bracelet now, but you can add them as you find them. I picked the globe so you'd always know this was from your trip of a lifetime."

"Oh, how perfectly lovely! Thank you, darling."

After several days, Mom finally asked the question I knew would arise. "So, what have you been doing?"

I started telling them about finding Max's notes and starting on the book. I told them all about Helen and Steve and Brooke. I even told them about Tad. But I didn't make the mistake of mentioning the presence of a certain very bossy ghost.

The day after Christmas, I heard Mom and Dad arguing. They almost never do that. In fact, I can hardly ever remember them disagreeing. But I heard Mom's firm tone and Dad's response.

However, when they emerged, they seemed okay.

"Come along, Nan," Mom said. "We have a very important errand to run." She gave Dad a rather pointed look and he nodded.

"I'm coming, too," he said. "Has Mitzi been out? Will she be okay by herself?"

"I took her for a long walk a little while ago," I said.

I was surprised when we pulled up to a big car dealership.

"We're buying you a car," Mom said firmly.

"But not a new one," said Dad. "The insurance will be cheaper, and a used one will be more economical for you to drive."

"You're kidding!" I shrieked.

"Honey, when I realized that you've been stranded, even though you were living in that lovely area, well, I just felt so guilty. Here we'd given away both of our cars without a single thought about our own daughter," Mom said and looked at Dad. "Your father said he was so proud of how you'd managed, and he didn't want to interfere. But I insisted we do this for you."

He hung his head. "Sorry, kitten. I guess we were just so caught up in everything that was happening when we left that we never considered how you'd get around."

I smiled. "I've done better than I ever thought I would," I said honestly. In truth, I'd surprised myself. Of course, without Max's money and Steve to take me to the store, I'd have had a much harder time. But I was sure Helen would have shown me how to get around by bus, and I'd have managed somehow. I had a sudden realization that I was proud of everything I'd accomplished.

"Well, we're getting you a car. And that's all there is to it," Mom stated firmly.

And they did. It was two years old, a small compact Chevy Cobalt in deep blue like its name. They paid for the insurance and registration, too. And as a final gift, they filled the tank!

I had my own wheels! I was with my parents, and I had freedom again! I couldn't imagine a better Christmas.

DURING MY STAY AT THE HOTEL, STEVE CALLED A FEW TIMES. I was glad to hear his voice, and we had long conversations about nothing in particular and everything in general. He was in New York with his family, but phoned on Christmas Day to wish my folks and me a happy holiday.

He called again on New Year's Eve. "Are you doing anything special tonight?" he asked after our usual rambling discussion.

"No. Mom and Dad and I have reservations for a late dinner, but we'll probably get to bed early since they're leaving tomorrow."

"I'm not doing anything either, but maybe we can celebrate together next year."

"That would be nice," I replied. And I realized I'd really missed him and would have enjoyed spending New Year's Eve in his company.

"I'll get back on the second, so I'll see you soon. We'll visit Helen this week," he said.

"Great. I've missed her. See you then." In my mind, I added, "I miss you, too." But I didn't say it aloud.

On New Year's morning, we packed. My folks were flying to Papeette. About noon, Mom started to get anxious about going to the airport, even though they wouldn't leave until four-thirty.

"I want to be sure we have enough time to check in," she said. "Air Tahiti Nui isn't too large, so it may take longer."

Dad laughed. "You just want to get back to traveling."

Mom smiled and nodded. "It's true. There are so many places to see and I want to go while we're still healthy. Besides, this upcoming experience is one I've been looking forward to. After we land in Tahiti, we'll catch a connecting flight to Rarotonga where we'll board the boat for the tour of the Cook Islands." Her eyes lighted up as she spoke.

"All I remember when reading about this little adventure was that the accommodations were primitive," Dad told me with a scowl.

"But, honey, that's what makes it fun and different. I don't know anyone who's gone there. We'll probably have some great stories to tell when we get back."

"Yeah. That's what I'm afraid of." Dad grimaced.

"I think I'll go on ahead since I have my own transportation," I said. I don't like farewells, and I wasn't sure exactly when I'd see them again. "Thanks for everything. I wish you'd been able to meet Steve and Helen."

I'd called Helen's a couple of times to see if we could stop in so she could meet Mom and Dad, but Susan said her aunt was sleeping, and she didn't want to disturb her. Helen seemed to be doing that a lot. I hoped it was because she was healing.

"We'll see them both next time," Mom reassured me and gave me a hug.

Our goodbye seemed to last forever and we were all in tears by the time I climbed into my little blue car. I waved for as long as I could see my parents in the rearview mirror. Mitzi had settled on the passenger seat, but when a tear trickled down my cheek, she stood up and licked it away.

"Thanks, girl. I still have you, don't I?" I patted her head.

As I came through the door, I called out, "Hi, Max. I'm home. Miss me?" I heard a harrumph. "It's about time," he grumbled.

"I thought you liked the peace and quiet and couldn't wait until I left."

"I also believed I preferred solitude. However, I discovered that I missed your furry companion."

"But not me?"

He didn't answer, but Mitzi ran to the chair by the fireplace.

"That's okay, Maxie. I missed you." I smiled. He'd missed me, even if he wouldn't admit it.

When I walked into the living room, I noticed the large microwave box on the table.

"Oh, no! Dad was going to help me unpack this thing."

I tried calling Mom's cell phone, but she'd probably turned it off in anticipation of the flight. Mom's not very technically adept. Neither is Dad. Since they'd have to turn the phone off on the plane, I was sure she'd done it ahead of time.

"Drat. Guess I'll have to do it myself."

Max offered no suggestions. The box mocked me.

"I'll tackle it later, Mitz," I said. "Right now, let's go for a run and work off some of that good food we've been eating."

As soon as she heard 'run,' my dog headed for the door.

I laughed. "Hey, wait for me."

It felt really good to get back to our routine. I was reminded how much I loved the cove. I'd enjoyed the hotel, but this was now home. The sea breeze lifted my spirits as I'd hoped it would and the exercise seemed to energize both of us.

I noticed the slider at Tad's place was open and his board was missing. I looked out and, sure enough, I spotted him on a wave. Grace in motion. I was mesmerized as I watched him glide across the water.

While I still thought he was beautiful (yes, beautiful), I also realized that he had no clue who I was and probably never would.

I sighed as I tore myself away from the lovely vision on the sea.

"Come on, Mitz. We have a lot to do."

When we got home, I showered and unpacked.

With all the gifts I'd received, I came home with quite a bit more than I'd taken. Mom and I had also gone shopping, and she'd bought me a bunch of new casual clothes. My closet was filling up. I had to push the hangers aside to make room for the new stuff. The best part was that I hadn't paid for most of the bounty. It was sure a change from the small pile of shirts, shorts, jeans, and sweats I'd moved in with.

"I'll be set for a couple of years," I told Mitzi as I forced a new blouse onto the rod.

She cocked her head as if she understood.

I knew I couldn't avoid the microwave much longer. "Come on, girl. Let's do this thing."

Of course, I made a detour to fill the dog's water dish and give her a treat. I drank a big glass of water and grabbed an apple. After two weeks, it was slightly past its prime, but edible. *Have to make a store run.* Then it occurred to me that I could. *I have a car!*

I was truly free but felt no real need to leave. Besides, it was New Year's Day, and most places were closed. *It's only three o'clock. I could take a drive later on.*

Before I went anywhere, though, I had to address the big box.

I walked around it to try to figure out the best way to get it open.

"What do you think, Max?"

"Precisely what is that monstrosity?"

"It's a microwave. You remember. I ordered it months ago."

"And you've fared quite nicely without one of those new-fangled and unnecessary devices. Why, in my day..."

I laughed. "In your day, you rubbed two sticks together to start a fire, caught your own game, and ate it on a stick."

"Don't be ridiculous."

"Oh, yeah, I forgot. Helen cooked for you."

He harrumphed again.

I'd never have told him, but I'd missed that sound.

I saw a flap and decided to just grab it and pull. To my surprise, it came away from the box easily and I lifted the top.

"Hey, this isn't so hard."

Actually, the carton was designed so that the front folded down once the top was opened.

"I can just slide this thing right out," I announced to Mitzi.

Max remained silent.

I turned the box so the front flap faced the table, then pushed the oven. It slipped out easily, dragging its cord behind it like a tail.

"That wasn't so bad."

Once the box was empty, I noticed the Owner's Manual taped to the bottom. I pulled it loose, intending to look at it later. It appeared to be primarily a cookbook, and I figured since I'd spent most of my life using the equipment, I probably didn't need instructions.

There was a plastic protective cover on the glass door and a couple of other labels stuck to the top. One of them said 'Warning' but it didn't look too important. I took them all off and positioned my new energy-saving device next to the coffee pot.

"Okay, girl, time for a test."

Mitzi wagged her tail.

I filled a mug with water, making sure not to use one of the china cups with the metal trim.

I opened the door and put the test container inside. Before I set the timer and pushed the Start button, I carefully unplugged the coffee pot.

"No blown fuses this time," I proudly told my audience of one. Well, two, if you counted Max. I decided not to.

I took a deep breath and pushed the button.

Poof! I saw a big flash. Everything went dark and an acrid smell filled the room.

"Oh, damn! What the hell happened?" I asked no one in particular.

"I presume you have precipitated a crisis beyond a mere fuse. However, it would be prudent to investigate the condition of the electrical box."

I ran through the kitchen and flung back the door. I didn't even have to open the cabinet to know it was serious because black soot and scorch marks extended up the wall from the metal enclosure.

"Holy crap! What now?"

I had a tough time prying open the warped door. What met my unbelieving eyes was nothing short of a disaster. Inside the blackened and burnt interior, no sign of any pennies, much less fuses, remained.

My heart pounded, and I panicked.

I need to get help! Good thing I charged my phone before I left the hotel. And my computer battery is still full.

The smell grew worse, so I threw open all the windows to air out the house. *I hope this isn't toxic. Who knows what materials they used when this place was built?*

I quickly booted up and searched for electricians in the area.

I called the nearest one, but only got a machine. I left a message that I had an emergency.

"Of course, with my luck, I not only nearly burn down my house, but I do it on New Year's Day," I mumbled as I called the second number.

No answer there or at the third or fourth ones. I finally located a guy in Tustin.

"It'll cost you a minimum of two hundred for me to drive all that way, especially on a holiday. And any work will be extra."

"Okay, okay," I said. I wasn't sure where I'd get the money. I'd have to use plastic and worry about paying for it later. But this was my home.

It took the guy over an hour to arrive. Meanwhile, the sun was setting and it was growing dark.

I was glad I'd bought some candles for Aunt Netta's beautiful candle holders. I lit them, and they helped a bit. I wished I'd gotten some wood for the fireplace. *I can always collect some driftwood later on.*

Whenever I thought about the damage to the cottage, my heart pounded so hard I thought it might come right out of my chest. But I kept telling myself the problem could be fixed. Everything can be fixed. Right?

The electrician arrived about the time I was ready to give up on him. "This better be a real emergency," he growled when I answered the door.

"Oh, it is," I replied.

"Geez, it smells like you fried the wiring in here. What the hell did you do?"

I was leading the way to the panel by the back door. "I just plugged in that microwave."

"Didn't you read the instructions?" he demanded. "This needs a dedicated circuit, and I'm sure this old place doesn't have one."

"Well, I did unplug the coffee pot..." I started.

He sneered. "This entire dump probably only has about two circuits, one for the lights and another for the outlets."

I hadn't liked the guy from the moment he walked in, and when he called my precious cottage a dump, I decided I hated him. In fact, I'd have told him to leave if I'd had any choice. But I'd already committed two hundred of my scarce dollars to him and, by golly, he was going to fix the wires.

He took one look at the burned electrical box. "Oh, no. Don't tell me you put pennies in this thing."

"Well..."

He mumbled under his breath. I thought I heard the words 'dumb ass' and 'broad,' but decided I didn't want to know for sure. If I acknowledged his name calling, I'd have to reply in kind. And since he was my only hope, I decided to count to ten—or twenty—and try to keep my cool.

"Oh, good lord, this is knob and tube wiring. I haven't seen this junk in years. You were just lucky you didn't burn down the house, not that it would have been much of a loss."

By this time I was biting my tongue to keep from telling him off.

He turned and looked at me.

"Can it be fixed?" I asked timidly.

"Lady, you don't have enough money to get me to work on this piece of junk. Tear it down and build something decent. This is a fire trap, and it sits on prime real estate. In fact, if you want to sell it cheap, I might be willing to take it off your hands."

Okay, that was enough.

"How dare you!" I shouted. "I asked you to come here to fix my wiring, not to criticize my house. This is my home, and it's not going anywhere no matter how much you or anyone else thinks it should." I pulled my credit card from my pocket where I'd put it before he arrived. "Charge it. Now write up the bill and then get out."

"Geez, lady, I just told you the truth. If you can't take it..."

"It's not true, and I don't accept it. Now give me my receipt. And I don't ever want to see you again."

He quickly wrote out the information. "I'll need to run the card in the truck."

"I'll come with you," I said. I didn't trust him to charge me only the amount he'd quoted.

I watched as he ran the plastic through some kind of electronic scanner then handed the device to me. I signed it quickly and took my card back, then turned on my heel and marched through the door and slammed it.

Only then, did I allow myself to slump to the floor and sob. What am I going to do?"

Twenty-nine

I REMAINED SITTING ON THE FLOOR, MY BACK TO THE FRONT door, sobbing, too defeated to move.

"Oh, Max," I wailed. "I can't let them tear down my house. I love this place. How can I afford to get it fixed, even if I can find someone to do the work? I know Mom and Dad would loan me the money, but I can't reach them. And I can't pay for it, even if an electrician is willing to make the repairs."

Mitzi came to me and licked the tears coursing down my cheeks.

"I believe this will require a screwdriver," said a calm British voice.

"Don't be silly. I can't fix this by myself. Believe me, I would if I could..." I was still gulping and crying.

"As I recall, you will find the required implement in the drawer next to the refrigerator," he replied, ignoring my increasing meltdown.

"Okay, I get it. You're trying to make me mad enough to stop crying. Well, it won't work." A new flood of pity and helplessness overwhelmed me, as well as annoyance. "What did I do to deserve this?"

Once again, Max spoke in calm, patronizing tones. "The solution to your dilemma will require the use of the implement I mentioned."

I got up from my seat on the floor. "Okay. I'll humor you. But this better work!"

Not only was I angry at the current situation, I was now mad at Max. I grabbed a candle, stomped into the kitchen and flung open the drawer. There were two screwdrivers. I picked up both of them and marched back to the living room.

"Okay, here they are. Which one do I need, the flat one or the other one?" I was still choking back the sobs and sniffling.

He ignored my question. "Next, you will require a torch."

"A torch? You want me to set fire to my house? No way!"

"I believe the item is called a flashlight in your vernacular," my aggravating ghost replied, still in the oh-too-patient tone one would use with a stubborn child.

I set the screwdrivers down on the coffee table as hard as I could. Unfortunately, the wicker made little noise in protest. Then I walked into the bedroom and retrieved the flashlight from the nightstand drawer. Dad had insisted I keep one next to the bed in case of emergency. He'd also put new batteries in it when I moved in.

The flashlight provided more light than the candle had, so I returned it to the mantle.

"Okay, Max. What now?" I asked sarcastically.

"Focus the light beneath the frame on the oil painting."

I suddenly got it. "Oh, Max. You're brilliant! I hadn't thought about selling it! Thank you, Aunt Netta."

"You will require the star-headed screwdriver. I believe it is called a Phillips-head."

Hope began to creep in. *I can sell the picture and save the cottage.*

I knelt on the floor, directed the light under the frame and saw two screws.

"Brilliant, Max," I said as I positioned the screwdriver and started to loosen the first one. "This a great way to protect the artwork from being knocked off the wall during an earthquake."

The screw came loose easily, but the second one took a little muscle. It finally gave way and fell into my hand.

"Now," Max directed, "Raise the bottom of the frame away from the wall."

I did as he ordered, being careful not to damage the beautiful painting. I knew I'd grieve its loss, but my home was more important.

The frame slid away from the wall and I lifted it off, then turned to set it on the floor beside the sofa. I don't know what caught my eye, but I swung back to the wall and was stunned to see a safe had been concealed behind the artwork.

"Max, is that what I think it is?"

He chuckled.

"Did Aunt Netta know this was here?"

"No one else was aware of my modification to the structure except for the installer, and he long preceded me in death."

I noticed that the safe had a combination lock. It reminded me of the one Dad had given me for my bicycle when I was little. It had been his when he was a child and for some reason, I liked using it.

I positioned my fingers on the round knob. "Okay, Max, what's the combination?"

He remained silent.

"Come on, Maxie, you're not going to let me get this close without telling me."

He still didn't say a word.

"Is this a game? Do I have to figure it out for myself?" I thought about it for a minute. "Oh, no. You didn't do anything that obvious, did you?"

He chuckled again.

I was ready to test my theory. "Right or left first?"

"Right."

I turned the knob twice to the right and settled on the number four. Then I went past the four to the left, stopping on the number one. I finally moved it again to the right and stopped on two. I heard a distinct click and laughed out loud.

"Your birthday? But Max, it's so obvious." Then I remembered that Wikipedia had it listed incorrectly. "No wonder no one ever opened this. They all had the wrong date."

"Nary a soul ever discovered this place of concealment," Max said.

As I reached for the handle, he interrupted me.

"Before you gain access, I wish for you to be aware that it was my intention to reveal this location to you as soon as you returned from your recent holiday."

My hand stopped in midair. "You were going to tell me about this even before the electrical disaster?"

"I was indeed. I no longer require material items in my current state. I had decided that you deserved to receive the bounty of my life's labors. After all, you completed my final work and did so in a superior manner."

I suddenly felt all mushy toward my resident ghost. "Have I told you that I love you?"

"I believe you might have mentioned it a time or two."

"And I know you love me too, even if you never tell me."

"Your assumption would be correct," he said softly. "But the time has come to provide you with the wherewithal to accomplish the restoration of your home."

Max had finally acknowledged that he cared about me and that the cottage was now my home.

With a satisfied sigh, I returned to opening the safe. The handle was hard to move, but I finally forced it to turn. The door swung open.

I picked up the flashlight and shone the beam into the opening. The light reflected off gold. Stacks and stacks of gold coins filled most of the opening. I picked one up.

"What are these, Max?"

"Most are South African Krugerrands. I began purchasing them when they were first minted and continued until my death."

"But, Max, there are so many..."

"There are also other international gold coins, including some American ones."

"But, why..."

"As I previously revealed, my parents lost their entire savings during what you yanks call the Great Depression. I never again trusted banks, or traditional investments. Instead, I began acquiring currency. When that proved to be quite bulky, I turned to gold."

"How..."

"How did I amass this quantity? I located dealers throughout the world who purchased for me. Not too many at a time, so as not to draw unwanted attention."

"Did they send these things through the mail to you?"

"Of course. And occasionally I arranged for a packet to be transported by courier."

My mouth must have hung open. I looked back into the safe. Pile after pile of gold met my unbelieving gaze. Then I noticed a few more things.

Along one side were several piles of bills extending from the bottom to the top of the enclosure. When I picked up one of the bundles, I discovered they were all hundreds.

Then I reached in and pulled out three velvet bags. Each of them was about four inches square.

"What are these?"

"Be most careful with those," Max warned solemnly.

I felt the outside and the soft little packages appeared to be filled with small rocks. I moved to the table and carefully opened one. Then I poured some of the contents into my hand. They caught the light from the candles and flashlight and threw rainbows around the room.

"Diamonds," I whispered.

"Investment quality," Max replied. "The other pouch contains colored gemstones."

I carefully poured the jewels back into their velvet container. Then I allowed myself to breathe again.

"What about this one?" I asked about the last bag.

"Open it," Max suggested.

Inside was a simple man's ring, set with a black stone. A small diamond sat in the center. The shank was twisted and worn so thin it looked as though it was ready to break.

"What's this?" I asked.

"It is the ring I wore for years. It belonged to my father and was the last item of value he owned when he died. It became damaged not long before my demise. I had intended to have it repaired, but unfortunately, I left this mortal coil before it could be restored."

I looked at the ring for a moment. "I think I know someone who would love to have this," I said.

When Max didn't comment, I looked at the photo on the mantle. Sure enough, the same ring I now held appeared on Max's hand.

I continued. "If you wore this every day, then Helen would recognize it. She'd probably appreciate having something of yours."

"I have recently recognized my love and appreciation for my secretary as a woman. I only wish I had acknowledged those emotions while I was still with her in life." He paused for a moment. "I would be very pleased if you would convey it to her with my deepest affection."

I smiled, happy at the thought that I could give Helen something she would value. Something from Max himself. I knew it was the greatest payment she could receive for everything she had done to help me.

My phone rang, startling me. It was the first electrician I'd called.

"I can be there in about five minutes. Don't worry about a thing," he said.

"Wow, Max. This guy sounds a lot more positive," I said as I closed the safe and re-hung the painting.

And he was. When he arrived, he immediately put my fears to rest.

"I grew up in this area," he said, looking around. "I love these little cottages. Far too many have been torn down. I'm always happy when I see that one's survived."

He knocked on the wall. "They don't build like this anymore. Nice thick lath and plaster."

I showed him the fuse box and explained about the microwave. He looked at the blackened mess and frowned. "I know lots of people used to put pennies in these old boxes, but it was a really dangerous practice. You're lucky you didn't have a fire."

"Can the house be saved?" I asked timidly.

"Sure," he answered quickly. "I can install a new panel and rewire the house in the next couple of weeks. Meanwhile, I'll loan you a generator. You'll have a couple of lights and an outlet or two. But no microwave or coffee pot until I can add some circuits."

"Deal." I shook his hand and my heart filled with joy.

He quoted me a pretty hefty price, but with Max's fortune at my disposal, I had plenty to cover it. And the electrician promised to return the next afternoon after he'd had a chance to pick up the generator and get some materials.

"Thanks for making this possible, Max," I said after I closed the door. I flopped down on the couch, too emotionally exhausted to stand any longer.

"I just couldn't bear the thought of losing my home." I looked around the room. "I love this place."

"I became aware of your attachment some time ago. That was why I wished for you to have sufficient funds to care for it properly. It also occurred to me that saving this precious abode may be the real reason I have been unable to leave."

"I never thought of that," I replied. It made sense, in a way.

"But I now realize it was something else entirely."

"What do you mean, Max?"

"I have finally become aware that during my entire span of years walking the earth, I was self-absorbed. You have brought to my attention my lack of awareness of the needs and feelings of others."

"But, Max..."

"Please hear me out, my dear. Being blind to Helen's affection as well as your aunt's was a manifestation of my selfishness. During our brief acquaintance, you have taught me to recognize others' feelings. Now I realize that my continued presence in your life does you an enormous disservice."

"What do you mean, Max? I love you, and I love having you here. I admit, you were a royal pain in the butt at first, but we've developed a great relationship, haven't we?"

"Indeed we have. And that, Nannette, is entirely the problem."

I knew he was serious. He'd never called me by my full name before. "But how could it be a problem?"

"My lovely Helen has had many conversations with you about the affairs between men and women. And I have learned a great deal as well. Her devotion to me has been instructive."

"But we get along really well. I don't see the problem."

"Ah and that is precisely the issue. We have grown quite fond of one another, and you do not seem to realize the necessity of forming an emotional attachment to a flesh-and-blood man. I fear that our mutual affection may prevent you from discovering the very real love simply waiting for your acknowledgment."

"What are you talking about?" I wasn't sure where this was going, but I was positive I wouldn't like it.

"Your young man displays many admirable qualities, and his deep affection for you is quite apparent."

"What young man? I don't have a young man."

Max sighed. "That is my point exactly. Your Steven loves you, and you pretend to ignore his very real ardor. He is always supportive, just as Helen was always present for me. I did not recognize her devotion either."

"But..."

"I fear that as long as I remain in your life, you will continue to deny the potential of your own happiness with a living being. You deserve much more than I can ever provide."

I started crying again. "Oh, Max, please don't leave. I need you here. I need you to talk to. And who will teach me how to be a writer if you're gone?"

Max chuckled. "My dear girl, you have already absorbed all the knowledge I am able to impart. Your young man is perfectly capable of guiding you through the finer points of the current state of publishing."

"I don't want you to go." I realized I sounded like a petulant child, but I'd become accustomed to his presence. "What will Mitzi do without you? She loves you, too."

"I am deeply fond of both of you. But you reside in the physical world, and I no longer do, nor have I for some time."

"But I thought you were stuck here." A small glimmer of hope rose within me.

"I now believe I could have moved on at any time. But I was so attached to this place and my work, I would not allow myself to entertain that possibility."

"Please stay, Max. I need you. Helen needs you." I was grasping at straws, but I couldn't imagine my life without Max in it.

"You will live a full and wonderful life, my sweet. But only if I depart."

"No Max!"

Somewhere deep in my heart I knew he spoke the truth, but I felt as though I'd be lost without him. I began to sob. As I closed my eyes, I thought I felt a gentle kiss on my cheek.

At that moment, I knew that Max was gone.

Thirty

"MAX! COME BACK!" I CRIED. BUT I KNEW IN MY HEART HE WAS gone for good. "Oh, Max," I wailed.

Mitzi climbed into my lap and whimpered.

"I know, girl. I know." I buried my face in her fur and sobbed until I thought I had no tears left.

When I finally checked my phone, I was surprised it was nearly midnight. The emotional rollercoaster I'd been on all day had totally drained me. I needed to talk to someone, but I couldn't call anybody that late.

"Come on, girl," I said to Mitzi. "Steve will be back tomorrow." I was glad. At least he'd understand.

Then it struck me. "Oh no. We'll have to tell Helen." The thought of her losing Max twice in her lifetime overwhelmed me, especially since I'd be the one to tell her he was gone. I dragged myself to the bedroom and lay down. My dog cuddled next to me as if she understood. Or maybe she needed comfort as much as I did.

As exhausted as I was, I couldn't sleep. I kept drifting off, only to wake with a start remembering that Max was gone. Then my tears began anew.

Mitzi remained close and seemed to want to help, but I couldn't find solace.

I must have fallen asleep just before dawn, because I woke with a start. The sun streamed into the window. It was after seven, and I felt as though

I'd finished a marathon or was coming down with something. I ached all over.

I hoped a run would help. But I had little confidence.

I pulled on my old college sweats. They were comforting, like being held in the arms of my past, when life was much simpler.

"Come on, girl. Let's go."

Mitzi followed me to the back door without her usual enthusiasm. I knew exactly how she felt.

The morning heralded one of those perfect Southern California winter days. I breathed in the crisp, clean air. But the sun shimmering on the ocean and the aquamarine blue sky were lost on me.

I set a blistering pace, and my dog kept up, her fur flying. We ran all the way to the end of the cove. The tide was high, so we couldn't round the far point.

I was breathless when I stopped and bent over to catch my breath with my palms on my knees. All the crying the day before seemed to have depleted my lung capacity.

Mitzi appeared to be happy I'd stopped.

We headed back at a brisk jog. My head felt clearer, but my heart was still shattered.

I loved Max. He was my friend, my teacher, my companion, my mentor. He'd become the most important person in my life. Well, he wasn't really a person anymore, but he'd become as necessary to me as breathing. And he was gone.

I thought about stopping at Tad's, even though I knew I couldn't talk to him about Max. But when we passed by, he was lying on one of his lounges, soaking up the sun next to yet another of his collection of beauties. He was like a fine painting—lovely to look at, but without much depth.

I waved as we passed, but he never acknowledged my presence.

I showered and dressed, then fed the dog.

It was eight-thirty. I knew I'd have to call Helen, but didn't want to disturb her until after nine.

However, at about eight-forty-five, my phone rang. When I answered, I heard weeping.

"Oh, Nan." I recognized Susan's voice. "Aunt Helen passed away. I got here this morning to check on her and she was already gone. I thought you'd want to know."

I felt as though I'd already gone a full ten rounds, only to be punched hard in the gut.

"Oh, no," I whispered. Then, through my own sobs, I told her about Max. "They're both gone," I said.

Susan's reply surprised me. "Why, that's wonderful," she said. "Don't you see? They're together. Maybe they both held on until they could finally reunite."

Somehow that thought made me feel a little better, but not much.

"Do you really think so?" I asked, sniffling.

"Aunt Helen didn't say much the last couple of days, but when she spoke, it was about Max. How much she loved him and what a good man she believed him to be."

I thought of Max's gifts to me and his ring. He'd wanted her to have it because he realized it would hold meaning for her. *What do I do with it now?*

"Thanks for letting me know. Steve's supposed to be back later today. Please tell us when you're going to have a service."

"Aunt Helen wanted to be cremated and have her ashes spread over the ocean. You and Steve will, of course, be invited."

I hung up the phone. "Oh, Mitzi," I said, completely defeated. "Helen's gone, too."

Grief flooded over me. I couldn't even cry. I felt so devastated.

I don't know how long I sat there with my little dog in my lap before I heard the knock. It took all the energy I could muster to stand and walk to the door.

I figured it was the electrician and that he'd come early, but I was stunned to see Steve.

"Sorry if I disturbed you," he started. "I caught a red-eye into John Wayne. I've missed you a lot."

I was never so happy to see anyone. Steve, with his too-long hair and rumpled clothes, looking tired and in need of a shave, was just what I needed.

He probably noticed my blotchy face and swollen, red eyes. "What's wrong?" he asked.

So I told him. Unfortunately, I found more sobs along the way.

"Oh, honey," he said and pulled me into his arms. He held me tightly and suddenly I wasn't alone. I felt protected. And I liked it.

After a while, I pulled back and met Steve's gaze. I wondered what he'd look like without his glasses. On impulse, I reached up and took them off. Clear eyes the color of a Southern California summer morning sky met mine. This time the love they held was unmistakable. It was very strange how Clark Kent, my Clark Kent, had somehow morphed into Superman. I decided I'd take Max's advice and keep him.

* * * *

The service for Helen was held the week after her death. It was simple and perfect for the woman who'd become my surrogate grandmother and dear friend. Steve and I were the only other people on the boat besides her family. Her ashes created a silver sheen on the surface of the water, and the pink and red rose petals we threw created a lovely mosaic. I swear I could almost sense her presence, along with Max's.

On the way back, I spotted my little cottage and recalled seeing it from another boat. The day we spread Aunt Netta's ashes, I recognized it as the cottage where the 'famous writer' had lived. I'd felt drawn toward it, as if by some unexplained magnetic force. That day, I realized I loved the place, even before I knew it was mine or about Max or Helen. And I felt such gratitude for it and for having had those two special people in my life.

* * * *

True to his word, the electrician, whom I now call 'Super Joe,' had arrived with a generator so I had some lights and one outlet, but it was enough. Within two weeks, he'd installed a new panel with real breakers and rewired the cottage. His appreciation for my home was his best gift.

"This should last you for many years, but let me know if you ever need anything," he told me when he was finished. "This is a great little place."

* * * *

The next few weeks were busy with preparations for the book's publication. And I felt grateful for the distraction. Steve barely left my side.

I'd been distraught when he arrived after Helen's death, and it was apparent, even to me, how concerned he was. It felt good having him there to lean on and to share my grief. And it felt even better knowing he was with me for the long haul.

As a thank you gift, I had Max's ring repaired for Steve. He seemed touched when I gave it to him.

The actual publication of the book was a bit anticlimactic after the publicity ahead of time. But, just as he'd promised, Steve was right there with me every moment. On the actual release day, I made yet another appearance on a local TV show with a popular morning host.

When we arrived back at my place, I fell onto the sofa, exhausted. Steve sat next to me, and Mitzi lay across our laps. Both of us petted her and she started purring. It was the first time she'd done it since Max left.

I knew how she felt. I was actually content just to be in this special place with her and Steve.

"You know," Steve said, looking at the ring on his finger. "I've been thinking about Max. Leaving you may have been the only truly selfless thing he ever did."

"I hadn't thought about it that way." I was stunned and then realized he was probably right. And maybe that was the real reason he hadn't been able to move on. In my head I whispered a final good-bye to Max, with a prayer that somehow he and Helen had found each other in death as they hadn't in life.

"So," Steve continued. "What's your next book?"

"Next book? This one's barely published."

"Yep. That's the time to start the next one."

"But Max had the creativity. All I did was finish for him."

"And if you want to truly honor his memory, you won't stop writing. He taught you well, and you're very talented. Believe me. I know."

"But I don't have the slightest idea what to write about."

"You know the saying, 'Write what you know.' Well, what do you know?"

I stopped to think about it. What did I know?

"You owe it to Max to continue writing. And besides, I'd love to introduce my wife as a multi-published author."

Wife? Did he say 'wife'?

I looked at him and he grinned. It wasn't Tad's thousand-watt killer model smile. But somehow it was more endearing, especially since I had no doubt it was intended just for me.

He kissed me thoroughly and with feeling. He'd been doing that a lot lately. I planned on getting very used to it.

"I'd like that, too," I whispered when I my breath returned.

"Then get to it." He grinned, shoved me off the loveseat, and patted my butt.

Suddenly I knew the story I'd tell. In fact, I had to tell it.

I went to the desk and booted up my computer. Then I started to type:

I don't believe in ghosts...

About the author

LORNA COLLINS WAS RAISED IN ALHAMBRA, CALIFORNIA AND attended California State University at Los Angeles where she majored in English.

Between 1998 and 2001, she worked in Osaka, Japan on the Universal Studios theme park with her husband, Larry. Their memoir of that experience, *31 Months in Japan: The Building of a Theme Park,* was published in 2005 and was a finalist for the 2006 nonfiction EPPIE award and named as one of Rebeccas Reads best nonfiction books of 2005.

They have written two mysteries together: *Murder... They Wrote,* published in 2009, and *Murder in Paradise,* published in 2010, a finalist for the 2011 EPIC eBook Award in 2011. They are currently working on at least two more in this series.

Along with authors Sherry Derr-Wille, Luanna Rugh, Christie Shary, Lorna wrote several romance anthologies: *Snowflake Secrets,* finalist for the Dream Realm Award and Eric Hoffer Award, published in 2008, *Seasons of Love* in 2009, and *Directions of Love* in 2010. *Directions of Love* received the EPIC eBook Award for best romance anthology of 2011. The group added debut author, Cheryl Gardarian for *An Aspen Grove Christmas,* published in December of 2010. The group is currently working on three more anthologies.

Ghost Writer is Lorna's first solo effort, and her favorite book so far.

Today she and Larry are retired and reside in Dana Point, California.

Made in the USA
Charleston, SC
11 July 2012